The DEATH of OBSESSION

RAY FASHONA

Mechanicsburg, Pennsylvania   USA

Published by Sunbury Press, Inc.
50 West Main Street, Suite A
Mechanicsburg, Pennsylvania 17055

www.sunburypress.com

NOTE: This is a work of fiction. Names, characters, places and incidents are the product of the author's imagination or are used fictitiously, and any resemblance to actual persons, living or dead, business establishments, events or locales is entirely coincidental.

Copyright © 2014 by Ray Fashona.
Cover copyright © 2014 by Sunbury Press.
Sunbury Press supports copyright. Copyright fuels creativity, encourages diverse voices, promotes free speech, and creates a vibrant culture. Thank you for buying an authorized edition of this book and for complying with copyright laws by not reproducing, scanning, or distributing any part of it in any form without permission. You are supporting writers and allowing Sunbury Press to continue to publish books for every reader. For information contact Sunbury Press, Inc., Subsidiary Rights Dept., 50-A W. Main St., Mechanicsburg, PA 17011 USA or legal@sunburypress.com.

For information about special discounts for bulk purchases, please contact Sunbury Press Orders Dept. at (855) 338-8359 or orders@sunburypress.com.

To request one of our authors for speaking engagements or book signings, please contact Sunbury Press Publicity Dept. at publicity@sunburypress.com.

ISBN: 978-1-62006-373-6 (Trade Paperback)
ISBN: 978-1-62006-374-3 (Mobipocket)
ISBN: 978-1-62006-375-0 (Epub)

FIRST SUNBURY PRESS EDITION: February 2014

Product of the United States of America
0 1 1 2 3 5 8 13 21 34 55

Set in Bookman Old Style
Designed by Lawrence Knorr
Cover by Lawrence Knorr
Edited by Jennifer Melendrez

Continue the Enlightenment!

DEDICATION

To Holly, Sarah and Becca, my lifelines.

ACKNOWLEDGMENTS

Diane and Ned Ticcony were the first to read this manuscript in its raw form, and their encouragement and suggestions kept this novel from dying before it was born.

After reading this manuscript, my dear friend Dr. Renee Downey demonstrated such enthusiasm that I began to believe others might find it interesting, too. When my own energy was flagging, she kept my hope afloat. For that, and for her friendship, I am grateful.

My friend and, now I can say, fellow novelist Jim DeFelice was instrumental in this project. More than once, he offered helpful ideas and, more important, wouldn't let me quit when getting this manuscript published seemed impossible. His message was clear and concise: Be persistent and keep sending it out. He believed in the book and in my writing. I owe him a debt I likely won't be able to repay.

Chapter One
Return to the Never

The one charm of the past is that it is the past.
—Oscar Wilde

1.

"Did you kill her?" the detective asked.

Michael Zinarelli snapped his head up, looked him in the eyes.

Detective Steve Delson stared back. Said nothing.

"What makes you think she's dead?" Z said.

"Then where is she?"

"How should I know?"

The detective sucked on his cigarette and blew a cloud of smoke into the air. There was no smoking in the building but he didn't give a shit.

"Mr. Zinarelli, let's cut the crap, OK? You tell me the truth and we can both get the hell out of here. We found her car parked near the riverfront. But no sign of her."

"I don't know what happened to her," Z said.

Delson leaned backed in his chair. His hawkish nose was pointed at Zinarelli and he looked him up and down with cold gray eyes. He said nothing.

"I haven't seen her in thirty years," Z said.

Delson stretched forward and put his elbows on the table that separated them. "That right?"

"Yeh. That's right."

Delson grinned darkly. "You're a liar, Zinarelli. We know you two talked recently. We have the phone records. Want to try again?"

"Should I call my lawyer?"

"That's up to you. You're not under arrest. We're just talking."

Z grunted at him. It was supposed to be a laugh. "Just talking, huh?"

"Sure. You can walk out of here any time you want."

"Yeh, and that would make me your top suspect."

Delson smiled slightly, the cigarette jutting up toward the ceiling. "Maybe you already are."

"I'm telling you, I haven't seen Crystal Cassidy in thirty years."

He shrugged. "You want to leave right now?"

Z shook his head. "I've got nothing to hide. Let's get this over with."

"Tell me again how this all started," Delson said.

"Christ Almighty! Are you not listening?"

"I just need to be sure," he said. His eyes grew darker.

Z squirmed in his chair, glared back at him. "What the hell do you want from me, man?"

"The truth."

Zinarelli laughed. "You people are all the same. The truth. Do you have any idea what the truth is?"

Delson looked at him without blinking. "No. Not yet. But I know a lie when I hear one."

"How old are you?"

"What?"

"How old are you?"

"None of your business."

"Around forty, right?"

"Around."

"Did you go to Poughkeepsie High School?"

"Lourdes."

"Ah."

"What's that supposed to mean?"

"Nothing. You just didn't strike me as a good Catholic boy."

Delson seemed amused by that. He smiled and blew smoke out of his nose. "My mother made me go there. She said there were too many ... undesirable characters at Poughkeepsie High."

"She meant blacks."

His face went totally neutral. "We're not here to talk about my mother, Mr. Zinarelli. Let's stay on point. When was the last time you saw Crystal Cassidy?"

The DEATH of OBSESSION

"I don't know. Maybe 1977 or '78."

2.

I know thinking about Crystal still makes Mike uncomfortable. Their whole relationship was embarrassing. He once told me it made him feel like a fool: "These things burn themselves into your psyche. I still remember dropping a pop-up in Little League that cost my team the game. It still hurts." What I can't understand is that, although Mike's on the other side of 50 and what happened between him and Crystal was in his sophomore year of college, he can't seem to let it go. I hate her for what she did to Mike.

When I first met Mike, he was still a wreck from what Crystal had put him through. She had taken something from him, something he thought I'd never recover. Back then, he spent most of his time getting drunk and stoned, trying to get away from himself. I saw a good guy through all that, a guy who needed somebody to really love him. I didn't know if that could be me, but maybe. He wanted to go slow, and that was fine with me. I didn't have much experience with serious relationships or with sex, for that matter. I knew he'd slept with a lot of girls, but that didn't bother me. I was glad one of us knew what we were doing.

What does bother me is that after twenty-seven years of marriage and two kids and everything we've been through, it still hurts him to think about Crystal. He should be able to put that behind him, finally. But that's not Mike. He holds on to everything that's ever happened to him.

3.

Delson's smoke was making him a little sick, but Z didn't say anything because he figured pissing him off was not a good idea. But he wanted to take that cigarette and shove it down the detective's throat. He wished lung cancer on the bastard.

"What do you know about this kid, David Kaplowitz?"

"Z" shrugged. "Never heard of him."

He raised an eyebrow at me. "He's Crystal Cassidy's son. Says he's desperate to find her."

"I've never met him."

"He seems to know you."

"Yeh?"

Delson took a drag off his butt and trained his cold eyes on Zinarelli. "He knows *of* you, anyway. Says you and his mother had quite a relationship. Apparently, she talked about you a lot over the years."

Z bit down on his anger. With a tight jaw he said, "That's her issue, not mine. I haven't had anything to do with her in thirty years. What is it about that you don't understand, detective?"

He tilted his head slightly to the right. "I guess there's a lot of things about it I don't understand. Like why you're lying."

Z pounded his fist on the table. "I'm not lying. Jesus Christ! Why do you keep saying I'm lying?"

"Mr. Zinarelli—"

"Will you call me Mike? My name's Mike."

Delson pursed his lips then smiled on one side of his mouth. "Listen, Mike, I know you talked to Crystal Cassidy recently. And I think a lot more than talked to her. Maybe you were trying to relive your college days ..."

"You are full of shit, Delson. OK? I love my wife. I've been married to Anna for twenty-seven years and she means everything to me. What the hell makes you think I've had anything to do with Crystal?"

"Mike, let me ask you something. Did you ever really get over her? Sounds to me like you loved her all your life. Twenty-seven years of marriage or not. And then she walked back into your life ..."

"You're nuts, Delson."

"Yeah?"

"Yeah," Z screamed at him.

He leaned back, looking smug. "Your wife doesn't think so."

"Why do you have to bring my wife into it?"

Delson crossed his arms over his chest and looked satisfied. "I didn't bring her into this, Mike. You did. By sleeping with your old girlfriend."

"That is a lie."

Delson pulled a ratty notebook out of his back pocket, flipped it open, and fingered through several pages. "Let me read you what your wife told my partner," he said calmly.

Z had seen Delson's partner and pegged her as a dyke with short, bottle-blonde hair and a physique that could make a wrestler envious. Z knew she could kick his ass and was pretty sure she could kick Delson's, too.

"Honestly, I don't want anything to do with Crystal Cassidy," Delson read. "That girl has been a cancer in Mike's life. Mike's been a good husband and good father. Our girls, Sophie and Tasha, love him—even though sometimes he drives them crazy because he's always trying to be funny and they're not in the mood to laugh all the time." Delson trained his eyes on Z then returned them to the notebook. "I love Mike. He's my life. But lately, he's been kind of distant. Preoccupied. I know he's got a lot on his mind with work and sending Sophie to college. Things haven't been easy for him. To be honest, I just want this Crystal Cassidy thing to go away."

When he stopped Z gulped back the lump in his throat and said, "So you interpret that to mean I've been having an affair." He clapped his hands with an exaggerated loudness. "Bravo, Detective Delson. Brav-O. You're a real fucking Sherlock Holmes."

Delson shook a new cigarette from the pack, put it in his mouth but did not light it. He said nothing.

"Yeh, I've had a lot on my mind. I don't have a guaranteed fucking government job like you. I'm under a lot of pressure."

Delson put a lighter to the cigarette, took a deep puff. "When's the last time you made love to your wife, Mike?"

Z felt his skin turning to fire. "Fuck you, man. I'm gonna talk to the chief about you. You are a sonofabitch."

"It's a simple question ..."

"When's the last time you screwed your wife, Delson? Or do you get off on that lesbian partner of yours?"

He grinned at that. "Actually, I'm divorced," he said. "There's a lot of that in this business. In yours, too, I suppose."

Z glared at him, taking breaths in slow, calming paces. When he felt he had control of himself, he said, "I know what you're doing, Delson. You're pushing buttons, trying to get me to say something I shouldn't. But you're wasting your time because there's nothing there. Understand? I love my wife. I haven't seen Crystal Cassidy in thirty years. End of story."

Delson took a drag off his cigarette and blew a cloud of smoke at the ceiling. "By the way," he said, "Detective Barone isn't a lesbian. You shouldn't be so judgmental. She's got a boyfriend who's a tae kwon do instructor. And if he heard you call her a lesbian he'd rip out your spleen without leaving a mark. Now, let's get back to you and Crystal Cassidy."

Z shook his head. "We're done," he said. "I'm going home now unless you plan on charging me with something."

Delson stubbed out his cigarette. "How about taking a polygraph?"

"No. No way."

"Why not?"

"Because I don't trust those things."

Delson shrugged. "You're free to go, Mike. I know where to find you."

4.

The newsroom of the *Hudson Valley Sun* was a strange combination of desolation and relentless activity. Half the work stations were empty, a result of corporate cuts and consolidation of functions. Z could look around the room and name the people who were gone – all of them hard workers, all of them deserving of their jobs. Maybe they were the lucky ones, he often told himself, starting over while there was still a chance.

The *Sun* boasted a long, proud history in Poughkeepsie, and even though it had changed names more than half a dozen times, it was known as the area's longest-standing newspaper. The 21st century had been cruel to newspapers, however. The billion-dollar communications conglomerate that had purchased the *Sun* in the 1970s was hemorrhaging money. Newspapers had once been a license to print money; those days were gone. Classified ads, help wanteds, car ads, all of the staples that had made publishers and stockholders rich, had been stolen by online sites. Newspapers had little to offer anymore that was unique.

So as profits plummeted, corporate newspaper owners did the only thing they could: slashed expenses to keep the bottom line from sinking through the floor. That meant obliterating people who had devoted their lives to the business, and piling two or three jobs on the ones who survived the cuts. It was an ugly time. Z had hung on somehow, although he wasn't sure how. He suspected the executive editor, Molly Thaves, felt sorry for him, had a misplaced loyalty to someone who had spent so much time in community journalism. He had been the manager of his own department, running the lifestyles section and its eight employees. But the cuts had gutted the section and Z had faced extinction. Instead, Thaves had laid off the assistant city editor, a sexy twenty-something named Delia Shelley who all the men in the newsroom drooled over, and installed him in the position. Thaves had never liked Delia, who spoke her mind too often and had no fear of the executive editor.

Z's new job required a cosmic shift in responsibilities and lifestyle. As a section editor, he usually worked Monday through Friday, 8 a.m. to 6 or 7 p.m. Now he worked nights and Saturdays. His family hated the change has much as he did, but he had no choice but to take the position. Where would he find another job at his age? And anyway, there were no jobs to be had. He sucked it up and threw himself into his new duties.

The problem was he had little left in the tank. The unyielding demands of the assistant city editor job overwhelmed him. The only explanation he could give Anna as he sank deeper and deeper into depression was, "I'm exhausted." Compounding his woes was the fact that he no longer reported directly to Molly Thaves, but was working under the city editor, Otto Hellinger. Hellinger was a huge, gruff-talking man of German descent, nearly twenty years Z's junior. He had a sometimes violent temper, possessed no patience for anything short of perfection in his employees, and was constantly complaining about "the reporters" as if they were some sort of necessary evil. Hellinger had never liked Z and had always looked on running the lifestyle section as a vacation. He made no secret about the fact he was displeased about him replacing Delia Shelley.

The rumor around the newsroom was that Hellinger was hopelessly infatuated with Delia, although she never encouraged it and took every opportunity to talk about her current boyfriend when Hellinger was around. The reporters universally disliked the city editor. Z knew this because they were constantly coming to him with complaints, feeling he offered a sympathetic ear. He would listen and try to offer constructive advice, but never took part in bashing Hellinger. In spite of everything, he felt that would be disloyal. Z hated the man but knew he had a very difficult job and was doing it the best way he knew how.

When Z got to his desk just after noon, he started going through the dozens of e-mails that had arrived overnight. His stomach quivered with each one. There was often a time bomb waiting to go off, a question about a story he'd edited or a mistake he'd let through or a story that was missed on his shift. His nerves were so tight these days he often vomited before leaving for work, wondering what new horrors would await him in the *Sun* office.

Hellinger, who had been out getting a sandwich for lunch, came blustering into the room, looking grim. His flat, oversized face was twisted into a mask of displeasure. He was not a person who disguised his emotions well. As he passed Z's desk, he growled, "I need to see you in the conference room. Now."

Z felt his knees go weak. He wanted to walk down the back stairs and never look back. Instead, he followed Hellinger into the conference room like a lamb to slaughter. As soon as the door closed, the city editor's voice dropped to a fierce near-whisper and he said, "What the hell happened last night?"

Z had no idea what he was talking about. "I don't know. What happened last night?"

"Have you been on our site today?"

He felt his face turning red. "Not yet, no."

The DEATH of OBSESSION

"Well there's a story on there about a fatal fire in Poughkeepsie that started at 6 last night. That's plenty of time for us to get it into today's paper. Only guess what, I open today's paper and there's nothing in there about the fire."

"Otto, nothing came across the scanner ..."

"I find that hard to believe. Especially since the Middletown paper had it on page one today." He threw a copy of the competitor's paper in front of him. There, on the front page, was a screamer that said "Fatal Poughkeepsie fire, story on page 3." Z felt sick. He had no idea what to say. He waited for Hellinger to continue.

"Didn't Quinn make the evening cop calls last night?"

Again, he felt his face burning. "I thought he did."

Hellinger slammed his hammy fist on the table. "You can't think, Michael, you have to know. That's your job. Do you realize how stupid this makes us look? Middletown gets a Poughkeepsie fatal and we don't. Jesus! Molly was all over me this morning. And what am I supposed to tell her? Michael *thought* the cop calls were made. Michael *thought* nothing came over the scanner."

"Otto, do you realize how many things I have to do to put this paper to bed every night? It's insane."

"If you can't handle it—"

"I didn't say that."

He glared at Z through cold blue eyes. Z had the impression that if he could, Hellinger would have grabbed him by the throat. "Priorities, Michael. It's up to you to make sure all the bases are covered before this paper goes to print. Missing a story like this is not acceptable. Delia would never let something like this slip through the cracks."

Ah, your precious Delia. "Otto, that's not fair. Things are different now. We're down so many people—"

"Excuses! God damn it, excuses don't get the paper out. Excuses don't cut it with our readers. Either you can do this or you can't."

Z felt the room twisting around him and thought he might puke right in front of Hellinger. Instead he said, "It won't happen again."

"It *can't* happen again," Hellinger spewed. "I'm writing you up for this."

"I understand," Z said lamely.

5.

Z sat alone in the kitchen drinking Jack from a thick glass with the company's logo etched into it. He downed several fingers of bourbon and refilled the glass. He was enjoying the late-morning quiet; the television and radio were all off. The only noise came from an occasional car whirring past on the wet street. The rain had stopped about a half hour earlier. He liked rainy mornings because they often matched his mood.

Despite the fact that he had to leave for work soon and should be getting in the shower, he continued sitting at the kitchen table and gulping Jack. The thought of facing the newsroom made him sick. His hatred for Otto Hellinger bubbled to the surface and he leaned back in the chair, staring at the ceiling. How could he possibly go on? It seemed impossible. Anyway, how long would it be before he became a casualty of the *Sun's* corporate cuts?

His only consolation was that Sophie was going to do better than him, be smarter than him. She was going to become a special education teacher and work for twenty-five years and retire with a nice pension. And she was going to do something that made a difference to people. He wondered now if anything he'd done as a journalist had accomplished any good. When he got into the business, Watergate was still fresh and being a reporter seemed like a way to make the world right. But the new century had been unkind to newspapers and they had fallen out of favor. They were like dinosaurs, waiting for the comet to hit.

As he drank more bourbon, his mind wandered to the issue that was truly gnawing at him: Crystal Cassidy. He couldn't get their lunch meeting out of his head. The memory made him want to vomit. How could he have agreed to see her? Then again, how could he have turned her down? He needed something from her that he had never been able to get: answers. Why he thought things would be any different thirty years later was a mystery. And what goddamn wound in his soul was he trying to heal by getting her to explain why she had ripped out his heart? It just *was*. He had moved past it, had made a good life with Anna and his girls. But then came Crystal's phone call and he felt their past gnawing at him again. He had not learned anything in his long, twisted life.

She drives up in a sleek, silver Mercedes and makes a show out of getting out of the car. My heart is pounding, waiting to see what she looks like. As she approaches me, I take a quick assessment. Her black hair is cut stylishly short, accentuating her angular face. She is dressed in a black business suit with rose silk shirt underneath. Her ears are studded with diamonds, not the large gold hoops she used to favor. She's wearing low heels with open toes. As she gets closer, I notice she's gotten plumper over the years, but she isn't fat. It's obvious to me that she's had a boob job. Her big sloppy tits are now pressed tighter to her body, but are still prominent. Overall, she looks good for a fifty-something woman who, by all accounts, has lived a somewhat hard life. Externally, she seems to have it all together.

"Hi, Mikey," she says as she reaches me at the front of the restaurant. She gives me a big hug, which is awkward at first but then becomes more relaxed. She smells nice, clean with just a hint of perfume. As she pulls back and looks at me, I can see her big brown eyes are as lively as ever.

"You look great," I say.

She smiles. Her teeth, obviously reconstructed for a great deal of money, are perfect and white. "So do you," she says.

"Yeh, bullshit."

She laughs. "Mikey. It's good to see you."

I realize as we walk inside that I would fuck her in a minute given half a chance. It makes my head spin, thinking about getting her into bed again. I've never forgotten the intense orgasms she gave me. Anna and I had great sex when we were younger, but it's been years since our lovemaking has been anything but bland and mechanical.

Sex with Crystal was always amazing. At least that's how I remember it.

It's a cool, sunny day, and we decide to sit out on the deck overlooking the lake. The water is tranquil and silvery. It makes me feel calm. When the waitress comes, I order a draft beer and ask Crystal what she wants.

"Seltzer with lime," she says. When the waitress leaves, Crystal smiles at me and adds, "I don't drink much anymore. Never during the day."

"Good for you," I tell her.

"I got tired of living like that. How are you doing?"

"If you mean am I still smoking pot every day, no. I got tired of that, too. I haven't touched it in years. I have to admit I still miss it sometimes, though."

"You miss living in J Suite and having no responsibilities."

"That too."

6.

The Zinarellis' neighbor, Earth Farmer, wished in her early years that she had a normal name: Michelle Farmer or Samantha Farmer. Kids laughed at her name and because she hated meeting people for the first time ("What's *your* name?") she stayed mostly to herself. Her worst days were the first day of class, when the teacher would go around the room taking that initial attendance: James Ellington ... Here; Lisa Exeter ... Here; Earth Farmer ... laughter. She especially despised those progressive teachers who made each kid stand up and offer a personal introduction. "Tell us your name and a little bit about yourself." Faced with such a prospect in the third grade, she had fled the room in tears when it was her turn, refusing to return to class until her mother came to the school and calmed her down.

Slowly, she grew immune to the snickers and taunts. She was smarter than most of her classmates and she knew it—this began to give her a boldness and sense of invincibility beyond her age. By fifth grade, no one made fun of her—or her younger sisters, Air and Water—for fear of being caught in the crosshairs of her acid tongue. *Bob.*

The DEATH of OBSESSION

Wow. That's such an original name. Your parents must be poets.

Her parents, in fact, were poets—and artists and avid gardeners and a dozen other things. She had never known either of her parents to have a "real" job. For one thing, the Farmers lived a spartan existence. They grew much of their own food, made their own clothes, didn't even own a television or a single cell phone between them. And then there was Max Farmer's financial acumen. What started as a tragedy—the sudden death in a car crash of Cyndey Farmer's parents—turned into a life-changing opportunity for the Farmers. Max took some of the sizeable life insurance check and invested it in gold just before it went from about $100 an ounce to nearly $700 an ounce. He cleared more than $100,000 after selling at the perfect time about three years later. And although he'd never again make a single strike so large or so quick, he was inspired to become an investor, earning enough to keep his family independent and allowing himself to remain out of the mainstream.

It was ironic that Max Farmer supported himself trading in the maw of capitalism. As a rebellious teen, he had violently denounced the "international financial tyranny" as corrupt and oppressive. He and his friends would smoke joints and talk about bombing the Stock Exchange, about seeing all the suits stumble out of the wreckage charred and choking. But now he had no qualms about playing their game and winning it. He was glad to take their filthy money and do something life-affirming with it. Their filthy money allowed him to spend hours a day tending to the tomatoes and cucumbers and peppers in his garden, allowed him to write an epic poem for each of his daughters, which he planned to give them in his final days, allowed him to make love to his wife at mid-morning or early afternoon or whenever the mood took them.

Cyndey Farmer still enjoyed making love to her husband, even though they were both in their 50s now. He held her with arms strong from digging and hammering, entered her with an ardor that made her feel 22 again, knew how and when to position himself to make her see stars. She could not imagine her life without Max. She could not conceive how things might have unfolded if she'd never met him. There'd be no Earth, no Air, no Water, no small and perfect corner of the world she could call her own. She loved watering her flowers, creating clothes from scraps of material, baking carrot cake from carrots she grew herself. She was mostly happy, a quiet and steady kind of happiness, and her most stinging moments of pain came when she wished her parents had lived to see how she had turned out, how her family had blossomed. But her parents knew somehow. She believed that.

Earth didn't think about her grandparents very much. They were dead before she was born. Cyndey never talked about them much, seemed overwhelmed by the subject. As for Max's parents, there was even less to tell. His mother died when he was an infant—it was horrible, he had heard from voices quivering with terrified excitement even years later, the picture of health one day and the walking dead a few weeks later. He swore to himself he recalled her moaning and weeping and cursing God, but that was impossible, he was too young, and he had no memory at all of her actual death.

Funny thing was, he didn't remember much about his father's death, either, even though Milo Farmer died of a heart attack when Max was sixteen. After that, Max was raised by his older brother until he graduated from high school and hit the road with a backpack and the money he'd saved from his job washing dishes at the hotel restaurant.

For Earth Farmer, history began when Max met Cyndey. Nothing existed before that seminal moment. The alignment of the planets Maxibus and Cyndeytia at the precisely correct moment in 1978 at the Saratoga Jazz Festival had been told and retold around family campfires, each in their turn—Earth, Air and Water—begging for it again and again just once more. Max delighted in telling the story at first, his brown eyes ablaze as he talked about tossing a Frisbee to a girl with straw-colored hair and watching her reach up to catch it and thinking as he saw her leg muscles ripple: *she's a goddess*. But after the first telling, and sometimes partway through, he would tire of talking and lean back against the ground and close his eyes.

Coaxed by her daughters, Cyndey would pick up the narrative, filling in the small details her husband often glossed over: How he had taken her aside and shared the last of a joint with her; how they had walked barefoot in the warm grass talking about Chick Corea and Larry Coryell and Flora Purim; how he had spent the last of his money buying her a plastic cup of wine and they had shared it under a tree, listening to music float up from the bowl of the amphitheater. They kissed—slowly, she remembered, softly. From there, their lives came together as if scripted. They were married three months later, although Cyndey's parents implored her to wait, to think it over, to get to know this Max character better. But they didn't wait. They knew from those first moments this was where it would lead.

For as long as she could remember, Earth had wanted a moment like her mother's, to feel the universe open and have someone step through and take her hand, lead her away on the stairs of a late-June breeze. In her more rational moments, she knew it was a ridiculous thought. Guys her age were morons. They couldn't talk about anything except sports, video games, and bad movies—and themselves, of course. That was a subject on which they were all well versed.

She'd had a few boyfriends—a serious one in high school, Jared, to whom she had lost her virginity, and a few in college that had started out promising but quickly fizzled. She was the one who always lost interest, who allowed the relationships to spiral down to nothing. Ultimately, she did not blame the guys. They were flowers without scent, stones with no density. It was not their fault. Truth was: she'd never been in love. Not really. Not like her parents. She wanted that.

But she was sure she'd never find it. The odds, after all, were against it. In her eyes, most guys were jerks. They couldn't get out of the way of their own pricks. Even a seemingly harmless man like Mr. Z looked at her with the glazed expression of lust. Even if he weren't older than her father and completely unattractive to her, she would never even consider sleeping with him. He was the husband of her friend, Anna, and she could never betray Anna that way. It made her shiver, thinking of Mr. Z fantasizing about her.

Anna loved him. Earth knew that. They were going through a rough patch right now, but things would work out. They had to. Anna loved him. And there were the girls to think about.

Chapter Two
The Incredible Intelligence of Pigs

I am fond of pigs. Dogs look up to us. Cats look down on us. Pigs treat us as equals.
—Winston Churchill

1.

I slept with Crystal Cassidy the same night I met her—within hours, actually. It was at a dorm party, a drunken, joint-worshipping ritual worthy of Dionysus. We were ready to tear human flesh from the bone with our teeth. I'm exaggerating slightly, but remember, this was a time of revelry: The Age of Aquarius was dead—we knew we weren't going to save the world with love and flowers—but Nixon had been fucked by Woodward and Bernstein and everything was up for grabs. Everybody had the Bomb and we didn't know if they'd use it and we didn't know if we'd live to be 30, so what the hell. Our parents bathed in their stability but we knew better, we knew stability was an illusion because if the goddamn Chinese decided tomorrow they were going to end the world (and this particular cycle of history), we were going to be a pile of ashes. So everyone was smoking pot and snorting coke, even geeks and brainiacs, even future judges and bank executives and United States senators. It was not a time of restraint.

I floated from room to room, my head expanding with each stop. A twisted mélange of music filled the halls; Little Feat meets the Beatles' *White Album* meets Pink Floyd. The corridor hung suspended in a cloud of smoke and the pungent aroma of burning cannabis. In Shank's room, I plopped down on the bed and watched him licking papers together so he could create a conduit for the spliff he planned to roll. Weather Report's electric fusion crackled through his speakers as Rick Cramer and Billy Thoms rocked their heads back and forth. Dave Shankman was the only guy I knew cool enough to own a Weather Report album, let alone play it at a party. He didn't care. His cool came from the deep.

"Shank, this is amazing," Billy said. Billy was an art major who drank in anything unconventional. His drawings were weird and unpolished, but kind of interesting: a praying mantis biting off the pope's head, a teenage girl being raped by Jesus.

"I don't get it, but I think I like it," Cramer said. That could have been Cramer's motto for life. He was a big old farm boy from upstate New York who pretended to love and understand beer and little else. He was a junior who had been on the verge of flunking out since his first semester, but had somehow survived. Everybody liked him the way you embrace a mascot.

"The Report," Shank said over his shoulder, as if that explained it all.

"The Report," Cramer echoed, chugging down the rest of the Molson in his bottle. He tossed the dead soldier into Shank's trash can and looked around for a replacement. He seemed dismayed.

I handed him my barely-touched Budweiser. "I'll grab another one later," I told him. "I'm fine for now."

He slapped my shoulder with his hammy hand. "Mikey Z, my buddy," he said, snatching the bottle from me.

"You need your nourishment," I said. Billy laughed.

Shank turned around, grinning and holding up a joint the size of a small child. "OK, boys, let's get high."

Billy laughed again and Cramer started bouncing on the bed, nearly knocking me on my ass. Shank held the joint in his mouth, raised a Bic in a ceremonial manner and torched the end of the joint until it began to glow. He sucked in smoke, held in a cough, passed the sacred spliff to Cramer, who accepted it with reverence and took a monumental hit. His face turned red and he clamped his mouth shut as his chest pounded up and down, trying to get the smoke out.

The DEATH of OBSESSION

Wendy Gallardo came into the room holding a half-full bottle of tequila. She smiled when she saw the monster joint. Wendy and Shank's on-again, off-again two-year thing was legendary. We all thought they were a perfect couple; they seemed to be the only ones who didn't realize they'd end up together. Wendy was so blonde her hair was almost white. She had pale blue eyes, porcelain skin, and a classically sharp-featured face, with perfect jaw and small, straight nose. Her body was thin and tight like an athlete's. She did not look the type to be walking around with a bottle of tequila.

"What do we have here?" she shouted as she entered the room. Walking in behind her was her freshman protégé, Liz something-or-other, who had latched onto Wendy in September and followed her around like a handmaiden. Ever the sweetheart, Wendy had allowed herself to be adopted.

I took a hit and passed the joint to Wendy, who sucked on it eagerly and held the smoke in her lungs like a pro. When she breathed out the cloud, she took a long draw on the tequila and handed the bottle to Shank.

"This shit'll kill you," he said before he took a swig. We all laughed. Everybody loved Shank. He was handsome and friendly and smart (but not in a showy kind of way); most of all he was interesting—he could teach you things if you listened to him. Beyond that, he rolled the biggest joints I'd ever seen. How could you *not* love the guy?

Weather Report was weaving a saxophone-keyboard tapestry around us, and I leaned back on the bed, taking it in. When the tequila bottle came to me, I took a sip and passed it on. I was in a good place; I didn't need to be any higher just then. For the first time in a couple weeks, I was somewhat at peace, enjoying the tunes and the company, and not thinking about Maggie. The sore spot was still there, but it was numb for the moment.

"You grew up around animals on the farm, right?" Billy was saying to Cramer. "You think animals got an extra sense, like some people say? Like they can predict earthquakes and tell if people are gonna die, shit like that?"

Cramer grunted. "Animals are dumb bastards. All they know is eating and shitting and fucking ... sorta like me." He finished his beer—my beer—and waited for the laugh. I obliged him and so did Liz.

"Seriously though," Billy persisted. "Aren't there dogs that can, like, predict when people are going to have seizures?"

"Pigs are smarter than dogs, and we eat pigs. So figure that out. My father's a farmer. He doesn't give a shit about diplomas. You know why he sent me to college?"

Straight-faced, Billy said: "So you'd stop fucking the chickens?"

Shank and Wendy howled.

"That was only once. I was just curious. No, my father sent me here so I could outwit the pigs. He wants me to take over the farm someday, and he's afraid the pigs are going to bury me."

Liz moved over and sat next to him on the bed. She was stoned and giggling at everything he said. *Big man has a chance tonight*, I thought. Liz was no great beauty, she was kind of mousy and had no striking features (she often disappeared when she came into a room), but she was certainly worthy of a one-nighter and I couldn't imagine it would amount to more than that. At that moment, Liz was looking at Cramer like he was Apollo, her watery green eyes shining. Billy took the cue, stood up and wandered out into the hallway. Watching Wendy nestle on Shank's lap and Liz and Cramer eyeballing each other brought the Maggie sore spot to life; I started to feel the ache of her being somewhere else with someone else.

"I'm going to grab another beer," I said, bouncing off the bed.

"Bring me one," Cramer said.

"If I make it back this way."

Shank waved at me as I left. He was smiling broadly, stoned and snuggling with Wendy. All was well in the world.

Music still pounded the hallway, and people loitered about, holding drinks or beers or joints, talking in small groups or meandering in search of the right room to drop in on. There were a number of rooms and conversations I would have been welcomed into, but I still felt alone. Mags. That bitch I loved or thought I loved or thought loved me. My spirits leapt immediately when I saw Elise Mathieu walking my way. She was gorgeous in a white sweater and tight jeans, curly caramel hair falling around her bright, smooth-skinned face. She kissed my cheek and punched me in the arm.

"You look so sad, Z-man," she said. "Knock it off."

"I'm fine. Just spacing out."

She leaned against me, smelling of pot and soap and other delicious scents. I wanted to put my arms around her but knew better. "Bullshit. You're thinking about her again. Listen, I love Maggie, but there are other girls on this campus, Mikey. Stop feeling sorry for yourself." A nasty comeback crossed my mind, but I would have never said it to Elise. She had earned the right to say whatever she wanted. She had sat up with me for two straight nights when I was too upset to sleep, walking with me to the snack bar and eating stale candy and drinking greasy coffee. She listened a lot, offered sympathy when I needed it, tried to make me laugh when I started to cry. Her boyfriend, Frank Dutton, wasn't too happy with me spiriting her away in the middle of the night, but he was a friend and he understood my pain. Maggie was my first sleep-in girlfriend. During the three months we dated, I slept in her room several nights a week (she didn't have a roommate). It was amazing to have sex at my fingertips whenever I wanted it, to roll over and put my nose in her hair and feel myself getting hard against her thigh. No stupid come-ons or persuasion required. Just her open to me and pulling me in. And afterwards we'd fall back to sleep curled into spoons. This bliss lasted for three months before she unceremoniously dumped me. She gave no reason. That was the part that ate at me. I knew there *were* reasons and I wanted to know them, wanted to analyze them and poke my fingers into them. But she was finished with me and felt no need to discuss it further.

"El, I want her to love me again. Is that too much to ask?"

She rapped her knuckles against my forehead, as if knocking on a door. "Yes, Michael Zinarelli. It's way too much. Maggie has moved on, honey. That's what Maggie does. Face it. You're not the first underclassman she seduced."

Seduced I was. Maggie was a junior and I was a sophomore transfer, a year younger and a lot less experienced in the ways of love. When I arrived, I knew no one at the school, had transferred blindly to get back to New York state from a ridiculous Florida school. Mags picked me out of the pack and I was instantly accepted into her circle. I went from anonymous newcomer to part of the in-crowd with head-spinning swiftness. What she saw in me I'm not sure, but to this day I'm glad of it because those were among the happiest months of my life. Until our abrupt split.

"I'm sure I won't be the last," I said, unable to come up with something wittier.

"Oh, you're not the last Z-man," Elise told me, her words heavy with meaning.

"Who?"

"Todd Braden. She's been to bed with him three times this week."

"That prick? Jesus, El." I felt more deflated than ever. Braden was a freshman lacrosse player with the kind of preppy good looks I hated and a brash, get-out-of-my-way attitude. I avoided being in his company whenever possible. My high began to spiral down into depression.

She squeezed my arm consolingly. "That's why I'm saying move on. She's not worth the heartache. If it helps, she really did care about you when you guys were together. She told me you were one of the sweetest guys she ever dated. And she always bragged about how good you were in bed."

"Get out."

"I'm serious."

I should have been flattered, but the emptiness wouldn't go away. "I guess I wasn't good enough," I said.

She pushed me against the wall and put her hands on her hips. "You are pathetic, Mikey. Honest to God."

"I know."

She stepped closer and tenderly ran her hand through my hair. "I think I know something that's going to cheer you up."

"What?"

"I know somebody who wants to meet you. I was telling her about you and she said she'd be at the party tonight."

"Who is she?"

"Her name's Crystal. She lives across campus, so maybe you don't know her."

"Crystal what?"

"Cassidy. Crystal Cassidy."

"Nah, I don't think I know her."

"She's cute. Kind of wild, but smart, too, so I think you two would get along. And if she likes you, you won't be alone tonight. Trust me."

"Crystal Cassidy. Sounds interesting. Where is she?"

Elise smiled. Her smile was like sunshine after a storm. "Let's go find her." She kissed my cheek and we stared at each other for a few seconds. El. If only things had been different ... but things were what they were.

"What the hell is this?" Frank Dutton boomed.

Elise turned and threw her arm around Frank's neck, pulling him toward us until we made a tight little threesome. "I was telling Mikey about Crystal. We're going to go find her."

"I think I saw her in Chad's room." Frank's brown eyes were glistening and he was talking very slowly. Drunk or stoned or both. He put his hand on my shoulder and grinned. "You'll like her, man."

Frank was a short, stocky guy with a powerful chest and arms, long, scraggly brown hair (complete with unruly beard) and a twisted sense of humor that confused as often as it delighted us. Frank was a good guy, but I wondered if he deserved Elise. Nobody deserved Elise. Except me, maybe. But that wasn't where we were headed. We were cementing a lifelong friendship and I was pretty sure that's as far as it would go. What the hell. There were worse fates than having El for a friend the rest of my life.

She took both Frank and me by the arm and led us down the hallway, singing along to "Daddy Don't Live in that New York City No More," which was booming out of someone's room. I started to sing, too, and Frank finally joined in, totally off key and murdering the lyrics. We stopped in Charlie Maurice's room, where everyone was taking bong hits. Charlie was the only black guy in our dorm. He was a suave sonofabitch, thin but sinewy, with a finely sculpted goatee and chocolate eyes that could look right through you. He laughed when we came in and blew a cloud at the ceiling.

"Here comes the coolest white man in Sneaky Falls."

"Seein' the coolest black man anywhere."

Charlie and I had smoked a lot of weed together since September and had solved the mysteries of the universe many times, only to forget the answers the next morning. We shared a love of jazz and had done a little stoned jamming together—him on his electric keyboard, me on my bongos. For a few hours, everything else went away and we rode the music. We weren't very good, really, but good enough to keep ourselves amused.

"Try this," Charlie said, handing me the bong.

I filled my lungs with smoke while Charlie held the lighter to a small, hazel-colored rock and the water in the bong bubbled. The top of my head opened and laughter, light, and Miles Davis rushed in. I must have been paralyzed for a while, because the next thing I knew Charlie was yanking the bong out of my hand.

"Damn, bro, give it up."

We both started laughing our asses off for no apparent reason. Elise took the bong from Charlie and fired up a hit for her and Frank. The entire room was hazy with hash smoke. We nodded our heads to Miles' horn playing and said nothing, absorbing everything. Charlie's girlfriend, Sierra Enrique, sat in the corner reading Reinhold Niebuhr's *Moral Man and Immoral Society*. I told her it was an interesting book and she smiled a small smile. To me, she was fascinating: half Cuban, half Mexican, a bronze-skinned goddess with melon-shaped tits and a voluptuous ass and long black hair that tumbled around her head. Her eyes were huge, green-brown orbs and her lips were thick and moist. I wondered what they would feel like.

"An irrational society accepts injustice because it does not analyze the pretensions made by the powerful and

The DEATH of OBSESSION

privileged groups of society," Sierra read aloud, looking up at me when she had finished the sentence.

"The greatest ideal is unselfishness," I said. It was the only quote from the book I remembered.

"Highest," she said. "The *highest* ideal."

I waved her correction away. "How many times have you read that fucker?"

She flashed her white-white teeth and returned to the book.

I felt Elise's hand on my wrist. She pulled me to my feet and said, "C'mon, we've got people to see."

Back in the hallway, I was walking three inches above the carpet. Only Elise's grip kept me from floating away. I considered going back to my room and allowing the rest of the night to spin away into oblivion. The thought of meeting someone new and trying to seduce her seemed a monumental effort beyond anything I could muster. But El wasn't about to let me go before she implemented her plan. She was going to get me laid whether I cooperated or not.

Chad Patrick's room was relatively quiet. *Abbey Road* was playing softly and Frank started singing "Mean Mister Mustard" way too loud. The first thing I noticed when we entered was a short girl with long, glistening raven hair holding court in the middle of the room. Three guys were gathered around her and she was regaling them with a bawdy story in an assertive but slightly slurred voice. She had an enticing New England accent and gesticulated wildly while she talked.

"His dick's hangin' out of his pants and Martha is standin' in the doorway, screamin' 'What the hell!' I thought I'd piss myself. And he's tryin' to give her some lame explanation with his little peckah swingin' around."

She took a swig from a glass filled with gin or vodka and a few ice cubes. The guys were falling over themselves with laughter. Chad was one of them, and he kept rubbing her arm while she spoke. Didn't look good for me. If this was Crystal, I might have been too late. Undaunted, Elise pushed herself into the center of the circle and began talking to the short girl. El pointed toward me and Crystal (yes, it was her) glanced over her shoulder, appraising me with deep brown eyes. Her face instantly etched itself in my brain. Smooth olive skin; small, straight nose; wide, sensuous mouth. She turned back to Elise and said something.

A minute later, she was standing in front of me. That's how I met Crystal Cassidy. Not met as much as had her handed to me on a platter. We exchanged names and touched hands. Hers was small and warm. I couldn't help but notice her tits. They seemed too big for her short muscular body, pushing aggressively against her green sweater. Her dark chocolate eyes devoured me. My legs felt weak.

We made small talk for a couple minutes, asking about classes and professors without interest. I couldn't think of anything clever to say and I felt I was losing her quickly. Again, Elise stepped in. "You should see Mikey's fish tank," she said. "It's really cool."

"I love fish," she said. "Eat 'em every Friday."

I laughed nervously. "These ain't eating fish," I said. "These are looking fish. You watch them for a while and guaranteed it'll drop your blood pressure. Very soothing."

I felt a bit like a phony because the fish weren't even mine. They belonged to my ex-roommate, Bret Bradley, who had quit school at the end of the first semester, leaving me with a single room and bequeathing me his aquarium because he didn't want to bother taking it home.

"I could use some soothin'," she said.

"Let's go take a look. Calm you right down."

In a prodigious gulp, she downed the rest of what was in her glass and refilled it from a bottle sitting on Chad's dresser. She took my arm and said, "Let's go." *It can't be this easy,* I thought. The flesh of my arm was tingling where she touched it. She kept talking (about what, I have no recollection) as we walked down the hallway. My room was a floor below, and as we were walking down the deserted stairwell, she leaned over and kissed my cheek. I turned toward her and kissed her full on the mouth, a long, slow kiss with lips slightly parted. The kiss was moist and full of promises.

My room was relatively quiet, since most of the partying was on the third floor. We stood in front of the aquarium, pretending to look at the fish. I made up goofy names for

The DEATH of OBSESSION

them and she laughed obligingly. "And these two are Ralph and Alice," I said, referring to a pair of zebra fish.

"You like the Honeymooners?" she said, dragging out the end of the word so her accent made it sound like Honeymoonahs.

"You kidding? It's only my favorite show."

"Bang! Zoom!" She threw her fist through the air a la Jackie Gleason.

I kissed her again, this one longer and with our tongues searching for each other. When we disentangled, I said. "You wanna hear some music?"

"Yeh. Can I pick?"

Before I could answer, she dropped to her knees and started flipping through my albums, which were stacked neatly on the floor in a few milk cartons. While she ran her fingers through my music collection, I went to my top dresser drawer and pulled out my stash and a small stone pipe. I closed the door and locked it. She didn't seem to notice. I filled the bowl and took a hit of sweet Hawaiian weed.

"Yes," Crystal said, waving an album above her head, "I love Grovah." It was Grover Washington Jr.'s *Mister Magic*, a perfect choice for what I imagined (hoped) was going to happen next. I took the vinyl out of its sleeve and placed it on the turntable. I eased the needle into the groove and Grover's sweet sax playing filled the room.

I offered Crystal a hit from the pipe, and she took it without enthusiasm. She seemed much more interested in working on her drink, which was already half empty again. We sat next to each other on the bed and all pretenses disappeared. We were not here to look at fish or talk about old TV shows. We melted into each other simultaneously, lips and tongues fusing. I rubbed her side, her belly and then her huge tits, squeezing and massaging until her nipples were poking up against the sweater. She pulled away from me, yanked the sweater over her head and undid her bra. Two heavy, slightly drooping breasts tumbled out. I attacked them like a starving man, licking, sucking, running my hands all over them. She moaned and moved her hand along my thigh, rubbing my crotch until I thought I'd burst through my jeans. We threw off our clothes and crawled beneath the sheets, touching each other the whole time.

My hand went between her legs and I opened her gently, running my finger along the wetness. She had me in her hand and was pumping hard. I felt like I might come then and there, but I told myself *no, no*. I moved on top of her and slid inside like we were born to fuse. Her hips thrashed against me and she was making small sounds in the back of her throat. My cock was so swollen every drop of blood in my body must have been flowing into it. I leaned down and licked her nipples while I exploded inside her, a flash of white taking the top of my head off. She kept bucking against me, drenching my cock with her juice. Her pussy squeezed me again and again, until I finally went soft. I rolled off her and we snuggled quietly, both realizing, I supposed, that we had just experienced monumental lovemaking. She kissed the side of my face and drew her fingers along my flaccid cock. I understood we were not finished. We made love twice more that night, each time longer and more intense.

2.

I rose through several layers of contented stupor until I came awake. The first thing I realized was that Crystal Cassidy was not next to me. I looked up and saw her sitting in a chair, pulling on her socks. She was dressed in her green sweater and jeans, looking as if she were prepared to leave. A knot in my stomach told me I didn't want her to go, but I wasn't sure about the protocol of such things. Was it unseemly to show any affection or attachment after a one-nighter? Would she laugh at me if I said something even slightly sentimental about our fantastic night?

"Hey," I said, just to say something.

She jerked her head up and gave me a tiny smile. "Hey."

"Where you going?" I knew I shouldn't have asked, but the words just poured out of my mouth before I could stop them.

Crystal shrugged slightly and started putting on her other sock. "I thought I'd head over to the library for a while and study for my sociology test. I got a real nutcracker Monday."

In the soft morning light of February in the Finger Lakes, she seemed smaller and a little sad. Was she embarrassed? Unsure how I would react to her now? I jumped out of bed and stood behind the chair she was in. She was tying her shoe. I reached down and draped my arms around her from the back. She stiffened at first, then put her hands on my arms.

"Last night was amazing," I told her. I figured it was not the time to leave anything unsaid. If this was it, I wanted her to know how much the night meant to me.

She turned to look at me, her face blank. Then her lips twisted upward slightly. "You were a good boy," she said. Her black hair, uncombed and wild, tumbled around her dark, intense face and made my heart skip a couple beats. I wanted to carry her back to the bed, but instead leaned down and kissed the top of her head.

"It's Sunday morning," I said. "You don't want to go to the library now. Let's go to the dining hall and get some breakfast, and you can study later." I wanted to prolong our time together, though I wasn't sure what my goal was. To have her spend the night again? To have her fall in love with me? I was acting, not thinking.

"The dining hall? That crap?" Before I could respond, she said: "What the hell, at least I can get a cup of coffee." She stood up, grabbed her purse, and headed for the door without waiting for me. "I left my jacket upstairs. Be right back."

It seemed a long time before she returned. I filled my pipe and took a couple hits. Where was she? Maybe she changed her mind and decided to head back to her room. Finally, she stuck her head through the door and said, "C'mon." I followed and didn't bother to lock my door as I hurried after her. I watched her ass swinging back and forth before I caught up to her.

On the way across the snowy campus, we talked about our families. I told her my dad was an engineer at IBM and my mom didn't work any more. I had a brother and a sister, both younger than me. She said her father was involved in construction and she had an older brother who was doing masters work in mathematics. When she said nothing about her mother, I looked over at her and she said, as if anticipating my question, "My mom died when I was fifteen."

Our feet crunched through the snow. I tried to think of something to say, but could only manage: "I'm sorry."

She shook her head. "We never really got along. I mean, I loved her, she was my mom. But she didn't like me very much. She was always yellin' at me and my father. We wasn't perfect, like her. Only Conor lived up to her standards. God, he balled like a baby the day she died. I think I cried a little, but I don't really remember much. She'd been dying for a long time, so I was ready for it. She had cancer. It was so bad."

I put my arm around her and she neither pulled away nor moved toward me. She let me hug her as we walked. On the red wooden bridge over a small pond halfway to the dining hall, Woody Sweet sat on the railing, his freckled face burning red from the cold wind. "Z-maaaaaaaaaaaaaaan!" he shrieked, shaking his long, red hair like a primitive. I chuckled.

Woody was Raymond Sweet from Woodstock, hence his nickname. He had a well-earned reputation as a madman. Since September, I had seen him: put a pool ball entirely in his mouth; eat a candy bar from the vending machine without taking off the wrapper; and leap from a third floor window headfirst into a snow bank. He was not going to survive his freshman year, amassing a D average for the fall semester and off to a worse start for the spring. I was going to miss him.

"Woods, what's up?"

He launched himself dramatically from the railing and landed noisily in front of Crystal. She flinched. "And who do we have here?" he asked, and before I answered he took her hand and planted a kiss on it. "Raymond Sweet of Woodstock, at your service."

She couldn't help but smile. "Crystal Cassidy from the great city of Baastin."

"Baastin?" he mimicked her. "You know what's great about Baastin?"

"What?"

"Oh, you don't know either." He howled an obnoxious laugh. She glowered at him but he didn't see it because he had turned toward me. "That was some bitchin' party last night, huh?"

"Where were you? I didn't see you all night."

"We scored an eight-ball and spent most of the night snorting and smoking in Teddy's room. By the time we got to wandering around, a lot of people were gone. Including you." He glanced over at Crystal. "I see your time was well spent."

I ignored the remark because I thought it might embarrass Crystal. "You shit, why didn't you tell me you were getting blow? I would have gone in with you."

"We might do it again today. I'll let you know."

"Sounds good."

Crystal was tugging at my sleeve. "C'mon. I'm cold," she said.

I was a little annoyed at her impatience, but I let her pull me forward a few steps. "Off to the dining hall," I told Woody.

"I already had my swill."

"Catch you later."

As we got to the end of the bridge, Crystal mumbled, "What a freakin' A-hole."

"Ah, that's just Woods. He'll grow on you."

"Not likely."

We walked in silence for a few yards, the cold lake wind making us put our heads down. Abruptly, we were stopped in our tracks by a blood-curdling scream. I whipped my head around and saw Woody standing on the bridge railing, waving his arms above his head. He screamed again and then leaped into the air, churning his arms and legs until he crashed through the thin layer of ice on the pond and splashed into the water. Crystal stood there with her mouth open. I started laughing and clapping my hands. The handful of other people in the vicinity were clapping and hooting. Woody stood up—the water only reached his waist—and took an exaggerated bow.

"Refreshing," he shouted, and as everyone cheered again he raised his arms triumphantly.

"That boy has a problem," Crystal said, but her tone had softened and there was a hint of affection in it. Woody had that effect on people. You could be turned off by his loudness or his bizarre behavior, but something endearing about him shone through. In the end, how could you not like the guy?

The dining hall was sparsely populated by the time we arrived. A few knots of people were scattered at the tables, talking quietly, drinking coffee, eating rubbery eggs. Elise and Frank were sitting with Shank, Wendy, and Billy. I saw neither Cramer nor Liz. Had the big man scored? I filled a plate with scrambled eggs, a bagel, and some potatoes, drew a cup of coffee, and headed toward my friends. Crystal was close behind, carrying coffee and nothing else.

We exchanged greetings and sat at the end of the table. Elise and Crystal traded looks but said nothing. Frank was wolfing down a huge plate of eggs smothered in ketchup and barely glanced at us. Elise was picking at some sort of fruit concoction and drinking a glass of milk. Her skin was smooth and white in the harsh dining hall light, and I thought how lucky Frank was to be able to touch it whenever he wanted, wherever he wanted.

Crystal surprised me by opening her purse, taking out a pack of cigarettes and lighting one. It was the first time I'd seen her smoke. She dragged on it and sipped black coffee.

"God, I could use a smoke," Wendy said. "You mind?"

Crystal slid the Marlboros across the table to her, tossed her the lighter.

"Thanks."

I ate my eggs slowly, between bites relating the story of Woody jumping off the bridge. Everybody laughed and shook their heads—a typical reaction to Woods. Crystal didn't appear to be listening, in fact she seemed removed from everything going on around her. At one point, she reached onto my tray and, without asking, picked up my buttered bagel and took a bite. I was glad she felt so at ease with me already, but I was also a bit annoyed at her presumptuousness. I didn't like people handling my food. Never had. Did she notice I left the bagel untouched after that?

I was still a little lightheaded after my night of heavy partying and intense sex. The coffee was hot and strong and steadied me as I gulped it. "Where's Cramer?" I asked the table in general.

Elise smiled at me slyly and shrugged. "Haven't seen him this morning."

"I think the big guy hit one out."

"He left Shank's room with Liz," Wendy chimed in. "I think they'd be cute together."

"Yeh, she looks a little like a chicken," Billy said.

Crystal snorted out a laugh and Wendy reached over and punched Billy in the arm, but she was grinning. "You're such a cynical bastard," she said.

"I can just see them together," he said, warming to the audience. He started flapping his arms, squealing, "Bawk, bawk, baaaaawk, oh baby, fill my eggs, bawk baaaaaawk." The more we laughed, the more he exaggerated the flapping.

"Billy, you're so bad," Elise said, giggling.

"Don't do that with Cramer around or he'll drag you out to the chicken coop and make you his hen," I added.

The dining hall aides started flicking the lights off and on, letting us know it was time to clear out so they could start preparing for lunch. "What's everybody doing?" Elise asked, but no one was interested in continuing last night's party. There were groans about papers due, exams coming up, reading that had to be done. It was time for a day of quiet contemplation and taking care of some business.

"I'm going to play racquetball," Shank said. "I need to sweat out all the crap I've been putting in my system."

"You need, like, eight years of racquetball," Billy told him.

"Fuck you, Thoms."

We left the dining hall, heading back out into the biting wind. The cold snapped me wide awake, and I glanced at Crystal, who was walking quietly beside me, head down. "So what're you gonna do?" I asked her.

She shrugged. "What about you?"

"Come back to my room," I said on an impulse. "You can study there. I've got a shitload of reading to do, so I won't bug you."

"I need to get my books."

"So get your books."

She put both hands on my arm. "Come with me."

"OK."

Crystal's dorm was in the opposite direction from mine, so we shifted course and headed back toward the north side of campus. As we walked, she snuggled against me as if trying to warm herself. I felt myself growing to monstrous proportions, a bad motherfucker who had conquered this hot little mama. My arms were pythons, my legs tree trunks, my cock an unyielding piston. I kissed her hair, which smelled of stale perfume and smoke. More than anything, I wanted to get her back to my room. We talked quietly on our way across the frozen campus. She asked me my major, and when I told her literature she said, "Why?" I said what I really wanted to do was write short stories and someday a novel. I told her I'd gotten a story published in the campus literary magazine, but she didn't seem very impressed. Still, she asked to read it.

As we approached her dorm, she said, "I hope my roommate's not there."

"Why not?"

"Ah, she's all pissed off at me."

"How come?"

She shook her head. "It's stupid. She thinks I slept with this guy she likes. Dave Nye. They ain't goin' out or nothin', but she's gettin' all possessive about him."

"Did you?"

"Did I what?"

"Sleep with him."

She paused, debating whether to answer. "Like, six months ago. It was just once. I'm tellin' ya, he was nothin' to write home about, either. But, hell, I let it slip to Ruthie that it happened and she went ballistic on me. I didn't even know she liked him back then. It's just crazy."

Ruth George was a sweet little thing, about five feet tall, with a slim, tight body, chestnut hair and wide, azure eyes. I'd had a Chinese history class with her in the fall semester and had admired her from afar. In class, she was quiet and answered thoughtfully whenever called upon by Professor Chu. It was difficult to imagine her going ballistic on anyone. It was also hard to imagine *any* guy ignoring her overtures. Who the hell was this Dave Nye? I didn't know him, but he had to be an idiot not to jump all over Ruth George.

To Crystal's great relief, her room was empty when she opened the door. I could see her sigh visibly, allowing a small smile to curl her full lips. The room could best be described as spartan. There were no posters on the walls, no photos on the desks; a total lack of personal items anywhere. It was like they were biding their time here and refused to become emotionally involved. This ascetic space made me sad.

Crystal picked up a fat textbook, a notebook, and a highlighter and tossed them into an oversized canvas bag. "Shit," she said. "I wish I didn't have to come back here. Ruthie's makin' me feel so uncomfortable."

I saw my opening and plunged ahead. "Listen, why don't you spend a few nights in my room? By then, this'll all blow over."

She stared at me for a few seconds then said, "Yeah?"

"It'll be fun."

She had, I realized, easily manipulated me into asking, but now she hesitated as if saying yes too quickly might diminish her. "I don't know," she said slyly. "Do you think you can take me for another night?"

I put my arms around her, pressed my forehead against hers. "I'll take the chance," I said softly.

"I guess I better bring some things," she said, disentangling from me. She rifled through her drawers, tossing items into the bag. She worked quickly, knowing exactly what she wanted and needed. The last thing she grabbed was an unopened bottle of vodka from the top shelf of her closet. There was just enough room for it in the bag. "Let's go, baby," she said, voice full of tenderness. Her spirits seemed elevated by the promise of a new adventure. I had no clue what a ride it would be.

Chapter Three
Tricks of Time

Time, space: necessity. Fate, fortune, chance: all snares of life.
—Luigi Pirandello

1.

Michael Zinarelli's daughter, Sophie, wanted to be a teacher, and he approved of that. If he had it to do over again, he'd probably get into teaching. Had he done that, he'd be getting ready to retire with a nice pension. But no, he was seduced by writing for newspapers and seeing his name in print. He could write a story and, wow, there was his byline the next day. And often people would call to react to it—good or bad. He was in love with having people talk about his words.

Now he was a fading journalist in a profession that was dying. He felt like a Pony Express rider in the last days before the telegraph made the job obsolete. *In the end, what did we devote so much to?* He heard people say there would always be a need for storytellers, for news gatherers. It would just take a different form. Everything would be electronic and available right now—hell, it already was. Blogs and tweets and all other manner of instant communication. He hated it. He wanted ink and paper and the thought that went into sweating over a sentence, over a word—*le mot juste*. The world was losing that. It broke his heart.

He supposed he was a reactionary when it came to these things, but this was an instance when he hated progress. He should have been born at the beginning of the 20th century. His sensibilities were much more suited to those times. Instead, he was born at the tail-end of the age of typewriters and printing presses. Here was a secret he kept to himself: He didn't read blogs or tweets, even though he was supposed to keep track of them on his paper's website. To him, it was a lot of babble going nowhere. He didn't give a damn what someone was doing minute by minute. He was not even that interested in his own life.

The funny thing was he used to think of himself as completely modern. He had once even considered his tastes and perspectives avant-garde. He loved fusion jazz. American imperialism angered him. He did not consider recreational drugs dangerous. Interracial couples did not bother him. Sophie had dated a black guy for a while—nice kid, actually—and Z never said a word against it. But he was discovering that in many ways he was a throwback. Something had happened that he never anticipated. He'd gotten old. And the older he got, the more he dragged his feet, kicking and screaming into the new world.

Once, change had come in increments. It had happened over time. There was a warning. Now progress, newness, unsettling differences came at warp speed and there was no way to slow it down. He thought about Albert Einstein's quote, "The only reason for time is so that everything doesn't happen at once," but these days points in time seemed to be getting closer and closer together. Is that what happened to old people? Did time speed up for them?

Day after day he sat at his job, hating what it had become, hating himself for doing it. He could not put his hands on all the threads of what they wanted from him—and they wanted more and more every day. Edit stories, assign stories, keep the website fresh, check other sites to make sure they were not missing anything, discipline slacking reporters who were not making maximum use of every second, check the hundreds of e-mails that came in every day to see which needed immediate attention. From the moment he stepped into the newsroom, he was bombarded with demands, trying to answer the voices that had no compassion for the fact he had put thirty years into the business and was tired now, was living on borrowed time.

Time. Yes, he considered time his enemy. He remembered when the passion between Anna and him burned hot and they would spend long nights making love, sometimes three or four times in an evening, stretching into the early hours of the morning. Now they barely touched each other. If they did make love, it was short and perfunctory. He figured this, too, was a trick of time. He longed to be young again, to have another chance. In his own warped perception he was still 18, coming into his manhood; he was not a used-up old man.

He mostly lived in his mind now. He stole minutes in the front window, watching his 21-year-old neighbor across the street. Dressed in denim cutoffs, a baggy Marist sweatshirt, and leather sandals, Earth Farmer raked leaves on an unusually warm fall day as if it were her only mission in life. While he studied her, Z sipped Jack Daniel's from a Coke can he had emptied most of the soda from. He feared having his wife catch him drinking sour mash on a Sunday morning. He still cared a little about appearances. This was his favorite part of the week, feeling the mild fall breeze caress his face through the open window, letting the sour mash work its magic, watching Earth put on a show for him. He suspected she knew he was watching; he was convinced of it. He swallowed his guilt in gulps from the can. She was not much older than his daughter, Sophie, and yet here he was staring at her with evil thoughts.

"I am a sick man," he said softly into the can.

His imagination provided scenarios in which he and Earth were alone, isolated, and came together in a paroxysm of desire. It was, he knew, ridiculous. No 21-year-old girl would have any interest in a withering dinosaur like him. But imagination had always been his salvation, and it was the one quality of youth that had not abandoned him. He did not actually have to sleep with Earth. In fact, it was better that they remained light years apart. Mingling reality and fantasy was dangerous, and now he knew the difference; that had not always been the case.

2.

When Z awoke it was still dark out. Anna lay beside him, her slow, ragged breathing telling him she was sound asleep. His head felt thick with clouds and his stomach burned. Beside him on the night table was an empty glass that smelled of bourbon. He had used it and one of Anna's sleeping pills to end a hideous night during which his brain would not switch off. He was thankful today was Sunday and he could try to forget about the newsroom.

The clock told him it was 5:07 a.m. He had passed out for about four hours. Exhausted and empty, he turned over and tried to will himself back to sleep. He closed his eyes and thought about watching football today, drinking a few beers, and maybe making some chicken wings. *It's gonna be OK, it's gonna be OK,* he silently repeated over and over like a mantra. He kicked off the blanket because his body felt like it was on fire. Nothing helped; he could not sleep.

Carefully, he eased out of bed, making sure not to disturb Anna. She slept as if she hadn't a trouble in the world. Out in the hallway, he walked stiff-legged toward the stairs, popping his head into Sophie's room and then into Tasha's room to make sure they were sleeping, too. He made his way down the stairs, taking them slowly, his knees bending painfully. His body had begun to betray him. The knees were the most recent traitors. The years of high school football, of throwing his then-slender body around like a missile, had caught up with him. So had a thousand other things he had done to abuse himself.

It was cold downstairs. The heat was turned to sixty and the weather had turned bitter overnight. His bare feet froze as he padded across the kitchen tiles. From the cupboard he took down the Jack Daniel's and took a gulp from the bottle. It was warm along his throat and stomach. He took another pull, set the bottle on the counter. Grinding his teeth unconsciously, he pictured executive editor Molly Thaves and city editor Otto Hellinger sitting in her office, deciding his fate, devising an impossible list of improvements he must make. It felt as if they were taking turns clutching at his throat.

"I'm too old for this shit," he said out loud.

He had not told Anna about his encounter with Thaves on Saturday. She had come into the office on her day off to call him into her office and put him on three months' probation. He knew he must inform his wife at some point. How could he not warn her that his job was in serious jeopardy? Right now, though, he didn't feel up to it. Let her maintain the illusion that everything was fine. Jesus, he had failed her in so many ways. Now it felt too late for him to do anything about it.

He grabbed the bottle off the counter, took two huge gulps and almost threw them back up. But he hung on, choking noisily in the empty kitchen. Taking deep breaths, he sat down at the table. The sour mash did its work. He felt the tight muscles in his neck go slack. Soon comfort was oozing through his blood. He thought about sleep and felt he could close his eyes now.

He stood up, took another hit off the bottle, and put it back in the cupboard. He was beginning to feel drowsy.

"Mike, is that you?" he heard Anna whispering from the top of the stairs.

"No, I'm robbing the place. Go back to bed, ma'am."

She ignored the joke. "Is everything all right?"

He walked to the bottom of the stairs, looked up at her through the dimness. "Everything's fine. I just ... I was thirsty and came down for a glass of seltzer."

"Come back to bed," she said.

"I was just coming." He trudged back up the stairs, knees aching from the cold. How had he gotten so old so fast?

A few hours later, Z had just opened a beer and was settling in to watch the Jets game when somebody knocked at the front door. Anna was up in the bedroom on her laptop—Facebooking, no doubt. Sophie and Tash had run out to the mall, promising to be back shortly. Z groaned and pushed himself up off the sofa. *Now what?*

He was pleased to see Earth Farmer standing on the other side of the door. She smiled at him with big white teeth.

"Hey," he said. "Come on in, it's cold out there."

"Thanks," she said, and hustled inside. Her long, wheat-colored hair was pulled back into a ponytail and she was wearing faded jeans and a plain blue sweatshirt. Her presence seemed to cheer the room immediately.

"What can I do for you?" he asked.

She raised her eyebrows and said, "It's what I can do for you. Mom and Dad asked me to come over and see if you wanted to join us for homemade squash soup. It will be a tasty treat, Mr. Z."

He thought about the football game and was about to answer her when Anna came down the stairs shouting, "Mike, who's at the door? Oh, Earth, how are you sweetheart?"

"The Farmers are inviting us over for homemade soup," Z told her.

She narrowed her eyes at Z then said to Earth: "I love your mother's soup. What kind?"

"Squash. She's just finishing it up."

"Sound great for a cold day like today. Let me throw on some clothes and we'll be right over. I'll leave a note for the girls in case they get back soon."

"Where'd they go?"

"The mall."

"Ugh," Earth said. "I'd rather have a root canal."

"You ever had a root canal?" Z asked.

She smiled, shook her head. "Actually no."

"I didn't think so. Trust me, it's no fun."

A half hour later, the Zinarellis were gathered around their neighbors' huge wooden table, which Max had spent several weeks building from an oak tree in the yard that had been split by a lightning strike. It looked like a medieval feasting table, long and sturdy with thick legs adorned by intricate fluting. Z had admired the table for years but was also intimidated by Max's ability to make it.

The soup was hot and delicious, smooth yet hearty, filled with small roasted pieces of squash that served as tasty croutons and produced a wonderful texture. Z and Anna spooned it into their mouths with obvious enjoyment, complimenting Cyndey between swallows. The soup was accompanied by fresh-baked bread, still warm from the oven. This had been a collaboration by Earth and Air, and featured a crunchy crust and soft, delicate inside. Z had three slices and kept dipping it into the soup, declaring again and again, "God, this is good."

Sophie and Tasha showed up just as they were finishing the meal. Cyndey ushered them in, saying, "Don't worry, there's plenty more, girls." And there was. Water set places for them and Air spooned out the soup while Earth cut bread for them. Tasha, who had always been a picky eater, sopped up everything in her bowl and when Cyndey asked if she wanted more, she nodded and said, "Yes, please."

When everyone had had their fill and the bowls were cleared away (Sophie and Tash helped with that), everyone sat around the table, contented and chatting. The room was warm from cooking and from the fire in the woodstove. The Farmers burned nothing but wood for heat, no oil or gas. "Trees can be replanted," Max had once told Z. "When oil's gone, it's gone."

"You want some red wine?" Max asked Z and Anna.

"Don't tell me you made that, too," Z said.

Max laughed. "No, but it is made here in the Hudson Valley."

"Sure, I'd love a little," Anna said, and Z nodded his assent.

As Max filled glasses, Earth said, "Dad can I have some?"

He looked at her and said, "Just a bit."

Over drinks, Anna talked intently with Cyndey, telling her how wonderful the meal had been. Cyndey just smiled, showing her perfect teeth. She was a picture of Earth in twenty years. Same unruly, brown-blond hair, but with a few strands of gray. Same clear, arresting blue eyes, but with the beginnings of age wrinkles around them. Same frank, open face, unspoiled by makeup.

"It's really easy, Anna," she said. "I can give you the recipe if you want."

"Forget it," Z interjected. "Anna's not a homemade soup kind of girl."

His wife glared at him but Z pretended not to notice. Earth said, "I don't know about soup, but Anna makes the best magic bars in the world."

"Thank you, Earth."

The DEATH of OBSESSION

Z shook his head. "Women, they always stick together."

Max chuckled. "Tell me about it. Here we are, two guys in a house full of women."

"How lucky can you be?" Sophie piped up.

Max laughed more heartily. He picked up his wine glass, brown eyes twinkling. He was, Z knew, a happy man. He lived his life on his own terms. Z envied him that. Max did as he pleased, did things that made him happy. Dressed in worn coveralls (one strap undone) over a red and white flannel shirt, he looked like a throwback to another age. His long brown hair, which fell in fits and starts to his shoulders, was streaked with gray, as was his thick, reddish beard.

The adults sipped their wine and smaller conversations flowered. Sophie and Air, who were the same age, talked about the pressures of senior year and searching for colleges. Tasha and Water went into the living room and could be heard laughing hysterically about something on Water's laptop. Max, Cyndey, and Anna were engaged in a heated discussion about the approaching election for county executive.

Z was at the far end of the table with Earth. He was trying his best to feel avuncular toward her, but he couldn't help staring at her fresh, smooth face and inhaling the scent of bread and soap on her.

"So why did you decide to leave college?" he asked her.

She shrugged. "This is going to sound so conceited, but I didn't think I was learning anything. I felt like I knew as much as my professors." Her soft, full cheeks went rosy. "That sounds terrible, doesn't it?"

"Thing is, I'm sure it's true. You are ridiculously smart, Earth." He paused then added, "Still, you should get your degree. It's always good to have."

"Oh, I'll probably go back sometime," she said. "At this point I'm not even sure what I want to do."

Z considered that for a moment. "Anyway, college isn't all about learning in the classroom. You mean to tell me you didn't have any fun up there at Skidmore?"

"To tell you the truth, Mr. Z, I didn't like Saratoga very much. It's so commercial. It's like Woodstock, pretending to be all cool but just trying to sell you the fact that it's cool. You know what I mean?"

He nodded. "Once you say you're cool, you're no longer cool."

"Exactly. And they want to charge you three times as much for a bagel because you're buying it somewhere *cool*."

Z laughed. "OK, I get that. But what about the friends you made? You can't tell me you didn't meet some interesting people at a place like Skidmore."

Her pale eyes seemed sad, or maybe just filled with longing. "Most people my age are either crazy stoned and drunk all the time or so focused on making money when they graduate that they are total assholes. I can't say I made any real friends."

Z felt a genuine pang of loss as he said, "That's too bad, Earth. When I look back at college, it was probably the best time of my life. It doesn't always translate into the real world, but it doesn't have to if you take it for what it is. I made some friends I still talk to today, thirty years later."

"You're lucky."

Z sipped at the last of his wine. "So what are you going to do now?"

She leaned forward, lips turning up slightly. "You know, Mr. Z, what I really want is an adventure. Like when my dad hitchhiked cross country. Or when my mom and a bunch of her friends piled into a van and went up to New Hampshire to protest a nuclear power plant."

Max, who had caught the end of the conversation, said, "It's a different world now, my darling. Hitchhiking can get you killed. And demonstrations ... they aren't what they used to be."

"Nothing's what it used to be," Earth said glumly.

Max laughed. "You'll have your own adventures. Everything in life is an adventure. You can't live my life or Mom's life."

"My life is a bore."

"That can change in a heartbeat," Cyndey told her. "It happened to me when I met your father. Chance brings us opportunities if we're willing to go through the door."

Earth rolled her eyes, but she wanted to believe her mother. She wanted to believe it more than anything.

The DEATH of OBSESSION

Later, on the way back across the street to their house, the Zinarellis were full, warm, and feeling good. Being with the Farmers often had that effect on them. "That was nice," Anna said.

"I love the Farmers," Sophie said.

"They are so damn whack, but they're fun," Tasha added.

"Tash, that mouth," Anna scolded her.

Sophie laughed and slapped her sister on the back.

Z was not thinking about Otto Hellinger or Molly Thaves or the fact that his job was hanging by a thread. He was thinking about how much he loved his girls and about the gravitational pull of Earth.

3.

Z tried to visit his mother as often as possible. She lived a couple miles from him in the house where he grew up. The house, once filled with kids and noise, was empty now except for Antonia Zinarelli and the caretakers who spent several hours a day there, helping her bathe, dressing her, cooking a couple meals, making sure she took her medication correctly. Michael Zinarelli Sr. had died nearly fifteen years earlier, but Z's mother had refused to move from her longtime home, even after she was diagnosed with Parkinson's disease.

Seeing his mother these days broke his heart. Far from the robust, feisty woman she had once been, Toni Zinarelli was a shrunken shell of her old self, barely able to walk, feeding herself tentatively with shaking hands, hunched and unsteady even when sitting in her favorite chair. Worst of all was that Z was never sure what he would find when he arrived at his old house. Sometimes, because of the medication, her mind would be cloudy—she would forget things or mistake him for his younger brother. Occasionally, when the drugs were out of balance, she would hallucinate feverishly.

Parked in the sloped driveway of the blue and white house, Z sat in the car for a minute, collecting himself. His head pounded from morning bourbon and tension. He saw the outline of his mother looking out of the bay window, gnarled and pale like a tormented ghost. Had he done enough to help her? What would his father say? He had promised the old man on his deathbed that he would take care of Mom. He was not sure he had fulfilled that promise.

He walked up the three stairs to the front stoop and his mother yanked open the door. She smiled thinly and he stepped inside. "Hi, Ma," he said, hugging her gently. It felt as if he could snap her in two with no effort.

"Hi, sonny boy," she said. It was how she always greeted him and it made him feel warm remembering how many years she had called him that.

She waved him toward the sofa. "Sit down, sit down." Using her walker, she shuffled back toward her chair and plopped into it. She looked incredibly uncomfortable, slumped down at an angle in the chair. Z went over and carefully pulled her into a proper sitting position.

"That's better," he said. "Where's Emma?"

Emma was the woman who cared for her on Mondays. Toni said, "Oh, she'll be back this afternoon. She had some errands to do."

"Did you have breakfast?"

"Emma made me a poached egg and toast."

"Uh huh. Did you take your medicine this morning?"

She nodded.

He went from the living room into the dining area and saw her pill box on the table. There were little compartments labeled morning, afternoon, and night for each day of the week. Monday's morning compartment was empty. Z's brother, Joey, who lived two houses away, usually took care of doling out her drugs.

"Looks like everything's OK," he said. "You need anything?"

"No."

"You want something to drink?"

"I'm fine."

"Need any laundry done?"

"Emma took care of it this morning. Michael, sit down and talk to me."

"I'll be right back," he said. He went into the bathroom, closed the door, and took his flask from the pouch of his sweatshirt. After two big gulps of Jack, he walked back into

The DEATH of OBSESSION

the living room and sat on the sofa. His mother was staring at him. He wondered what she was thinking.

"I saw your father last night," she said finally.

"Oh yeah?"

"I was watching *Everybody Loves Raymond* and I fell asleep, and when I woke up, he was sitting on the edge of the bed. Only he wasn't sitting, he was kind of floating. He didn't have any legs or feet."

He watched her, said nothing.

"He told me, 'Toni, you're doing good. You're stronger than you thought you could be, right? You keep this house and stay here until you and me are together again.' That's what he said, Michael." Her eyes were glistening.

"Ma, you know that wasn't really him, right? It was the drugs."

She shook her head. "It was him. You live with somebody for forty years, you know. Don't say it wasn't him."

He leaned back against the sofa cushions, forced himself to smile at his mother. "What the hell do I know? It could have been him. You know Dad. He loved this house. He probably visits all the time."

"He does."

"You know, I dream about him a lot, even after all these years. Sometime he seems so real I feel like I could reach out and touch him. And when I wake up, I'm so disappointed I could almost cry."

Toni looked tenderly at her oldest child. She had too much of her own pain to soothe his, but they shared the realization that time was passing too quickly. Z felt that familiar twinge of wanting to start over, of wanting to return to a time when his father and grandparents and Uncle Charlie were still alive and they'd all gather for Sunday dinner and laugh and argue and drink red wine and play bocce on warm summer days. Those were the best times of his life.

"Michael, I know your father's dead," Mom said.

"Good, Ma."

"That doesn't mean he's gone."

"OK, Ma."

He stood up and went back into the bathroom. He took out his flask and emptied it in a few prodigious gulps. His stomach burned and his head pounded. He knew he was killing himself but found it difficult to care.

4.

Mornings were still strange for Z, even though he'd been on his new shift for some time now. By 8 a.m. the house was empty; his daughters were in school and Anna was at work. The silence accosted him as soon as his eyes opened. No radios playing, no TV blaring, no girls shouting at each other about borrowed socks. Alone, he began to gnaw at Saturday's lecture by Molly Thaves. The memory made his stomach roil: God damn Molly and the *Sun* and everything else.

He pushed himself out of bed and went down into the kitchen. The Jack Daniel's bottle waited for him in the cupboard. He filled a glass with four fingers and swallowed two burning mouthfuls. Almost immediately, the fist in his gut loosened. If Anna caught him drinking first thing in the morning, she would kill him. He hated himself for needing the bourbon, hated his job for making him need it. How, he wondered, standing in the cold kitchen, had his life gotten so far away from him?

Once, he felt his future held so much promise. He was going to be a writer and everyone told him it was possible, that he had the drive and talent to do it. But things had unwound *the center cannot hold of course it can't impossible*. He tried to pinpoint the exact moment when things came unhinged, tried to understand how it had happened, but he realized it had been a slow descent, not a going toward but a moving away from.

Without thinking, he went to his desk in the cluttered spare room and rummaged through a pile of papers and other junk until he found his address book. He looked up a phone number and kept his finger on it as he dialed with the other hand. It rang three times before he remembered it was not even 9 a.m. He hung up before the answering machine kicked in.

The quiet grated on his nerves. He drank more sour mash, went into the bedroom, turned on the TV, and watched cartoons. Dora the Explorer was counting to five in Spanish and he counted along: *uno, dos, tres, cuatro, cinco.* He had never studied Spanish—he had taken five years of French—but knew a few words because he had helped Sophie study when she had first started Spanish lessons. He had encouraged her to take Spanish because the Hispanic population was exploding and being bilingual could help her find a job after college. He had never had the foresight to worry about such things, but he wanted her to be better prepared than he was.

His head lolled forward and he drifted into a haze, half dreaming as the television kept him company. When he jerked awake it was almost 9:30. Back at his desk, he dialed the number again and got an answer after one ring.

"Red Hawk Consulting," said a bright, young female voice.

"I'd like to speak to Elise Mathieu, please."

"*Doctor* Mathieu isn't available at the moment."

"Well, can I leave a message for her? Please tell her that Michael Zinarelli from the *Hudson Valley Sun* is calling about an interview. I know she's a recognized expert in education issues and I'd like to ask her a few questions."

"Certainly. Can you spell your name for me and give me a number where she can reach you?"

He did so, thanked her, and hung up. Before he finished pouring himself another drink, the phone rang. The caller ID told him it was from Red Hawk Consulting. He picked up the receiver and said, "*Hudson Valley Sun.*"

"Z-man," said a familiar voice.

"I'm sorry, Doctor Z-man is not available right now."

"I know this is your home number, Einstein."

He chuckled. "How are you, El? How's Syracuse?"

"Freezing. How are you?"

"OK. You know."

"It's good to hear from you, Z. To what do I owe the honor? And don't give me that interview bullshit."

"I just wanted to hear your voice," he said.

She detected his sadness immediately. "Is everything all right, Z?" She let the question hang until he answered.

"Sure. I just hate my job and I'm wondering what I've done with my life. But otherwise, everything's great."

"Mid-life crisis. It'll pass. How are the girls?"

"Sophie's trying to decide where to go to college, which is causing us all a lot of stress. And Tash ... is Tash, thinking up new ways to drive us crazy."

Elise laughed and said, "Sounds like Rain. I caught her masturbating in her room the other day with the door wide open. I told her if she was going to do that, she needed to do it in private."

Rain was Elise's 8-year-old daughter, a late-life gift that El insisted was not an accident. "I don't need to know such things," Z said. Since he had first met her, Elise had always had a habit of revealing the most intimate details of her life. It hadn't changed thirty-some years later. "So is Cheyenne looking at colleges, too?"

"Anderson wants him to go to Dartmouth, but Chey has his eye on Bard. So we may be taking a trip down your way soon. I'll keep you posted."

"I'd love to see you," he said. Z had never met Elise's husband, Anderson, or any of her children. They had kept in touch by phone over the years, but had not seen each other since the first few years after graduation. Elise had met Anderson just after her breakup with Frank, and the two had married almost immediately in a small, quiet ceremony.

"Sure. How many times have I invited you to Syracuse?"

"It's always hard to get away," he said lamely. "Anyway, I'm always thinking about you guys. How's Maggie?"

"She's great. She and Josh just opened another coffee shop. It's their third one."

"She becoming a real tycoon," Z said.

"Best coffee in Syracuse. She caters all of my seminars."

"You ever hear from Frank?"

"Oh, sure, he calls every once in a while. He's become quite a fitness nut. Last I heard he and his wife, Suzie, were taking a thousand-mile bike trip into Canada."

"Frank?"

"Yeah, I know."

He took a deep breath. "El, I miss you."

"I miss you, too, Z. I miss J Suite and all the fun we had there. But life moves on, Z. It moves on."

"That's unfortunate, El. It really is."

Chapter Four
The Good Boy

What a good boy, what a smart boy, what a strong boy.
—Barenaked Ladies

1.

That first afternoon with Crystal was idyllic. We spent hours lounging on the bed listening to soft music while she studied her sociology and I read Thomas Mann's *Buddenbrooks*. I filled an occasional pipe from which she took a hit or two. We sipped vodka from plastic cups. Every now and then she reached over and stroked my beard. I gently kissed her ear, her jaw, her moist lips. As the sun slanted toward the horizon and the light faded into an early February night, we got undressed and made long, slow love, exploring each other's bodies. There was no hurry, only the urgency of lust.

While we climbed back into our clothes, I said, "We better get going. The dining hall's gonna be closing for dinner."

She made a face. "Do we have to go there?"

"I'm starving."

"You got a car, right?"

I did have a beat-up old Buick my father had given me. I didn't like to drive it much for fear it would not last the semester. When school let out in May, it had to get me all the way back to Poughkeepsie. Plus, I never had money for gas. I spent most of my cash on beer and pot.

"Let's go to Angelo's," she said. "We can get a couple slices."

I didn't want to leave the womb-like comfort of the campus, but I didn't want to disappoint Crystal, either, so I fished my keys out of my top drawer and we headed into town. It was five-thirty or so and almost completely dark. The wind was howling off the lake and I hadn't started the '64 Buick Special in a week. It coughed and wheezed on the first two tries but finally caught and began to warm up.

"Good old girl," Crystal said, rubbing the dash like she was petting a dog.

As we drove, I turned up the radio, which was tuned to the only decent station within miles. BTO's "Takin' Care of Business" was playing, and I sang along. Crystal tapped on the dash and started singing, too, her sound smoky and edgy. She reminded me of a blues singer whose voice was colored with dark emotion. Lady Day, maybe. Again, I got the impression there was something fundamentally sad about Crystal Cassidy. I wanted to make her happy.

"And if your train's on time you can get to work by nine, start your slavin' job to get your pay. It's the work that we avoid, and we're all self-employed. We love to work at nothin' all day ..."

The village was basically one main street with a few side roads that contained a business or two and old houses that had seen better days. It was a depressing place, hanging on stubbornly to long-dead grandeur, a typical upstate shell of a community barely disguising its deterioration—but smiling still as it slapped a coat of paint over its rust. Angelo's was on one of those side streets. Its windows glowed with neon, advertising various kinds of beer along with the claim: Best Pizza in the Finger Lakes.

The small parking lot had barely been plowed and the balding tires of the Buick crunched over the packed snow as we pulled in. I felt uneasy, but Crystal appeared buoyed by being off campus. She took my arm when we got out of the car and clung to me as if we'd been lovers for years.

Angelo's was nearly empty on a Sunday evening in February. A pimply-faced kid, 16 or 17, and his greasy-haired girlfriend, a bit younger, perhaps, were in a corner booth, eating slices, drinking Cokes and laughing at nothing. They were obviously stoned. Who could blame them? Growing up here, pot was likely one of the few salvations. A fat dude in his 50s sat at the counter, drinking a Budweiser and talking incessantly to the lone employee, a middle-aged guy who was rolling out dough for a pizza and nodding absently to the customer's chatter. He might have been the owner, Angelo himself; it was a sickening thought. Is this what you worked all your life for?

We peeled off our coats and sat in a booth. Despite the bitter night, it was ungodly hot in the pizzeria. I felt myself sweating immediately. Figuring there was no way we'd get table service, I asked Crystal what she wanted. Two slices, extra cheese, and a beer, she told me. As I approached the counter, she lit a cigarette and sucked in smoke contently. The fat customer and the guy behind the counter eyed me without interest. They were used to the comings and goings of college kids.

"Yeah?" the counter guy said.

I ordered four slices, two extra cheese and two pepperoni, and two Buds.

"ID?" the guy said.

I fished out my driver's license and handed it over. The counter guy, a chunky Italian with curly black hair grayed at the temples, studied it suspiciously for a few seconds (even though I was obviously older than 18) and finally slid it back across the counter. He reached into the cooler, extracted two beers and slapped them in front of me. "You want glasses?"

I shook my head, thinking that any glasses in this place couldn't possibly be clean. "Nah, this is fine."

He liked the fact that I hadn't made extra work for him and warmed up a bit. "I gotta heat up the slices. It'll take a minute or two. I'll bring 'em over."

"Thanks, man."

"Right on," the fat customer said, laughing at me.

I ignored him and took the bottles back to the table. I handed Crystal her beer and said, "You don't mind drinking out of the bottle, do you?"

"Hell no," she told me, and sucked down several prodigious gulps. We waited for the slices and talked about her beloved Celtics. She had no interest in baseball ("an old man's game") or football ("but I love those tight pants"). Her sports were basketball and hockey. More precisely, the

Celtics and the Bruins. When I told her I was a Knicks fan, she shook her head in fake sympathy.

"They got, like, what, two titles in their whole freakin' history. Look at the Celts. Domination. More championships than you can count on two hands. What do your Knicks have to say about that? And don't even talk to me about the Rangers. The Bruins. Bobby Orr. C'mon."

I didn't argue. I didn't want to argue. I just smiled at her passion. A girl who loved sports and could fuck like her was a find. Who cared which teams she rooted for?

I suppose I was grinning like an idiot, because she said, "What?"

"What what?"

She shook her head and tangled her fingers into my beard. "You're a nutjob, you know that?"

"I'm nuts about you," I said without thinking.

That caught her off guard, and she stared at me in silence. Had I gone too far? The counter guy was there, putting down two plates of pizza. He didn't say a word. Neither did I. Maybe I'd said too much. I bit into my pepperoni slice, burning the roof of my mouth but not feeling it. A gulp of beer was cold and soothing. I let a long silence pass because I couldn't think of anything to say.

Finally, she said, "Are you falling for me, Michael Zinarelli? Because if you are, you better be careful."

"I know what I'm doing."

"No, you don't."

As if on cue, we both stretched across the table and kissed. The two townies were fooling with the jukebox at their table, and the next thing we knew, "Takin' Care of Business" was blaring through the tinny speakers. We laughed and started singing along, our eyes locked on each other.

"And if your train's on time you can get to work by nine, start your slavin' job to get your pay. It's the work that we avoid, and we're all self-employed. We love to work at nothin' all day ..."

We didn't care if anyone was looking at us. We were alone in the world.

2.

Despite the icy cold, the old Buick got us home without a hiccup. For much of the drive, Crystal rubbed my leg, working her way up to my crotch. I could barely concentrate on the road. As soon as I parked, I turned toward her and we shared an open-mouth kiss for several seconds. I slid my hand beneath her coat and gently squeezed one of her nipples through her sweater.

"Are you gonna be a good boy tonight?" she said softly. "You gonna fuck me nice?"

I put my hand between her legs and she bucked her hips up toward me, moaning.

When I closed the door of my room behind us, we tore off our clothes and ran our hands all over each other. Her flesh was warm and smooth. We were standing next to the bed and she jerked off my underwear and took me in her hand, pumping up and down. I was tracing small circles around both of her nipples, which were hard as pebbles. Suddenly, she pulled away from me, dropped to her knees and took my cock her in her mouth. Her warmth enveloped me, tongue playing while she sucked. My knees trembled.

"Jesus, baby," I groaned. "Baby, stop, I'm gonna come."

But she didn't stop, and I felt myself explode into her mouth. She took it all and kept licking me. My vision went white. I was so turned on, my cock stayed hard. I lifted her onto the bed and entered her roughly. She was drenched and cried out, clawing my ass with her fingernails. I slammed into her and she spread wider, wrapping her legs around me and tilting up her hips. I felt like I was penetrating all the way through her. She came with a shudder, her pussy pulsing against my cock. A few seconds later, she came again, pounding my back with her fists and screaming, "Mikey, oh Mikey, fuck me, baby."

I pulled out of her, flipped her over and entered her from behind. She eased up onto her hands and knees and pushed against me, moaning softly the whole time. I grabbed her ass and moved her pussy back and forth on my cock. "Baby, give me your come," she breathed hoarsely. "C'mon, baby, come inside me."

The DEATH of OBSESSION

I did, curling against her while my entire body tingled and every ounce of energy I had went shooting out of the end of my cock. I collapsed onto the bed, panting and sweating, draping my left arm over my eyes. I felt her snuggle up against me, her hot breath brushing my chest.

"Good boy," she mumbled. I held her and said nothing. In a few minutes I could tell by her slow, regular breathing that she had fallen asleep. It had been an eventful weekend and I understood why she had drifted off by nine o'clock on a Sunday night. But I was nowhere near sleep, so wound up my mind raced in a dozen different directions. Crystal. Cryssie. What was I getting into with her? Whatever it was, I wanted more. Two nights into this, my relationship with her was twice as intense as my time with Maggie ever was. Maggie had been prim in bed compared to Crystal.

My mouth was dry and suddenly I was craving a soda. I fished through my pants pockets and dug out some coins. On the third floor, in the rec room, were two vending machines—one filled with soda, the other with snacks. An icy Coke sounded heavenly right then. I pulled on a pair of shorts and, before leaving the room, glanced back at Crystal, who was breathing deeply with her eyes closed, the blankets drooping off her shoulder, exposing olive flesh down to her right breast. I thought she looked like a tiny angel and that was probably the moment I realized I was falling in love with her. I closed the door behind me and walked down the quiet hallway. For one of the few times in my life I felt still and happy.

On the stairwell up to the fourth floor, I was stopped in my tracks by the hulking form of Rick Cramer sitting on the landing. When he saw me coming up the steps he turned away. His face was flushed and his shoulders were slumped, defeated.

"Hey, big guy, what's up?"

He replied without looking at me. "Ah, you know, nothing much."

"You OK?"

"Hell yeah, why wouldn't I be?"

I put my hand on his shoulder and tried to look him in the eye, but he kept averting his face. My floating feeling began to dissipate and I was dropping to the ground. I only wanted my soda.

"Cramer, what the hell, man?"

He finally looked at me and I almost shuddered. He eyes were red, as if he'd been crying, and his face was splotchy with angry scarlet spots. I noticed his sausage-like fingers were trembling slightly. I had never seen him so unsettled.

"Talk to me, big guy. What's wrong?"

He opened his mouth, closed it again, shook his head. "Z-man, I think I fucked up bad."

"What happened, man?"

He shook his head again. "I ended up with Liz last night. It was nice, really nice. But the next morning, Jesus, she woke up and started screaming at me about using a condom—I didn't 'cause I figured she was on the pill. She didn't say anything about it when we were getting down. She was all ready to go."

My stomach twisted, but I said, "Christ, Cramer, you can't blame yourself. It was mutual. She wanted you and you wanted her. Everybody could see that. You didn't do anything wrong."

He pursed his lips, closed his eyes. "What if she's pregnant? She's a goddamn freshman, a child for Chrissake."

"She can get rid of it."

"Get rid of it?" His brown eyes glistened. "What if that's the only son I'll ever have?"

I almost laughed at his melodrama. Instead, I put my hand on his arm, trying to calm him. "You're getting way ahead of yourself, man. You were with her one night. The chances of her being pregnant ... forget it. She's not pregnant. Stop worrying about it." Then I added: "You think your sperm's that robust, lad?" in a hokey Celtic accent.

He nodded unconvincingly, ignoring my attempted joke. "You're probably right," he mumbled, but he didn't move and kept staring at his feet.

I stepped past him, leaving him to his self-flagellation. The exchange had killed my buoyant mood. I just wanted to grab my soda and get back to Crystal to watch her sleeping in my bed. Unfortunately, the rec room was not empty. Woody and his roommate, Stan Holman, were playing pool, or some crazed version of it. Balls clacked and the two of them laughed giddily. I wasn't in the mood for conversation, but when they saw me they perceived a new audience and began to play to me.

"Z, Z, Z, what's up?" Woody yelled.

"Hey, guys."

Stan, Woody's perfect foil, rarely spoke, and when he did, it was gently. He nodded at me, took a shot, and had the six ball bounce off the corner pocket. "You suck," Woody told him. He lined up a shot and hit the cue ball so hard it flew off the table and into the wall. The two of them howled. I figured they were coked up and walked over to the vending machine, trying to ignore them. But there was no ignoring Woody. He let out a blood-curdling scream and started hurling pool balls against the brick wall. I slid coins into the slot and pushed the Coca-Cola button. A can clattered noisily into the opening at the bottom of the machine.

The nine ball bounced off the wall and came flying back toward Woody, nearly taking his head off. He and Stan collapsed with laughter. "Woods, you're fuckin' nuts," I said, and walked out of the room followed by their roars.

Cramer had disappeared from the stairwell. Was he back in his room wallowing in self pity? I didn't want to think about his pang of conscience. I had never asked Crystal about birth control. I had assumed—like Cramer—that she was taking the pill. We hadn't used condoms and I had no idea whether or not she was protected. A girl like Crystal, who had been around the block a few times, had to be savvy about things like that. But I didn't know for sure. When we had a quiet moment, I had to ask her.

Back in my room, I climbed under the covers and draped my arm over Crystal. She smelled of warmth and fading perfume. I squeezed her and held on like she was my salvation. She stirred, snuggled against me, ran her hand along my leg. "I love you," I whispered, so softly I hoped she didn't hear. She turned over, wrapped her arm around me, and kissed me gently on the lips.

"I'm so tired," she breathed. And then after a few seconds: "I feel safe with you."

My heart swelled and I almost laughed with delight. I suddenly realized I was tired, too—exhausted, in fact. I closed my eyes and started to drift away. Just before I dropped into oblivion, I was jerked back by a flesh-rippling scream from the bowels of the dorm. Woody. Crystal and I chuckled quietly and held on tight.

3.

I awoke to Crystal kissing the tip of my nose. The smell of her first cigarette mingled with mint toothpaste made me turn my face away. "C'mon, stallion, it's time to get up," she said softly into my ear. I groaned. Totally disoriented, I shoved my head beneath the pillow and growled, "What the hell time is it?"

"After 8:30, sleepy boy."

"Eight-fucking-thirty! I don't have South American lit until 11. You kidding me?"

She moved off the bed as if an electric shock had run through it. Her voice turned cold, but not in an angry way —more disappointed. "I've got my soc test at nine. I thought maybe you'd want to walk me over. That's what boyfriends do, you know."

Boyfriends? I sat up in bed, wondering when this quantum leap had occurred. I remembered murmuring something about love last night, but that was in the drowsy contentment of two nights of tantric sex. This whole thing was proceeding at warp speed, Captain. Still ... the idea of us as a couple made my breath come a little faster. Had she already chosen me?

"I gotta go, baby," she said. "If I'm late for Balinchek's test ..."

"Give me a couple minutes," I told her, throwing off the blankets and feeling my man parts withering in the cold air. "I have to finish that Garcia Marquez book before class anyway."

"I need a Coke. You want something?"

"Nah. I'll grab a coffee at the snack bar."

The DEATH of OBSESSION

As soon as she closed the door, I scooped my pipe out of the drawer, opened the window to the icy wind and took two monstrous hits of Hawaiian, blowing the smoke away. Then it was a mad dash to the bathroom for a quick whore's bath (that was what my mother called it: a soapy washcloth over the face, armpits and genitals) and a scrubbing of my nasty mouth. By the time Crystal got back I was tying my boots.

"C'mon, pokey, I'm going to be late."

I grabbed my coat and copy of *One Hundred Years of Solitude* and locked the door behind me. As soon as we stepped outside the dorm, I thought my eyeballs were going to fall out of my head. The wind was pounding off the lake ferociously. "Mothah F!" Crystal screamed, shrinking against me. Anyone with a few working brain cells avoided Monday morning classes—except, as with Crystal's sociology requirement, if it was impossible—so the campus was like the arctic on a February morning: nearly barren, razor-sharp wind, white white white dazzling the eyes. We walked without talking, huddled together. The snow was so frozen every step barely broke the surface but crackled like breaking glass. By the time we made it to the behavioral sciences building, our faces were stiff and raw.

"Got damn!" I screamed.

We held each other tightly until our bones began to thaw. Her body against mine. The smell of her hair. Her tiny hands squeezing my ass. "Cryssie, I'd only get out of bed this early for you," I said, kissing her forehead.

"I'll pay you back later," she said. She glanced at her watch. "Shit! Gotta run." She went tearing up the stairs, stopping on the landing to shake her ass at me. At the top of the staircase, she passed a brick shithouse I recognized as Trey Tuttle and she shouted "Tut!" He lifted her as easily as a rag doll, swung her around and kissed her on the mouth. My face and neck were burning.

"Where you been, baby girl?" he asked, finally setting her down.

"I'm late for Balinchek's class," she said. "We'll talk." And with that she disappeared down the hall. I watched all this from the bottom of the stairs, pulse throbbing at both temples. Tuttle, the bull elephant on steroids, stampeded down the steps and rushed past me as if I didn't exist. I'm not sure either of us knew if I *did* exist. I wanted to hurl Garcia Marquez at his block head, but I just stood there watching his concrete shoulders move away. Fuck you, man, fuck fuck fuck.

I plopped into one of those modern, U-shaped chairs covered in carpeting. A bolt of sunshine heated by the glass made the spot so comfortable I felt myself drifting between consciousness and dreamlike images. At one point, I shook my head violently and opened *One Hundred Years of Solitude* to chapter 19. "He tried to reconstruct in his imagination the annihilated splendor of the old banana-company town, whose dry swimming pool was filled to the brim with rotting men's and women's shoes, and in the houses of which, destroyed by rye grass, he found the skeleton of a German shepherd dog still tied to a ring by a steel chain ..."

My eyes closed and I didn't try to fight it. The sun was the Colombian jungle on my face and I floated above the banana trees. Images mingled in my mind, and then a delicate young face was smiling at me through the equatorial clouds. It wasn't Crystal or Maggie or even Elise —it was Christine Wendel. I hadn't thought about her in a long time, but the memory made my stomach tremble.

Christine Wendel. What does she look like now? Still excruciatingly cute, curly blond hair framing her soft-featured face, with the cool blue eyes completing the picture? I had been infatuated with her throughout junior high school and into high school, had shared honors classes with her—she was smart, as well as painfully pretty —but I had never gotten close to her. We had talked and joked and once I'd asked her to a dance, but she'd turned me down cold. I hadn't expected her to say yes. In my early years I was anonymous and mousy, intelligent but otherwise unremarkable. Christine was beyond me.

Then, without being aware of it, I somehow blossomed. I grew a bit taller and broad-shouldered. My swirling, unkempt hair became longer and stylishly chaotic. The mustache I'd been trying to cultivate finally filled in. During my senior year, I had several short stories published in the school literary magazine and became a minor celebrity among the artsy crowd. At age 17, I had my first long-term girlfriend, Devon Shea. I had emerged from years of emptiness. I was happy, perhaps for the first time since I was nine or ten.

During the summer after graduation, life was good. I was going off to college in Florida, the envy of many of my acquaintances. Devon and I became more and more intimate, though we hadn't yet had sex. Everything in life was moving forward. Still, in quiet moments, the old loneliness swirled around me, seeped into my veins. That pain was not so easily swept away—the parties I hadn't been invited to, the girls who had looked through me, the snickering as I'd tried to fit in.

In the middle of August, weeks before I was to leave for college, Christine Wendel hosted a party—a last fling before everyone went their separate ways. Devon and I were invited. Devon told me she'd be late; she had to work at the bookstore, helping with inventory. Now 18, I stopped off at a bar for a few beers with friends and showed up at the party in good spirits. I toured the room, making small talk in a way I had never been able to.

When I went into the kitchen for a beer, I found Christine standing in front of me, an exaggerated pout on her lips. "Got a few minutes for the hostess?" she asked. "You've talked to everybody but me."

"You were busy."

"I'm not busy now."

We sat at the kitchen table, chairs so close they were almost touching. We talked about college, about my writing, about the life that stretched out in front of us. The Beatles' "While My Guitar Gently Weeps" was playing on the stereo (I'll always associate the song with her). The words passing between us didn't seem to matter now. We were drawing closer and closer, as if by some irresistible gravity.

She ran a warm finger across my cheek, stared into my eyes. "I've been so stupid," she said.

"Stupid about what?"

"About you."

She leaned forward and kissed me softly on the lips. An electric charge ran through me. I was pleased and stunned.

Paralyzed. I had no experience in such matters, girls like Christine coming on to me. I decided I should kiss her back, and was bending my head down toward her when the front door opened and Devon came sweeping in. Instinctively, I jerked away from Christine, the moment shattered. Not now, goddamnit, not now, I thought. But it was too late.

Devon came into the kitchen, bent, kissed me on the cheek. "Hey."

"Hey."

Christine was already standing up. She gave Devon a quick hug and said, "Glad you made it." Then she walked with purpose into the living room.

"What was that about?" Devon asked.

"What?"

"That," she said, jerking her head in Christine's general direction.

I felt my face flushing, couldn't control it. "Nothing. We were just talking."

"Must have been a pretty intense talk."

I tried not to compare Devon's angular nose, thin lips and curveless body to Christine's gentle beauty. There was no sense chasing Christine. I had Devon. I was not alone and didn't want to be.

When I drove Devon home, we made love for the first time (my first time) on her parents' living room carpet. Just before I entered her, she said, "Are you sure I'm the one you want to be with?"

"I'm right where I want to be," I answered.

I never saw Christine again. I thought of calling her but did not. And before I knew it, I was gone to college. A few months into freshman year, Devon and I split up—which was best for both of us. But I regretted not knowing what that night with Christine might have led to.

4.

Sitting in the lotus position on my bed (was it *our* bed now?), Crystal dragged on a cigarette dangling between her lips, absorbed by John Stuart Mill's "The Subjection of Women." Occasionally, she would pick a yellow marker and thrash it across a sentence or paragraph. My class load was light that week, so I was smoking hits of weed and thumbing through an issue of the *Fabulous Furry Freak Brothers*. It was my favorite underground comic and I loved Fat Freddy because he reminded me of Cramer.

From time to time, I would catch myself staring at Crystal. The words I wanted to say to her filled the space between us like a comic book font, but I said nothing. I just kept hitting on the weed and returning to the adventures of Franklin, Phineas, and Fat Freddy.

"Mikey, listen to this," she said. "Really listen. 'The second benefit to be expected from giving women the free use of their faculties, by leaving them the free choice of their employments, and opening to them the same field of occupation and the same prizes and encouragements as to other human beings, would be that of doubling the mass of mental faculties available for the higher service of humanity.' He wrote that more than a hundred years ago, Mikey. Everybody needs to contribute if we're gonna get anywhere. That's what he's sayin'."

Her brown eyes were glistening with excitement and I couldn't help but smile—but it must have been a glum smile because she said, "What's wrong, baby?"

My brain threw together a raging reply—you fucked that sonofabitch Tuttle and you'd do it again if you had the chance I hate him for touching you, Cryssie. But all I did was shake my head.

She set her cigarette in the ashtray and picked up the half-filled glass of vodka balanced between her legs. After a few sips, she said, "C'mon, Mikey. Something's been buggin' you all day. What is it, baby?"

Did Tuttle fuck you better than me would you run back to him now if you got the chance?

"I was just wondering what was going on with you and Trey Tuttle today."

"Going on?"

"The big hug, the kiss ..."

She laughed as if to humiliate me. "Oh, Christ, Mikey, is that what's up your ass? Me and Tut are friends. That's all. Him and Emily are practically married." She took a couple more sips from her vodka and said, "Is my boy jealous?"

I know he fucked you and it burns. "Tell me everything."

She finished what was in her glass and rubbed her eyes with her fingertips. "You gonna tell me about every girl you ever fucked?" she said, almost snarling.

Before I could form an answer, she went on: "Emily's mother got sick last March. They thought it was pretty bad, so Emily went home for a couple weeks. Turned out to be nothing serious. The old lady's fine. So while Emily was gone me and Tut had a few drinks in his room one night and the next thing you know ... we had a little fling. It only lasted till Emily got back. And she never knew nothin'. Nobody got hurt."

What kind of person fucks her friend's boyfriend how cold-blooded are you Cryssie? "I thought you liked Emily."

She shrugged. "I like Emily fine. Me and Tut, we were just havin' some fun."

I stared at her, my eyes scorched from so much pot. I didn't know what to say. Crystal reached across the bed and grabbed my hand. "What happened then don't have anything to do with us, baby. You know what? Tut's got a cock big as a horse. But he doesn't know how to use it. It's like bein' under a jackhammah. You know how to treat a girl. You're sweet. You got finesse. That's one of the reasons I love you." She patted the bed next to her. "Now come here and show me what a good boy you are."

Without an alternative in mind, I obeyed.

Chapter Five
Talking to the Dead

I don't live today. Maybe tomorrow, I just can't say.
—Jimi Hendrix

1.

When the phone rang at 3 a.m. Z was almost immediately on alert. His first thought was that both girls were tucked safely in their beds, so that was not a concern. He reached for the receiver as the second ring died out. He put the phone to his ear and said, "Hello."

"Mr. Zinarelli?" said a deep, steady voice.

"Yes."

Pause. "This is Officer Paley of the Town of Poughkeepsie Police Department."

Oh no! Ma! "Yes?"

"I'm at your mother's house."

"Is she all right?"

"Yes. She called us because she said an intruder was attacking your father. I searched the house and there's nobody here. And it looks to me like your father is deceased." Officer Paley sounded almost apologetic.

Z sighed. "He's been dead quite a while now. My mother has Parkinson's and sometimes if the medication isn't exactly in balance she'll hallucinate. She's been pretty good lately, but obviously her meds are off today."

"Uh huh. Well, what would like me to do?"

Put her out of her misery. And mine, he thought. "I only live a few minutes away. I'll come over and get her settled back in bed. You can take off."

"OK, sir. Have a good evening."

"Thanks, Officer."

Anna was awake by this time and as soon as he hung up, she asked him what was wrong. He told her, trying to keep the frustration out of his voice. He said he would head over there as he pulled on a pair of pants and a sweatshirt. She told him to drive carefully and rolled over.

The car was cold and he let it warm up for a few minutes, listening to sports talk on the radio and sipping at the bottle of Jack he had pulled from the cupboard. He filled his flask. He had forgotten to ask the policeman why he had called him instead of Joey, who lived two houses away. Maybe he was working. He put in crazy hours at the IBM manufacturing line. Anyway, it didn't matter now. He was dressed and in the car. His night's sleep was destroyed.

"Hello, this is Salaam in Bayside."
"What's up, Salaam?"
"I want to talk about the Jets."
"Go ahead, buddy."
"I think a lot of their problems are caused by the offensive coordinator. He never throws the ball down the field ..."

Driving the deserted suburban streets, Z wondered how many times he had come this way without seeing. Or, more precisely, without anything registering on his mind. The development had been nearly new when his family had moved in forty-some years before. Not even half the houses that stood now had been built yet. There had been a freshness to everything. There had been an empty field at the corner of South Gate and Robin Road where he and his friends had played baseball. It was covered with houses these days, crammed so tightly together there was barely room for a side yard. Back then, most of the neighborhood was white. The ethnicity had changed dramatically over the years: blacks, Hispanics, Asians, Pakistanis, and Indians all populated the area. Z liked the mix. He didn't want his kids going to lily-white schools. Tasha and Sophie had to learn to get along with all kinds of people.

Z tugged at the flask of bourbon while he drove. No other cars were on the road. He was not endangering anyone, he reasoned. Still, he drove just under the speed limit in case a cop was lying in wait somewhere. He could not afford a drunk driving charge. That was all Molly Thaves needed to put the last nail in his coffin.

The front light was on at his mother's house. The policeman had obviously left because there were no cars in the driveway. He pulled in and sat in the car for a moment, trying to collect himself. He wanted to be calm. He wanted to demonstrate patience, even though he was angry that his sleep had been interrupted. She belonged in a nursing home. Everyone knew that. But she refused even to discuss it. He considered it incredibly selfish of her.

As soon as he reached the porch, the front door opened and his mother ushered him in. She seemed pale and nervous.

"Ma, what the hell's going on?"

"The police were here," she whispered.

"I know. They called me."

She put a finger on her lips. "Keep your voice down," she said. "They might still be around."

"The officer's gone. His car isn't in the driveway."

"Not him," she said with soft desperation. "Them."

"Them who?"

"Shhhh."

He put his hands to his head as if his brain might explode. He exhaled slowly. "Mother, there is no one here. There never was. It's just your medication."

"I know that," she said, but her eyes were empty and feverish.

Z put his arm around her withered frame and led her toward the bedroom. "Come on," he said. "Let's get you back to bed. You just need some sleep." More than anything, he wanted her to drop off so he could head home. His old house depressed him. It reminded him of his father's last days, propped on the couch. Knowing he was about to die. Wondering how Toni would cope. Extracting promises from his children. *Yes Dad we'll take care of her you know we will.*

With his help, she struggled into bed, but he had to pick her up and reposition her until she was comfortable. He could not imagine how she managed when she was alone. Did she just stay curled in a ball at the side of the bed? He pulled the blanket over her and she said, "I want to watch TV for a while."

"You should go to sleep."

"The TV helps me fall asleep. You can go."

He handed her the remote and sat on the end of the bed. At this time of night, there was little more than infomercials on. She settled on an old police drama and set the remote down. He waited. When it became apparent that she was not going to sleep right away, he said, "I have to get home."

She nodded. He kissed her cold forehead, pulled the blankets up around her, and walked out into the living room.

His father was sitting on the sofa, arms folded across his stomach. He looked the same: curly black hair peppered with gray, neatly trimmed mustache also flecked with gray, strong jaw and clear, alert eyes behind brown-rimmed glasses. When he saw Z, he cocked his head and said, "Hi, Bones."

Michael Zinarelli Sr. was the only one who had ever called Z by that nickname. Z offered a half-smile and patted his paunch. "I'm not exactly Bones anymore, Dad," he said.

"You'll always be Bones," he said.

Z took a step forward, wishing he could hug his father but knowing it was impossible. Much of his life he had feared his father, had thought of his father's word as law. Later, after Z had married and then Zinarelli Senior had gotten sick, father and son had become friends, had faced each other on equal terms for the first time. When the end came, Z cried as hard as he ever had, thinking of the time wasted fighting his father instead of appreciating him.

"Are you taking good care of your mother?" his father asked.

Z hesitated, stared at the carpet. "I'm trying. It's not easy."

"Neither was bringing up you kids."

"I know. I know now."

"You told me you were going to take care of her." His father's face was severe, almost angry. But behind it there was compassion.

The DEATH of OBSESSION

"I'm sorry. But, Dad, she needs somebody with her all the time. She needs to be in a nursing home."

His father sat forward, shook his head. "She needs to stay here, son. You don't put family in the hands of strangers. Jesus, she's your mother. Do you think she'd abandon you when things got tough?"

"You don't understand ..."

"*You* don't understand, Bones. Family is everything. You keep your mother in our house until she comes to join me. That's our house. You kids grew up there. She deserves to be there."

"I'll do what I can."

His father levitated off the sofa, rising several inches, and seemed to grow to twice his size. "That's a bullshit answer. You and the other kids, you do it. Don't try, do it. You do what's right." His father's brown eyes blazed behind his glasses.

Z stood silent, face frozen in a frown.

Zinarelli Senior floated back onto the couch and looked at his son with concern. "What's the matter, Bones?"

"Nothing. It's just ... life is hard, Dad. I hate my job. I seem to hate everything these days. I'm so tired. Sometimes I think it would be better to be where you are." He moved back a few steps and sat in the chair opposite his father, body slumping.

"Don't wish your life away. I miss being alive. I miss sitting in the yard on a warm day and drinking beer with you and your Uncle Charlie. I miss holding your mother. I miss tickling my grandchildren. Trust me, son, there's nothing good about being dead. Don't wish for it."

His father was just about gone. "Dad, don't go," Z said. He was talking to himself. The sofa was empty and there was no sign of Michael Zinarelli Sr. Z felt a vast emptiness and wanted to cry. But he did not. Instead, he took out his flask and sipped at the bourbon.

"Michael, are you still here?" his mother called from the bedroom.

"I'm just leaving."

"Who are you talking to?"

"Nobody. Go to sleep now."

He walked out of the house into the cold night. The air was crisp and he breathed it in like a starving man. The moon was shrouded by thin clouds, obscured except for a halo that made a silver circle in the sky. He stared at it. He wished he was a night bird that could soar upward and capture the joy of that silver halo. But he was just a man, weighed down by the world. He got into his car and drove home.

2.

Tasha came home from school, went up to her room, and threw her backpack violently to the floor. She turned her radio on loud and sat on the edge of the bed, staring at the wall. Her lips were pursed, brown eyes smoldering. Down the hall, Sophie was doing her calculus homework. She shouted something at her sister, but Tasha didn't hear. She punched one of her pillows.

Sophie came stomping down the hallway and stuck her head into her sister's room. "Jesus, Tash, turn that shit down. I'm trying to do my homework."

Tasha ignored her.

"Tash, goddamnit!" Sophie entered the room and punched the power button to Tasha's radio, shutting it off.

Tasha snapped her head around and glared at her sister.

"What the hell's your problem?" Sophie growled.

Tasha's face softened. "Can I ask you a question?"

"I'm busy."

"Please."

Something in her sister's voice made Sophie pause. Tasha often infuriated her, but Sophie also felt responsible for helping her troubled sibling. Family was family. That's a lesson their parents had preached forever.

Sophie leaned against the doorjamb. "OK, what?"

Faced with her sister's full attention, Tasha hesitated. "That girl, Taylor Cardone, is picking on me again."

"What'd she do?"

"She pushed me into my locker, hard."

"Maybe it was an accident."

"It wasn't an accident, Soph. And at lunch, when I got up to buy a milk, she threw my whole lunch in the garbage."
"You sure it was her?"
"That's what Gabby said."
"What'd you do?"
Tasha turned red. "Nothing."
Sophie ignored her sister's embarrassment. "Isn't she Liz Cardone's little sister?"
Tasha nodded.
"Her sister's a bitch, too. Nobody at the high school can stand her except her little group of thugs. They terrorize the freshmen and think it's funny."
"Liz ever bother you?"
Sophie shook her head. "I got enough friends to scare her. And my boyfriend's on the football team, so she doesn't want to mess with that. She only picks on people she knows won't fight back. Like any bully."
Tasha looked defeated. She didn't have a boyfriend, on the football team or otherwise, and really didn't have many friends who would stick up for her. In many ways, she was isolated by her social clumsiness. To her, friendship was an all or nothing proposition, like everything else in her life. She didn't understand compromise.
Sophie went into the room and sat next to her sister on the bed. "I think I can help you," she said.
"How?"
"You push a bully back and it freaks them out. I'm just gonna let that little bitch know that when she messes with you, she messes with me. And all my friends."
Tasha smiled. "Thanks, Soph."
"Don't worry about it."

3.

It was another glum Monday. After he prepared a tuna sandwich for his mother's lunch and made sure she took her pills, Z went home and fell asleep on the couch watching game shows. He woke up when Tasha came through the door, tossing her overloaded backpack onto the floor and heading into the kitchen.

Z sat up and rubbed his eyes. His head was cloudy and he felt empty, although he couldn't put his finger on why. Tash came into the living room drinking Coke with a load of ice.

"Mom doesn't want you drinking soda," he said.

She ignored him, plopped on the soda, and snatched the remote from the coffee table.

"Did you hear me?" he said.

"OK," she answered, but kept drinking. He wanted to scream at her but didn't have the energy. Instead, he struggled to his feet and headed toward the stairs. Tash turned on some teen cable show about a high school where everyone was either gay or pregnant or ready to commit acts of violence.

"Do your homework," Z grumbled.

"OK," she said but didn't turn the TV off.

A sense of hopelessness washed over him. It was like talking to the dead. He wasn't sure if he wanted to cry or slam her into a wall. But she knew too well that he would never raise a hand to her. Tasha had been emotionally unsteady for years, had been seeing a therapist since she was 8 years old. To the outside world, she seemed like a normal 13-year-old. The Zinarellis, though, knew her many phobias, her insecurities, her deep need for validation. Z had tried hard to make her happy, to be a friend, to do special things for her. What tore at his emotions was the fact that, when the mood struck her, Tasha could be the most kind and loving child in the world. One night, she might kiss his cheek and say, "I love you, Daddy," while going off to bed. The next she might stomp into her room and slam the door without saying a word to anyone. Often, there seemed to be no provocation for her anger.

He trudged up the stairs and was halfway to the top when the phone rang. "Grab that," he called, but the ringing continued. "Tash," he yelled. The ringing stopped. As he reached the second floor, his daughter screamed, "Daaaad! Phone!" Now what? He hurried into his bedroom and picked up the receiver.

"Hello?"

"Michael Zinarelli?" The voice was stern and official sounding. Definitely not a salesman.

"Yes." As he said it, he recognized the voice.

"This is Detective Steve Delson."

"Ah, Detective Delson. Calling to harass me?"

Delson chuckled darkly. "No, Mike, I am officially not harassing you. In case my boss asks."

"What do you want, Delson?"

"Well, I have a question for you. You called in sick to work two Wednesdays ago. Where'd you go?"

Z's stomach twisted. "Nowhere. I didn't feel well. I laid in my bed and watched television."

"Yeah? You sure about that?"

"Positive."

"'Cause I got a witness who swears you were at a motel in Carmel. And you weren't alone."

Z was sweating. His hands were trembling. He was glad Delson was not in front of him. "Your so-called witness is mistaken. I got a common face. People mistake me for other people all the time."

"So you weren't with Crystal Cassidy that day? You weren't screwing her in that motel?"

Z coughed. "You know, Delson, I wrote a nice feature on Chief Antonelli a few years ago. He likes me. If I tell him the things you've said to me, he's going to take a bite out of your ass. Understand?"

"The chief is very interested in this case, Mike. He wants to know what happened to this woman. She was here. We know that. And now she's disappeared. The chief don't like those kinds of loose ends."

"Crystal and I are ancient history. That's all I can tell you, Detective."

Delson's voice turned icy. "Is she dead, Mike? Just tell me that."

"I DON'T KNOW."

"I understand you had a lot of animosity toward her. The two of you had kind of an ugly breakup. That right?"

"That was a long time ago. I've been happily married for twenty-seven years. I've got two great kids. Why would I give a damn about Crystal?"

"I don't know," Delson said. "Maybe you never got over her. It happens. I've seen it a hundred times."

Z didn't answer. He wasn't going to add fuel to this conversation.

4.

Most mornings Z got up early with the rest of his family. He went down to the kitchen and made lunches for his daughters to save them time; Tash would only eat turkey and Sophie liked it, too, but would also take salami or peanut butter and strawberry jelly. He packed the lunches with care, making sure they contained juice boxes, chips, and cakes. He repeated the routine every school day.

The house was in chaos until about 8 a.m. as the three girls fought over the upstairs bathroom (the downstairs half-bath was a last resort), argued over whose clothes were whose, and shouted to each other from their various bedrooms about what the plans were for the afternoon: "I'm going to Britt's"; "I've got chorus"; "I'm getting out of work early."

When the stampede out of the house ended, Z sat in the quiet for a few minutes, reading or just thinking. Then he tried to go back to sleep for a few hours before work.

Sleep didn't always come easily, and when it did there were often interruptions. Salesmen called. His mother might ring him about a problem she was having. On this day, he was awakened by a persistent pounding at the door. Ascending through several levels of sleep, he became aware of himself. He looked at the clock: 9:11 a.m. Groaning, he struggled out of bed, pulled on his sweatpants, and headed downstairs. The knocking was strong and steady. He wondered if it was some bible thumpers trying to bring him to Jesus or the cops again telling him his mother had done something outrageous. Whatever it was, he resented the intrusion.

When he opened the door, he was confronted with a young man, about 30 or so, wearing a leather jacket and black jeans. He was medium height, slim, with wiry black hair cut close to his head and one of those scraggly, week-old beards women seemed to find appealing these days. There was something handsome about him. Maybe it was the smoldering brown eyes or the classically straight nose or the strong jaw. He wondered immediately how many hearts the man had broken.

"Yes?"

"Mr. Zinarelli?"

"That's right."

The young man smiled. His teeth were white and straight. "I'm David Kaplowitz," he said. "Crystal Cassidy's son."

Z stared at him for several seconds, not sure how to react. He was surprised and angry and remorseful all at once. His first instinct was to say, "I don't see what we have to talk about."

"If you'd just let me in for a few minutes, I can tell you." He smiled again. He was aware, Z suspected, of how ingratiating the smile was and probably used it often to get his way—with women and otherwise.

Z pushed the door open further and waved him in.

"Thanks," Kaplowitz said.

Glancing out into the driveway, Z noticed the young man was driving a newish BWM. It put his old Honda to shame. Z brought him into the living room and motioned him to sit on the sofa.

"Pardon my appearance," he said. "I was asleep."

Kaplowitz picked up on the scolding tone in Z's voice and said, "I'm sorry about that. I knew you worked nights so I wanted to get here before you left."

"Can I get you some coffee?" Z asked, although he didn't really want to make it. He wanted an excuse to go into the kitchen and grab the bottle of Jack in the cupboard.

"That'd be great," Kaplowitz said. "I take it black."

Z bustled around the kitchen, measuring out coffee and pouring water into the coffeemaker while taking hits off the bourbon bottle. While the coffee was brewing, he took one last gulp from the bottle and replaced it in the cupboard. Back in the living room, David was waiting patiently, hands folded in his lap.

Z stood in the middle of the room with his arms folded. "OK," he said. "I don't want to be rude, but why are you here?"

Kaplowitz's mouth turned up slightly, the same wry smile his mother had often employed when caught slightly off guard. "Right to the point, huh? Well, I guess that's the best way." He collected his thoughts, watched Z with his penetrating eyes. "Mr. Zinarelli, I'd do anything to find my mother. She's all I have."

"I understand that."

"And for some reason, I keep coming back to you. The stories she used to tell me about you—"

"Stories? What stories?"

Kaplowitz hesitated, mulled over his answer. "It's not important. What is important is that I know she cared about you, a lot. Even if she didn't always show it. She loved you, Mr. Zinarelli."

Z spat out a laugh. "Loved me, huh? Crystal had no idea what love was ..." He shook his head. "Forget it."

"I know what she was like," Kaplowitz said. "What she *is* like. I don't have any illusions about my mother. She likes men. I wish she were different, but there's nothing I can do about it. But she's my mother and she's always taken care of me. Always. I need to know if you have any idea where she is."

"What makes you think I do?"

Kaplowitz didn't answer. He stared at Z—through him—with those dark eyes. Under the probe of that gaze Z squirmed a bit and said, "I'll check on the coffee." He went into the kitchen and poured two mugs of coffee, filling one only halfway to the top. In that one he poured a large dose of bourbon.

He was just handing Kaplowitz his coffee when someone knocked at the door. "Christ," he muttered, and went to answer it. Earth Farmer was standing on the porch.

"Come in, sweetheart," he said. "What can I do for you?"

She stepped inside, cheeks red from the October wind. She looked beautiful with her wheat-colored hair tied back and her full lips smiling slightly. Again, he thought how the years had betrayed him.

"Dad needs to borrow your *Kind of Blue* album, Mr. Z. His has a scratch in it and he has to listen to Miles *immediately*. You know how he is." Her tiny laugh seemed to ask his indulgence.

"I'd never stand between a man and his Miles," Z said. "You should tell your father to buy a CD player. Then I could burn a copy for him."

"Oh, you know he'll never give up his turntable. It's the only way to listen to music, he says."

She followed Z into the living room and stopped short when she saw David sitting on the sofa. They looked at each other for a long time before he said, "Hi," and gave her that devastating smile. She nodded at him, deep blue eyes glistening with interest. When Z noticed them looking at each other, he said, "Oh. I'm sorry. This is my neighbor, Earth Farmer. This is David Kaplowitz."

Kaplowitz stood up and held out his hand. He was just slightly taller than Earth and probably weighed ten pounds less. "Earth Farmer. What a fascinating name," he said.

She shook his hand, smiled at him. "I didn't always think so."

"My albums are in the basement," Z told Earth. "I don't really play them much anymore. I'll be back in a minute."

As Z left the room, Kaplowitz said, "So you got teased when you were a kid?"

"Yeah, but I usually got the best of it."

He showed her his perfect teeth. "I'll bet. How long have you known Mr. Zinarelli?"

"Forever, it seems like. They've been our neighbors for a long time. How long have you known him?"

"All my life, I guess. But this is the first time we've ever met."

She cocked her head a bit. "Mysterious. How long are you going to be around?"

"A few days."

"Well, maybe we'll run into each other again."

"Let's make it definite," he said. "How would you like to go out for a drink with me tonight? I can solve the mystery for you."

"I'd prefer tea," she said. "I know a nice place."

"Sure, whatever you like. I'm staying at the Marriott up the road. Room 202. Call me there later and we'll settle the details."

She grinned. "OK."

Z came stomping up the basement stairs, waving a copy of the Miles Davis album over his head. "Found it," he said. He was a bit unnerved by how close Earth and David were standing to each other.

"Here you go," he said, handing her the album.

"Thanks. Now Dad can get on with his day." She turned to David and said, "Talk to you later." She disappeared out the front door with a bounce in her step.

"What'd she mean 'talk to you later'?"

Kaplowitz shrugged. "Nothing. It's just an expression."

Z picked up his coffee and drank several mouthfuls, feeling the bourbon in the brew. He wanted this young man to be gone. He did not feel comfortable with him in the house.

"When are you going back home?" he asked.

"When I'm sure that I know everything you do about my mother," Kaplowitz told him.

5.

Z opened his eyes in the darkness and felt that familiar squeezing in his stomach. Something was wrong. It was a few seconds before he realized that Anna was lying beside him crying. His first instinct was to ignore it and pretend he was still sleeping. But he couldn't. He had to know.

"Anna, what's wrong?" he whispered. Once in a while she would awaken from a bad dream, crying. But this had not been a dream.

After a moment, she said, "When did it start, Michael?"

"When did what start?"

"You and Crystal."

He mastered his voice before answering. "I don't know what you're talking about, Anna. There is no me and Crystal."

She cried quietly, making the bed shudder. "Michael, please don't insult me by lying to me. At least tell me the fucking truth. Can't you do that?"

He shut down like he often did when overwhelmed by emotion. He didn't answer. He stared at the wall through the darkness.

The DEATH of OBSESSION

"Did you call her first, or did she call you?" his wife asked him.

He felt dizzy and wanted to go back to sleep. He took a deep breath and said softly, "What difference does it make who called who first? The truth is we started talking a few weeks ago. But it was just phone calls. Nothing else."

He felt her staring at him in the dark bedroom. She had stopped crying because she was angry now, not sad. "How could you, Michael? After all the bitch did to you, how could you get involved with her again? Are you sick?"

He shook his head even though he knew she couldn't see. "I didn't get involved with her. I talked to her on the phone a few times. That's all."

"Why?" she breathed intensely.

"I was just curious. I wanted to know ... a lot of things. I wanted answers to questions I never got. I wanted closure —God I hate that word!" He turned over and tried to see Anna's face in the dark. "Can't you understand that? I needed to know why."

After a pause, she asked, "And did you get your answers?"

"No."

"Why not?"

He breathed in sorely. "She didn't have any answers. She never did."

She spoke hesitantly as if she didn't want to go on, but had to. "Do you have any idea what happened to her, Michael?"

"No. Jesus Christ, Anna, no. I swear." He reached out to touch her but she pulled away violently as soon as his fingers brushed her arm.

"Don't."

6.

Z could not stop thinking about his meeting with Crystal Cassidy. He kept running through it in his mind:

Our drinks arrive and we peruse the menu for a while. As we decide, she says to me, "Before this even becomes an issue, I'm paying. I insist. This was my idea."

I shrug. "Fine with me." I notice how perfectly her fingernails are polished as they rest on her glass. "Money agrees with you," I say. "You look fantastic."

"It beats the alternative."

"You wouldn't have been happy with me. I'm just a poor newspaper man trying to scrape by."

It's her turn to shrug. "You never know how things would have turned out," she says. "Maybe I would have inspired you to greater things."

The waitress returns and we order lunch. After she grins at us and walks away, Crystal and I talk about our spouses and kids. She brags about her husband, says, "Richard adores David. He gave him a BMW. He treats him just like a son."

The conversation inevitably returns to our days together. We reminisce about the night we met and about how it seemed fated that we would come together at that moment. My recollection is that night started a spiraling down in my life and it didn't end until I tore myself away from Crystal. She talks as if it was the heyday of her existence. I'm again struck by how differently we look at our time together—even after all these years.

"Why did you call me?" I ask.

She chuckles. "Honestly, I was bored. I started Googling names of people and up you popped. Still living in Poughkeepsie, working as an editor at the Hudson Valley Sun. It was so cute. I thought maybe we could renew our friendship. Maybe have some fun together."

I ignore the innuendo. "Whatever happened to us?" I ask her, trying to get at the question I need an answer to.

She sips at her seltzer, shrugs in a way that seems almost annoyed. "I don't think about that, Mikey. I like to think about the nice times we spent together, about the way you made me feel. Don't you think about those things?"

Chapter Six
Love and Rage

Why should I blame her that she filled my days
With misery, or that she would of late
Have taught to ignorant men most violent ways.
—William Butler Yeats

1.

At the end of February, I was a bachelor for the weekend. It was Crystal's father's 50th birthday and she had to be at the big gala in Boston. The plan was for her to leave after her last class on Thursday, skip Friday classes, and get back Sunday night. Her brother, Conor, who was working on his masters at RIT, was going to swing by to pick her up around 6 p.m. Thursday. I was kind of excited to meet someone in Crystal's family, but she said no, I wasn't going to meet Conor. Her brother was an asshole and would only try to screw things up between us. He was picking her up in front of the Dowd building and I was to stay away. "The less that shit knows about my life, the better," she said before slinging a backpack over her shoulder and kissing me goodbye.

Wendy had a major paper due Monday, so Shank and I planned a great night: smoke a fat joint and engage in a fierce backgammon match. Let me say modestly that I was a pretty good player, and Shank was a master strategist who was also lucky with the dice, so our battles were often monumental. We once played until 4 in the morning to a dead-even draw. We would have continued, I guess, except that we were out of pot, out of beer, and out of energy.

We were halfway through Shank's monster joint—which we'd stubbed out to save for later—and were in the middle of a classic game in which Shank had me hemmed into my own territory but had left two stones open for me to capture. I shook my dice in the cup while sucking down the rest of my Molson. As the die flew toward the board and clattered about, a meaty hand scooped them up and Cramer said, "I win."

"Jesus Christ, farm boy, where'd you come from?" Shank snapped.

"Looking for something to do," Cramer said pathetically.

"There's beers on the windowsill," I said. In the winter, those of us without mini-fridges would line up beers on the outside of the windows. In the dead cold of northern New York, you had to be careful not to leave them out too long or they'd become beer slushies.

Sensing my quiet evening with Shank was now ruined, I said to Cramer, "You wanna play the winner?"

He ripped the top off his beer and said, "Hell no. I hate this freakin' game. Hey, can I toast up this joint?"

"Help yourself," Shank said. He grabbed the dice from Cramer, handed them back to me and said, "Roll 'em again."

But it wasn't meant to be. A flesh-roiling scream interrupted me in mid-roll and Woods' shaggy red head popped through the doorway. "What's up, gentlemen? You too, Cramer."

"Fuck you, Woody Woodpecker."

Stan Holman followed Woody in and accepted the joint from Cramer. As Stan filled his lungs, Cramer said, "Nothing much happening tonight, you homos."

Woody took a hit from the roach. "That's about to change big time, farm boy."

Out of his shirt pocket he pulled a small plastic envelope and tossed it on the desk. It was half-full of white powder and nuggets.

"Sheeee-it," Cramer said.

"Looks like three grams, maybe more," Shank added.

"Woods, I'm broke right now," I said. "I wouldn't be able to pay you for a couple weeks." I stared at the gleaming bag and said, "But I definitely want in."

Woods pulled a small mirror from his pants pocket and laid it on the desk. "Never fear, my brothers, it's on me tonight. This is my birthday present from my brother."

"Your birthday was last month," I said.

"Yeah, well, my brother is a slow ass, but when he comes through he comes through."

"Fucken-A," Stan screamed (Stan never screamed), and we all laughed. Shank kicked the door closed while Woody shook a pile of coke out onto the mirror. The powder sparkled like a magic potion.

"So much for a quiet night of backgammon."

"Fuck backgammon."

Woody started cutting up five fat fingers of blow. Shank rolled up a crisp dollar bill and tucked it in here and there until it made a perfect straw. I started flipping through my albums and decided on *Fillmore East*, the Allman Brothers live classic; as soon as Berry Oakley's bass thundered through the speakers, everybody whooped. Woods offered me the first snort and I sucked it down. It was clean and fierce, and when I felt the drippings hit the back of my throat I knew it was going to be one of those nights. Woods went next, then Shank and when everyone had had a hit, we stood nodding our heads to the Brothers. We finished Shank's joint and he rolled another before we realized the first was gone.

"Let's play some spades," someone said.

"Five's too many."

"Fuck it. I'll sit out," Cramer said.

Woods passed him the mirror and said. "You got a more important job, chicken-lover. Cut us up some more lines."

We played a couple hands, smoked the rest of Shank's joint, did five more plump lines and drank all the Molsons on the windowsill. "A song Dickey Betts wrote from our second album, *In Memory of Elizabeth Reed*," Gregg said through the speakers, and we all moaned in anticipation. The back and forth of ripping guitar riffs between Duane and Dickey had everyone bending their heads back, eyes closed in ecstasy.

"Man, dig on those two drummers," Shank said.

"Jaimo and Butch Trucks, two bodies and one mind," I said.

"Man, I'd love to eat some pussy right now," Woody said out of nowhere.

"I'm sure Stan's mom ain't busy," Cramer said.

I thought Holman was going to have a seizure. He started laughing so hard he fell off the bed and rolled on the floor, kicking his legs spasmodically and howling. We all went into hysterics. When the laughter finally died down, we realized we were out of beer. Someone suggested heading into town to buy more, but I said, "Let's go down to the Tail." The Moose Tail was a local dive, within walking distance from campus, all wood and animal hides and perfect for the yahoos who lived along the lake. Pitchers were two-and-a-half bucks, filled right to the top, and bowls of snacks, mostly pretzels and nuts, were spread along the bar. The crowd was a mix of shit-kicking townies and students looking for a few cheap laughs. But despite the unlikely combination, there were few fights at the Tail, mainly because the manager, a lumberjack-looking mass of muscle named Gord, took shit from no one.

"One more line before we go," Woods said.

"Small ones," Shank whispered over his shoulder. "We might need a boost later."

Woody wagged his shaggy orange mop. "That's my man, Shank. Always thinking about the next high."

I rolled a small joint from my Hawaiian—it was almost gone by now—and we sucked up our last lines and headed out. The night was bitter, but we weren't feeling a thing. By now the coke was racing through our veins like pure adrenalin, dripping down the backs of our throats in alkaline rushes. Woody and Shank were arguing about who was a better guitarist, Duane Allman or Jimi Hendrix. Woody's contention was that Hendrix revolutionized guitar playing while keeping it true to its blues roots. Shank said Jimi was all glitz and technique and you could feel the way Duane loved the music by the way he laid it down.

"Don't get me wrong, I admire Jimi's playing, but I'd rather listen to Duane any day."

"My man Jimi don't get enough credit for his finesse. Everybody thinks he's all pyrotechnics and a thousand notes a minute, but he's got *touch*, too."

"Who gives a shit?" Stan shouted. "They're both dead."

The DEATH of OBSESSION

"Your mama sure ain't," Woody said.

Cramer and I hung back a few paces, enjoying the crystal February night and the huge, argent moon. Everything seemed alive with the exact moment of life—not yesterday, not tomorrow—but right now as the cold air filled our lungs and pumped our hearts. I asked him how his "little problem" was working out and he stared at me blankly.

"With Liz, man."

He grunted. "Oh, that bitch. She ain't pregnant. Didn't even bother to tell me, either. I had to ask Wendy. Now that little freshman whore won't even look at me. Like it was all my fault. I don't get it, Z. Maybe she's just embarrassed that she bunked down with a farm boy."

I was not exactly the guru of romance to be handing out advice, but Cramer wanted something and I was crackling with wisdom I had to share. "Cramer, I think she just got caught up in the moment, you know, Wendy and Shank together, all these couples melting all over each other and the music blaring and the booze and weed—she got carried away. So the next morning she wakes up next to you and she doesn't know what to think. She's what, 18, and obviously ain't been around the block. Then she realizes you didn't use a rubber and she flips. Big guy, I'm telling you, it's nothing personal. Just look at it from her point of view."

"Mostly, that's what women want," Stan, who had been listening in without us knowing it, interjected.

"What's that?"

"To have guys look at things from their point of view."

"Stan Holman, philosopher of love," Cramer screamed at the icy moon, his breath like an explosion of clouds being pumped into the sky.

2.

The Moose Tail, we figured, was mostly held together by beaver shit and a handful of nails manufactured by the original nail cutting machine in 1796. The screened-in porch sloped down toward the lake and it wasn't uncommon for a glass or plate to slide off the table when sloppily placed by a waitress who was unaware of the delicate balance. Inside, it was everything you'd imagine: stools lined up against a long bar, sticky tables scattered around the room surrounded by plastic-covered chairs in a variety of colors and configurations (some tables had six chairs, others one), a TV over the left side of the bar that was never turned on, three pinball machines in the corner that were constantly making noise whether anyone was playing them or not. Some comic genius had mounted a moose's (or some other animal's) behind on a varnished plaque right above the bar.

The place was tearing-it-up loud when we walked in. The sound system was playing the usual schlocky pop music beyond aural endurance, and the place was packed with people jabbering and laughing. It must have been a slow night on campus, because tables were filled with friends. Elise, Frank, Maggie, and Billy Thoms were at one table. Sitting close by were Charlie Maurice, Sierra, Chad Patrick, and Liz. I glanced at Cramer as if to say, "Be cool, big guy," but he ignored me. Everybody whooped hellos and we all pulled up chairs and pretty soon we were all in one big conglomeration. I used my last three bucks to buy a pitcher (Gord barely grunted at me) and Shank pitched in and pretty soon the tables were filled with pitchers and we were knocking them down and the coke kept us hovering just a few inches above the room.

I walked up behind Frank and Elise and put an arm around each of them. "Let's step outside in a few minutes and have a hit or two."

Frank smiled and Elise's pool-blue eyes lit up. Maggie was watching us, but I didn't say anything to her. The noise level in the room continued to escalate as conversations competed with the music. Chad Patrick was chatting up Liz and Billy Thoms was explaining the validity of pop art to Maggie and declaring Lichtenstein a genius. Shank was trying to convince Charlie Maurice that *Kind of Blue* was Miles' masterpiece, but Charlie insisted *Bitches Brew* had eclipsed it. Sierra, who was in one of my philosophy classes, and I were debating Kant's true legacy to the advancement of philosophy.

The DEATH of OBSESSION

"His arguments were so brilliant they nearly silenced philosophy for decades," this gorgeous, caramel-colored girl was telling me. "He made it impossible to circumvent his argument."

"Aw, Christ, Sierra, it was all a parlor trick," I said, slamming down another beer. "It was clever as hell, but what did it mean? We can't know reality because we function in time and space and reality is beyond time and space. So, what, all philosophy should stop? It's clever, clever bullshit."

"There was more to it than that and you know it, Z. He was trying to say reason alone won't get us there ..."

The night wore on and beers went down throats and onto tables and across chairs. Groups of four or five slipped into the parking lot for a smoke, and at one point Woody dragged me into the bathroom for my last line of coke, a chubby thumb that sent me spiraling again beyond the shackles of who we were and what we were doing. Miles and Kant and Lichtenstein had nothing on us.

All the while, the sound system rolled on and on, and we suffered through songs likes "Please Come to Boston" by Dave Loggins, "Seasons in the Sun" by Terry Jacks, and "Sunshine on My Shoulder" by John Denver. Still, we enjoyed a few head-boppers like "Rikki Don't Lose that Number" by Steely Dan, "Radar Love" by Golden Earring, and "Hello It's Me" by Todd Rundren. When "Tell Me Something Good" by Rufus came on, Charlie reached out his hand and Sierra took it and they started dancing. I could see the red eyes of the few townies left in the place turn redder. Man, that Charlie Maurice could move. His bones seemed to be made of rubber and he swayed and slithered through the whole song while Sierra complemented his every move.

We all started clapping when the song ended and then "Jungle Boogie" by Kool and the Gang came blasting through the speakers and everybody stood up looking for a partner. Shank grabbed Elise (Frank never danced), Billy cornered Maggie and Chad made off with Liz. I wondered what Crystal was doing.

"Jungle fuckin' boogie is right," I heard one of the townies grumble.

Everyone was jumping up and down and twisting to the primitive beat. Chairs were bumping up and down and half-filled beers were toppling off tables. Cramer grabbed Stan by the wrist and dragged him into the middle of the floor and the two of them started dancing like a water buffalo and a prairie dog. Everyone was roaring and laughing. When the song ended, one of the townies said, "How about playin' some white people's music?"

Everyone froze except Charlie Maurice, who turned his back on the guy as if to dismiss him in the rudest way possible—without acknowledgement. There was some scuffling at the stools where the two townies were sitting, but before things got any further Gord stepped around from the back of the bar, huge arms folded across his chest. "I pick the music here," he said, not shouting but loud enough for everybody to hear. "Who don't like it, there's the door."

The townies seemed to be measuring their odds, but even if they thought they could take all of us, there was Gord to consider, and no one was sure what peacekeeping implements he kept behind his bar. Conjectures varied: a baseball bat, an axe, an AK-47 he'd captured in Vietnam and had somehow smuggled back into the country. No one was anxious to find out. The townies settled their tab and left without another word.

I said, "Thanks, Gord," but he ignored me. He hadn't done it for us but because this was his territory and it was his job to keep order.

Things quieted down after that as we settled into our various highs. Frank and Elise were the first to leave, Elise laying a fat kiss on my cheek. Charlie and Sierra were next. Somehow, Cramer had ended up next to Liz and they were talking quietly, Cramer's thick hands moving in gestures that seemed to signal some silent language. Shank, Stan, and Woods headed back to finish off Woody's coke, but I stayed behind. Maggie was still sitting there. Mags. Chad Patrick and Billy Thoms were sitting nearby, but no one was saying much.

Gord was standing over us with a pitcher. He slapped it on the table and said, "Last one. On me."

The DEATH of OBSESSION

I filled a cup and drank unenthusiastically. Maggie sipped and stared at the door. Cramer and Liz stood abruptly and walked out hand in hand. Knowing now their night was over, Chad and Billy hammered down two beers each and staggered out the door. There were several awkward moments between Maggie and me until I finally said, "Let me walk you back. I promise I won't try anything."

"You don't scare me, Z."

"I know."

As we fumbled into our coats and headed out the door, I said, "Thanks, Gord," but he didn't say anything. He was already busy wiping down the tables with a soapy rag. Maggie and I stepped outside and walked in silence for a while. I wanted to take her hand. I wanted to stop and kiss her. Instead, I said, "I got a few more hits on this joint. Want some?"

"Sure."

The roach was tiny and it took me three or four tries—and a scorched finger—to get it lit. I took shallow hits, having had enough for the night, but Maggie got three big lungfuls before the Hawaiian was gone. The lights of the campus were yellow against the silver moonlight, and it reminded me of the night in October when Maggie and I first went to the Tail together and floated home in a beer and cannabis lather and made love for the first time. I'll never forget her saying, "I want to feel you inside me." I was already in love with her before I ever touched her, but when she said *that* I knew I'd die for her if she asked me.

"How are things going with your lacrosse player?" I asked. It was a mature question, right, a Cary Grant question to a woman he loved but lost.

"That's finished," she said. "Lacrosse is a stupid game and it's the only thing he thinks about."

"I'm sorry."

"Forget it. Just another one of my many screw-ups. I don't make a lot of good decisions when it comes to romance."

Was she talking about us? Was she saying she'd made a mistake breaking up with me? My heart was pounding so hard I felt like I'd done another line of coke. I thought my best strategy was silence, so I said nothing.

"Anyway, I guess things have worked out for you, huh? Crystal's already living in your room, I hear."

I shrugged. "It happened fast, but I like it. I like being with her. I like her being there in the morning."

She laughed, shook her head with a hint of sadness. "Mikey, you wanted everything all at once. You wanted me to love you the day I met you. I told you to slow down. But you wanted me to ... I don't know ... validate you."

"What the hell does that mean?" My cold breath was hissing across her face like steam. Someone had fed her that line. Elise?

"I'm not even sure. I just ... I don't want you to get hurt."

"That's funny, coming from you."

Maggie was not a beautiful girl. She had a straight, unremarkable nose; watery brown eyes behind round glasses; chestnut hair that fell unswerving just above her shoulders and taut, uncompromising lips. Her body was a conglomeration of wide hips and narrow chest and storkish legs that seemed to run to her throat. But my heart bled with a thousand little blades every time I saw her.

"Michael, go slow with Crystal. That's all I'm saying." Her soft, white fingers pushed the hair away from my forehead. "As a friend."

"Come back to my room," I said without thinking.

"We both know that's a bad idea. If Crystal finds out she'll kill us both." She giggled in the slightly goofy way I found so endearing. I reached over to kiss her and she slithered to her left and gave me her cheek, then walked into her dorm. I stood alone in the cold for a long time. *I want to feel you inside me* say it just once more *I want to feel you inside me.*

3.

Hail battered the window like barbarians assaulting the fortress. The wind screamed so ravenously I could feel the cold penetrating the glass. I thought about Poughkeepsie and the cool, early-summer breezes blowing up off the

Hudson, about how perfect that felt. I wondered how my father's sore back was doing in this spine-wrenching cold. I wished I knew how to say things to my mother I could never express. I wanted to know where Devon and Christine were.

I was hovering between a few hits of pot and a couple beers when the door crashed open and Crystal was standing there dripping with frozen rain. Her face was set in a mask of anger and I knew immediately she had returned from Boston in a pissy mood. She threw her duffel bag into the corner and said, "Christ Awmighty, never again!"

I tried to kiss her but she brushed her lips against mine and pulled away. I told her I'd bought her a present and pulled out a bottle of vodka, and that temporarily elevated her spirits. She hugged me, then tore the top off the bottle and gulped down several mouthfuls. "What a freakin' nightmare," she said after the vodka had settled in.

While I chipped away small pieces of my last bud of Hawaiian, I listened to her bitch about her brother, about her father's new girlfriend named Candace ("who thought I was gonna be her best friend and whose hair supported, like, two bleach factories"), about her father's obnoxious friends and, of course, about some guy named Jeremy.

"God, Mikey, he was all over me every minute. He's my dad's partner's son, and when we was young he was always grabbin' me and askin' me to show him my titties—and nothing's changed. He's still a freakin' perve."

My stomach turned to ice right then and I knew she had fucked him. I listened to the tiny balls of ice clatter against the window and waited.

"Thing is, the little shit turned into quite a hunk. And he goes to Brown, so he's got a couple brains in his head. If I wasn't in love with this great guy, I might have given him a tumble."

You fucked him you lying bitch you gave him what you gave me and maybe more maybe things we haven't even thought of. I took two hits of pot and held them until I thought my lungs would burst. I wondered if the hail and wind could obliterate me into something without memory.

"Do you always have to be sucking on that pipe?" Crystal said suddenly. "I mean, Jesus, Michael you're gonna be a junior soon. It's time to start getting your head on straight."

I snatched the vodka from between her legs and slammed it onto the desk. I thought the bottle might shatter. "Yeah, Crystal, let's talk about growing up and not being drunk every night of your life and fucking every guy who's willing to crawl between your legs." The words came out so forcefully they seemed to quiet the hail. I wanted to take them back but there was no way now; they were out there solid as metal. Her face turned to stone, like a statue of Kali mocking the destruction of the world.

"Cryssie," I said, but she was already in motion. She scrambled off the bed and picked up her duffel bag. "So that's what you think of me?" She swung the bag and clipped the side of my face. I might have been bleeding. "I don't need you, loser."

She stormed out the door as I yelled after her "Cryssie, come back. Cryssie!"

I fell back onto the bed, wanting to chase her but unable or unwilling to move. The hail laughed at me.

4.

Elise sipped her coffee, made a face, added a couple sugars, and stirred vigorously. It was after 2 a.m. and we were the only two in the snack bar. I gulped my own coffee, black, no sugar, and savored the bitterness. I hadn't seen Crystal for 32 hours and I knew there was a good chance I wouldn't see her again—except passing in the hall or at some random party. I tried to reconstruct what happened but all I could think about was her fucking that preppie from Brown.

"Déjà vu, Z-man," Elise said with a lopsided grin.

"I know. I'm sorry, El."

"You need to find a stable girlfriend or I'm going to develop insomnia."

"I'm such as ass."

"No, Z, you and Crystal are not meant to be. That's all the sense it makes. When I set you up, it was for a one-nighter. Maybe for the weekend. But this moving in together, this girlfriend-boyfriend thing ... there's no plane of reality on which it makes sense. Face facts, boy."

I drank more coffee, feeling my stomach grumble with the nausea of too much caffeine and not enough nourishment. "But I love her, El."

"You love the sex."

I stared. I couldn't deny what she was saying.

"Look, Z, a couple weeks ago you loved Maggie and were gonna drown yourself in Cayuga Lake if you couldn't have her. Now you can't live without Crystal." She took my hand and held it gently. "Take a step back, take a few deep breaths, and figure yourself out. You're a good guy, Z. For Chrissake, have some fun and let the rest take care of itself."

"Is she making a chump out of me, El?"

Elise's ears went red and she tried to ignore the question, but I kept staring at her until she said, "You know where she's been the past two nights? Joey Bocca's room."

Joey Bocca was a wannabe bad boy with thick black hair that flowed past his shoulders and a perpetual scowl on his face. He wore nothing but black: black jeans, black T-shirts, black army boots, even a black wristband an old girlfriend had braided for him. I'd seen him staring at us more than once in the dining hall.

"Freshman year Crystal and Joey had a hot thing going for a while, but it went to hell quick," Elise said. "But every so often when the mood strikes, they'll hit the hay for old time's sake."

"She's got these old time's sake motherfuckers all over campus," I said.

Elise just looked at me.

5.

All through my Greek Tragedy class I kept thinking about Agamemnon, the king of Argos, whose queen, Clytemnestra, spent the better part of a decade screwing some thug named Aegisthus while the king was away fighting the Trojans. The two lovers had other things in mind for Agamemnon once he returned, but maybe in the end they were doing him a kindness. Maybe a quick, sharp blade to the chest is less painful than feeling the sting of faithlessness every hour of every day Jesus Crystal spread across his bed legs splayed taking him saying his name begging him to fuck her fuck her fuck her.

"Mr. Zinarelli, maybe you can give us an intelligent answer to this question," Professor Chilocetta said.

"The Greeks ..." I coughed, my voice sounding strange to my own ears. "The Greeks weren't really concerned with evil when it came to drama. Things unfolded as they were scripted by the fates. People were just ... caught in the middle. Sometimes heroically, sometimes tragically."

The professor perched on the edge of my desk. "Thank you, Mr. Zinarelli. That's all for today, everyone."

As we piled into the hallway, I heard Thoms behind me: "Thank you, Mr. Zinarelli. May I kiss you, Mr. Zinarelli?"

"Stick to your art history classes, Billy. Greek Tragedy is for the big boys."

Just then I saw the blackness that was Joey Bocca. His long hair was tied in a ponytail and his boots clomped down the hallway. He was headed right toward me. I wanted to turn off into an empty classroom, but there wasn't any time so I did the only thing I could: I stared him down. His brown eyes were dead, not smug, not even satisfied, just flat. *Having a good time with her you dick how many times have you fucked her already you going back to your room to fuck her right now?* It took every ounce of my concentration to keep walking because what I really wanted to do was wheel around and split the back of his head open with anything I could get my hands on.

"That's it," Thoms said. "Don't even blink. Don't give him the satisfaction."

"I want to kill him."

"No you don't. It's not his fault... . C'mon back to my room and smoke a joint. You'll feel better."

"Can't. Got shit to do."

He kept walking straight and I took the staircase to the right, which led out into the gloomy afternoon. The sky was low and the color of old metal. I felt like I was in a cell. Winter never ended in the Finger Lakes. I thought about the raw days I'd sit on the rocks by the Hudson River, listening to the water lap against those ancient banks and thinking how, even in winter, this river valley was the most beautiful spot in the world with its soft hills and slow curves that led to the sea.

"I want to go home," I whispered to the steely sky.

Crystal was sitting in front of my door, her back up against it as if preventing some great evil out from getting out. I looked at her and had nothing to say. I just stood there. "Can I talk to you?" she asked softly.

"Talk."

She shook her head, dark hair floating around her face. "Not here. Can we go inside?"

"I don't want you inside."

She reached out for my ankle but I moved away. I didn't want her to touch me. "Please, Mikey," she said, her voice cracking. People were watching from the doorways of their rooms and the last thing I wanted was a public scene. I unlocked the door and kicked it open. "Go on," I said.

She stood up and went inside. I closed the door behind us.

"All right. What is it?"

Her eyes were glistening. "I want to come home," she said.

Home? I had no answer to that.

"I want to move back into our room and go back to the way things were. Please, Mikey, I love you."

I still had no words. *Love me?*

She sat on the edge of the bed. "Baby, I'm sorry."

Sorry! A tight cord at the back of my brain seemed to snap. Everything went white for a second. I grabbed a handful of her gorgeous black hair and dragged her across the bed until our faces were inches apart. She didn't struggle, didn't make a sound. "You're sorry, Crystal? Sorry for what, exactly? Sorry for fucking that Ivy League faggot? Sorry for sucking Joey Bocca's cock for the past two nights? Sorry for fucking Emily's boyfriend while her mother was in intensive care? What are you sorry for? Some of it? All of it?"

I released her and stepped back because I was afraid of the rage in my hands.

"Baby, I didn't touch Joey. I swear. I slept on his floor. He wanted to, but I said no. I said you were my baby."

"Uh huh."

"And I didn't sleep with Jeremy, either." She tried to laugh. "He's from Brown, for Chrissake. Mikey, please. Mikey." Tears were spilling from her eyes, but they left me cold. I grabbed her by the throat and shook her.

"Stop fucking lying, Cryssie. I may be a hick from Poughkeepsie but I'm not an idiot. What happened? Joey Bocca get sick of you already and throw you out? Is that why you're back here? I know you fucked Bocca and I know you fucked that Brown bastard. Stop lying for once."

She opened her mouth and I slapped it closed.

"Say it!"

She stared at me. There was an ugly red mark on her left cheek.

"Say you fucked them. Say it!"

She stammered, tears still running down her face. "I fucked them," she said quietly.

"Louder."

"I fucked them," she screamed.

"Was it good? Did it feel good when Ivy League boy put his cock in you? Did he know some fancy moves they only teach at Brown?"

"Baby, please, I love you."

"Stop saying that. How about Bocca's cock? Was that nice too? Did it feel big in your mouth? Was it better than my cock?"

"Mikey, I love you."

I grabbed another handful of her hair and shook it back and forth. "Don't say that again or I swear I'll beat the shit out of you. Don't say anything about love. I want to know if Bocca fucked you better than me. I want to know if his cock made you crazy."

"I only care about you, Mikey. You're the only one I care about."

"Yeah, is mine nicer?" She nodded her head as I unzipped my pants and pulled my cock out. "Is mine better?"

She reached out for it but I slapped her hand away. "Don't touch it until I tell you."

I dropped my pants below my knees. "Put it in your mouth." She did, gobbling it down. She was so turned on I thought her nipples would burst through her black and gold Bruins T-shirt.

"You like it better than Bocca's?" She nodded as she kept sucking and licking me.

Everything became a blur. I tore her clothes off and entered her as savagely as I could, but she was drenched and accepted it easily, moaning at the violence while I hammered her *you love this cock yes baby you gonna fuck it whenever I tell you yes baby you ever gonna touch anybody else's cock no baby no just you.*

I don't know how long we made love (love?), but at one point I turned her over and she rose up on her hands and knees. My cock was so hard I thought it would never go down. Instead of sliding it into her pussy, I jammed it into her ass. She made a few small sounds of pain but didn't protest, kept herself open to me.

I pounded until I gushed into her, everything—rage, love, embarrassment, pain—flowing out of me. Dizzy, I pulled away from her and sprawled across the bed. I couldn't feel anything except my heart jamming against my chest.

After a moment of white light and tingling skin, I stood up.

"I've never done that before," Crystal said, as if offering me some form of virginity. I could see small streaks of blood on the backs of her legs. I saw her nut-brown body rippling with goose pimples.

"Can you cover me, baby? It's chilly in here."

I dragged the blanket over her and she said, "That's my good boy," before curling into a ball and starting to doze.

I stood naked next to my dresser, my limp cock smeared with small stains of red. I took out my pipe and slowly sucked in several hits of pot.

My entire body was trembling. The pot couldn't calm me. I thought I was going to implode.

Chapter Seven
The Inevitable Attraction of Earth

*The days are bright and filled with pain
Enclose me in your gentle rain.*
—The Doors

1.

    David Kaplowitz walked close to Earth without touching her, smiling now and then at her words. He was listening carefully, paying attention to the exact content while also drinking in the nearness of her, enjoying the smell of soap and warm bread. The Farmers' yard was showing the signs of late October in the valley: colorful leaves scattered about, glinting in the afternoon sun; vines withered in the garden awaiting the last cleanup of the season; half-naked tree limbs poking toward the sky like skeletal fingers. He took it all in and felt cozy about where he was at the moment. Still, he was well aware of something hanging over his head.
    Earth was satisfied with the meal she had cooked for David. He had obviously enjoyed it and, she thought, was even impressed by it. She was glad to impress him. She had never met anyone quite like him. He was his own man, seemed to act on his convictions and passions. Yes, she found him handsome, but there was more to her attraction than mere looks. She liked him.
    "What's it like being a singer?" she asked him as they walked around the yard.
    He shrugged. "Not as glamorous as you might think. I'm nobody, really. I play small clubs for a few bucks a night. That's it. Actually, it can be very humbling. I'm up there playing the guitar and singing my heart out, and

people are laughing and talking and clinking glasses, hardly paying any attention to me."

"Sounds painful."

He laughed softly. "Oh, it has its moments. I mean, once in a while, there's a moment when everybody's quiet and listening and I'm hitting every note perfectly and I can tell I'm getting through to them. That's when it's special."

"How do you live on what you make?"

He seemed a bit embarrassed and she immediately regretted asking it. "That was a terrible question. I'm sorry."

"No big deal. My mother helps me out. She's the one who bought me the Beemer. She's married to a rich investment banker and she likes spending his money."

She didn't reply to that. They walked in silence for a minute, feet crunching through the leaves. His life seemed exotic to her. The stories of singing in clubs and visiting the world's greatest museums on a whim thrilled her. Living in New York City, away from her sheltered little valley, must be an adventure.

"Your family is amazing," he said.

She didn't know how to answer. "I love them," was all she could think of, and it sounded so hackneyed she was sorry she said it.

"I'm sure. How could you not? Your mother is charming and your father is an absolute hoot. And both of your sisters are great. I'm glad you asked me to dinner."

"Tell me about your family," she said.

He hesitated, his sharp-featured face registering something between pain and confusion. "There's no short answer to that," he said finally. "My father was a college professor and he met my mother when she was a graduate student."

"Is he still teaching?"

Kaplowitz shook his head. "Nah, he retired a few years ago."

"Living the good life, huh?"

"Not exactly. My mother left him a broken man. I don't like saying it, but it's true. She humiliated him beyond belief. She slept with other professors, with students. God knows who else. Janitors, maybe. By the time he finally got the guts to throw her out, he was a wreck. He's never really recovered from it."

"Do you see him much?"

"Nah. We left him when I was five, and for a while I got to see him a couple times a year. Even when I was young he'd tell me how horrible my mother was, how she had been an unfaithful bitch. I didn't understand it then, really, but as I got older it all became clear. After a while, he couldn't stand looking at me anymore. I haven't talked to him in years. He sends me a letter once or twice a year, but I rarely answer."

She reached out and took his hand. "I'm sorry," she said. "It must be horrible for you."

He shrugged. "I've gotten used to it. Of course I blame my mother, but, you know, my father was such a wimp. He knew what she was doing and he let her get away with it until it ate him alive. Maybe if he'd confronted her from the start, things would have turned out different ... or maybe not."

They sat on the stone bench at the back of the yard, still holding hands. Her sky-blue eyes searched out his brown ones, and they stared at each other for a few seconds, not needing to speak. He wanted to kiss her but held back, waiting for a sign from her. He did not want to push it. Things were going smoothly enough.

"You must really love her, in spite of everything," Earth said. "The way you won't let go of her."

"I'm going to find her," he said. He changed subject abruptly. "It seems like you're pretty close to the Zinarellis," he said.

"I don't ever remember them not living across the street."

"What do you think of them?"

She considered that, and wondered briefly why he asked it. "They're good people," she said after a moment. "I mean, they have their issues, like any family. Mr. Z drinks too much. Sophie is way too hard on her sister. And Tasha, well, Tasha has a lot going on. I love that girl. She's one of a kind."

"Interesting," Kaplowitz said.

"Why do you think Mr. Z knows something about where your mother is?"

"Just a feeling."

"Did your mother ever talk about him?"

He chuckled. "Yeah, quite a bit the last few years. When people start getting older they can't let go of things in their life they regret. I think she really loved him back then. Maybe she thought her life could've been different if they got married. But that was a fantasy if you ask me."

"Sounds romantic."

"I think they were just two desperate people looking for the same thing everybody else is looking for."

"What's that?"

His brown eyes twinkled as he looked into her angelic face. "The real thing."

2.

Tasha Zinarelli sat straight up in her bed and looked wildly around her room. A chill ran along her spine despite the two stout blankets covering her. Eyes wide in the darkness, she looked into every corner trying to find what had unsettled her. There was nothing but piles of clothes and scattered papers and random pens and colored pencils. Nothing ominous. But that didn't comfort her. It had always been difficult for Tasha to find comfort.

She swung her feet around to the carpeted floor and then remained perfectly still, listening. The October wind rattled the half-naked tree limbs, making them creak and scratch the side of the house. There was noise beyond that, however, something faint and sinister. *It's my imagination it's nothing it is a trick of night.* Silver moonlight streamed in through her window. She wondered why she had forgotten to close the blinds. She always closed the blinds when she slept.

For as long as she could remember, fear and uneasiness had been her companions. She did not understand how it had started, and her therapist had never been able to get to the roots of it. Her parents, as far as she could recall, had always blanketed her with a sense of security. They had loved her, she thought, had tried to build up her ego and her sense of wellbeing. Why did she detect evil everywhere? Where did that come from?

Tasha drew a deep breath, held it for a few seconds, let it out slowly. Dark wings beat just above her head, making her tremble. So many things tore at her it was difficult to pinpoint a single threat. Her grandmother was very sick and slipping away. Something odd and frightening was going on with her father. Ever since Sophie had threatened her, Taylor Cardone had menaced Tasha silently; she had glared at her without getting too close, had hovered around her locker without even brushing against her. Tasha was afraid for herself and afraid for the people she loved—though if she were asked to put her fear into words, she would retreat into the sullen silence that infuriated her parents.

In Tasha's eyes, death seemed to hang over everything. Death terrified her. She had no understanding of it and had not been offered comfort against it. Her parents had never taken her to church and rarely talked about religion except in a philosophical sense. They had never said, "God will take care of you," or "When you die you'll be reunited with God and be filled with joy for eternity." Anna Zinarelli was indifferent to religion and Michael Zinarelli was an enemy of organized religion. "More people have been murdered in the name of God than any other reason," he'd said more than once. He did not fully understand how such proclamations affected his younger daughter.

Mike Z had some complex, convoluted theory about God and the universe. If pressed, he would say that he did believe in some sort of creator, some ultimate overseer of life. "It's hard to believe all of this is an accident," he had once told Anna after he had downed several glasses of wine and was staring at a pink and orange summer sunset. He had no idea Tasha was listening and did not know she had absorbed the statement. She drank in every word he said about God and creation and reality because she had no formal training in theology. She had never studied Genesis and how in the beginning God had created the heavens and the earth. She thirsted for answers; simple, straightforward answers to what dogged her. But there was nothing to fill the emptiness and she could not articulate her cosmic isolation, would never say "I feel alone in the universe" because, after all, what kind of corny thing would that be to say.

Just as she stood up to go to the window, clouds moved in front of the moon, blocking the argent light and throwing the backyard into deep darkness. She stared through the glass. Shadows within shadows seemed to twist and slink toward the house. The tree at the back of the property, the one she had climbed happily as a 5 year old, sprouted a black figure that looked at her with blank eyes. She pressed her face against the pane, trying to get a better look. The thing stole in her direction.

"What the hell," she whispered.

For an insane moment, she thought it might be Taylor Cardone trying to sneak into the house and kill her in her sleep. She shook her head, smiled grimly. That was too much even for Taylor. The bitch wanted to humiliate her, but murder? No. Still, something or someone was out there. The clouds swept away from the moon and the silvery light returned, giving Tasha a clearer view of the yard. The shadowy figure was gone from the tree. Perhaps it had been her imagination. She scanned the yard and felt a pinch in her stomach. There by the bushes, perfectly still but not completely concealed, was a shape. She could not tell if it was an animal or a person. But it was there. It had eyes.

Tasha moved slightly away from the glass. She was terrified. The eyes met hers, glared at her with purpose. They exchanged looks for several seconds, Tasha's heart beating so fast she thought it would surely explode.

Unable to tolerate the eyes any longer, she threw open the window and screamed, "Who are you? What do you want?"

The eyes did not move but answered with menacing silence.

"What the hell do you want?" Tasha shouted again. "Go away."

The eyes mocked her. A cold night-breeze sifted through the screen.

Z came running into the bedroom and flicked on the light. When he saw his daughter huddled near the window, he said, "Tasha, what's wrong?"

She jerked her head around to look at him. "Someone's watching the house," she said with something approaching calm.

"What?"

He came to the window and shut it against the cold. Then he asked Tasha to switch off the light so he could see better into the yard. Anna and Sophie were in the room now, too, and they both crowded near the glass, staring down. "Tasha said someone's watching the house," Z said.

After a few seconds, Sophie said, "Well, there's no one there now."

"There *was*."

"There's not now," Sophie repeated.

"Damn you, Soph—"

"All right, all right," Anna said. She hit her younger daughter lightly on the shoulder. "Tasha, that mouth."

Z had been staring out the window during this exchange and was not sure he didn't see something moving at the far end of the yard where the tangle of brush and scrub led down to the creek. It might have been the wind or a skunk or even a stray coyote. He could not be certain if it was anything at all. He switched the light back on.

"OK," he said to Tasha. "I'm sure it was nothing. Maybe you were dreaming."

"Next to the window?"

"Your mother once went down into the kitchen while she was asleep and came back upstairs with a quart of milk. Why, I have no idea. And neither does she. Sometimes weird things happen when we sleep."

"Weird things happen to weird people," Sophie mumbled.

Tasha threw a punch that nearly clipped her sister's jaw, and Sophie tumbled back onto the bed to escape the blow.

"All right, girls—that's enough!" Z snapped. "Everybody back to bed."

As Anna snuggled beneath the blankets, Z curled up against his pillows but did not close his eyes. He wondered

The DEATH of OBSESSION

if what Tasha had seen was his father, watching over the house. If so, why? What was the old Sicilian worried about?

3.

Anna was splashing cold water on her face in the upstairs bathroom. The girls were both out, Michael was at work, and she was glad to be alone. Her eyes burned and she was bathing them to cool them down. She felt slightly sick and could not fully understand what was wrong.

She heard the front door handle waggle, the door open. Were one of the girls home? She had to make everything seem normal.

"Anna," a voice called. "Hey, Anna."

It was Earth. Anna took a couple deep breaths and called down to her young friend, "Up here, honey."

Earth came thundering up the stairs, her strong legs bouncing with the strength of youth. She popped her head into the bathroom and was immediately taken aback by Anna's appearance. Her eyes were rimmed in red and her face was ashen. Earth stepped into the room and hugged her neighbor without saying anything.

"Earth," Anna said, holding back tears.

"What's the matter, Anna?"

Anna pulled away from her, turned back to the sink, began running the cold water again. She splashed her face once more.

"Anna?"

She snapped off the water, turned abruptly. At first she seemed defiant; then her face sagged. She looked very old right then. "Everything's coming apart, Earth. Everything I've worked for all these years."

Earth hugged her again, pulling her against her chest. She rocked her slowly as one might comfort a baby.

"Oh, God," Anna wailed.

"Anna, listen to me," Earth said, her voice authoritative. "Mr. Z loves you. He does. But he's a man and you know men are asses."

Anna laughed through her tears, squeezed her friend. "I don't know what to do."

"Don't do anything right now," Earth told her. "See how it all plays out."

Anna sucked in a shuddering breath. "The police think he might have killed her."

Earth shook her head. "We both know that's not true, Anna."

Anna held on and started crying again. "Earth, I love you, honey."

"And I love you and your family, Anna."

4.

Tasha was shooting baskets at the hoop in her driveway, snapping her wrist and squaring up like her coach had taught. The ball sailed through the net, making the satisfying swoosh sound. Tasha expected to be on the high school's JV team this year, even though she was only an eighth-grader and attended the middle school. She had excelled last year on the modified squad—the team designated for seventh- and eighth-graders. JV tryouts were in the next couple weeks and she needed to be ready. Doing well in basketball was important to her because, on the basketball court, she felt special.

The day was gray and chilly, with a wind gusting from the east. Tasha would have rather been in the house, sitting in front of the television. Instead, she dribbled the length of the drive, switching hands to strengthen her ball-handling skills. She had a reputation as a hard-nosed player—a good defender and tenacious rebounder. Where she needed improvement was on the offensive end. If she could handle the ball and shoot better she would make the JV team. To do so as an eighth-grader was a high honor.

The driveway was empty, since both of her parents were working. Sophie wasn't home, either. She had a National Honor Society meeting which was probably going to run until dinner time. Being alone when it was light out didn't bother Tasha. In fact, she welcomed the solitude. Dealing with her mother and sister was often difficult, although she couldn't put her finger on why. The truth was, she didn't always like people very much, even the people she was closest to—especially the people she was closest to. She could not understand why she was often so annoyed at her family. She *did* love them, in fact couldn't imagine her life without them. But something she was unable to describe gnawed at her, made her angry and petulant for no apparent reason. She wanted to be a nicer person but did not know how.

Starting at the end of the driveway, she dribbled toward the hoop, cut left and switched hands, cut back to the right and looped the ball up off the backboard. It rattled around the hoop and fell through the net. If she could do that at the tryouts, with somebody draped all over her, she would surely make the team. OK, so maybe she didn't have mad skills, but she was tough and knew the game and those were things coaches appreciated. Being on the JV team as an eighth-grader would elevate her cool. And even though she pretended not to care about that, it was important to her. She wanted desperately to belong to something.

Tasha dribbled back out for a fifteen-foot jumper when a car came screeching into the driveway, rattling her completely. She did not recognize the car, a newish Honda, and could not see at first who was inside. She stood and stared. Both doors opened and out popped Taylor Cardone and her sister, Liz Cardone. Tasha's knees trembled and she thought she might vomit.

Bravely, she shouted, "What the hell do you want?"

Liz stayed near the car and Taylor moved forward, her face twisted into a sneer. "I want to fuck you up," she said with soft menace. "You're not so tough now that your big sister's not here to do your fighting."

"She'll be back in a minute."

Taylor laughed angrily. "No she won't."

Liz added, "She's at that meeting for the smart bitches. It's supposed to be going on for a while."

Tasha stood her ground, even though her stomach was fluttering. "So what do you want?" she asked again.

Taylor took a few steps toward Tasha. Her voice tightened into an inexplicable rage. "You gonna see what I want, bitch."

Liz laughed. She skipped toward Tasha, shaking her head back and forth as her dyed yellow curls bounced around her head. "You gonna see, bitch," she repeated, her voice mocking everything.

"Fuck you," Tasha said to both the Cardone girls.

Liz howled as if she might rip Tasha apart with her bare hands. She pulled a knife out of her pocket and opened the blade. It was not big but looked very sharp. Jesus, would she really use it? Liz giggled crazily and said, "Who's fucked now, you little bitch? Huh? Who's fucked now?"

Tasha said nothing. She had no idea what to do. She was afraid and did not speak. She wondered how much a blade in her flesh would hurt. Somehow she had seen this moment in her nightmares. At least now it would be over. She would not have to be afraid anymore. She was so relieved she smiled.

"Something funny, bitch?" Taylor asked. She closed in on one side of Tasha while her sister moved in on the other. Trapped, Tasha stood silent and emotionless. The Cardones mistook her frozen terror for bravery.

"You think you're tough?" Liz sneered. "We'll see how tough you are." She held up the blade near Tasha's face.

"What's happening, girls?" a voice said casually.

Liz and Taylor whipped their heads around and saw Earth Farmer standing a few feet away. Her arms were folded across her chest and her blue eyes seemed to blaze. She stepped forward and pointed to the knife. "You better put that thing down. It could be dangerous."

Liz turned and made a move toward Earth. "Well, well, if it isn't hippie chick. You better just mind your own business or you're gonna end up getting hurt."

Earth smiled dangerously. "You don't scare me, airhead. Get back in your car and go home."

Liz snarled and thrust the knife forward. It might have cut Earth except that Air Farmer, as if appearing out of nowhere, protected her sister by bringing her folded hands down across Liz's arm, delivering a blow that made her stumble. The knife clattered to the driveway and Earth scooped it up quickly. Liz turned on Air and tried to punch her, but Air was too fast. She ducked away from the fist and shot her foot out into Liz's stomach. Liz doubled over, gasping for breath. Air grabbed her by the shoulders and threw her against her car. Liz leaned there, panting.

Taylor looked at her sister, uncertain now what to do.

"You came here to do something," Air told her. "Finish it."

Earth got between Tasha and Taylor. She moved Tasha back and looked into her eyes. She saw the fear. "She's as scared as you are," Earth whispered. "You want to end this once and for all? Remember one thing: bullies are all cowards. You understand? They're all cowards."

She stepped away and left open space between Tasha and Taylor. "Well, go to it," she said to Taylor.

Liz seemed as if she might try to join the fray, but Air grabbed her by the hair and pulled her back against the car. "You stay put," she said. Liz obeyed. She could not believe how strong Air Farmer was.

Taylor mustered as much ferocity as she could and charged toward Tasha, screaming wildly. Tasha stood her ground and took one powerful swing. Her fist slammed into the side of Taylor's face, dropping her instantly. Eyes wide, she stared in disbelief at Tasha. A dribble of blood ran down her cheek. Tasha stood over her. She was trembling and her fists remained tightly balled as if ready to deliver another blow.

Earth helped Taylor to her feet. "Go home," she said. "And don't come around here again." As a peace offering, she added, "I'm sure Tasha isn't going to say anything about this."

Tasha shook her head.

"Let this die here," Earth said.

Head down, Taylor got into the passenger side of her sister's car. Air opened the driver side door and ushered Liz inside. Earth was still holding the knife. She closed the blade and put it in her pocket.

"You'll get this back when I think you can handle it correctly," she told Liz.

The Cardones' car squealed away, their speed a last act of defiance. When they were out of sight, Tasha came forward and hugged Air, then Earth.

"Thank you," she said softly. She was crying.

"We take care of our own," Earth answered, embracing her gently.

5.

Z was raking in his front yard before going to work when he was aware of someone crunching through the leaves. He looked up to see a short, powerfully-built woman heading his way. His insides twisted. Jesus Christ, when was this going to end? He leaned on the rake and waited.

"Hello, Mr. Zinarelli."

"What is it now? You and Delson taking turns hounding me?"

Her mouth twisted into a wry grin. "Delson's off today. But I wanted you to know a new development in the case."

"What's that, Detective Barone?"

She folded her arms across her small chest. She was dressed in black pants, a black jacket, and a red shirt. She looked very sharp, Z thought. He still imagined her as a lesbian, though. Her short yellow hair and fierce expression told him so. No matter what Delson said.

"We found Crystal Cassidy's pocketbook between some rocks along the river," she said. Her voice was enticingly gravelly.

"OK."

"Your name and phone number was in it, written on a piece of paper."

He shrugged. "So? I already admitted we talked. But that's all. We *talked*. I never met with her."

Detective Barone was chewing gum and she snapped on it hard. "The funny thing is the pocketbook was wiped clean on the outside. No fingerprints. Her fingerprints were all over the inside, of course. But nothing on the outside."

"And that means what to me?"

"What it means to me is that somebody planted that pocketbook near the river to make us think, what, that Crystal Cassidy jumped in and committed suicide?"

"Is that what you think?"

Detective Barone shook her head slowly. "No." She stepped uncomfortably close to Z. "I know you were with her in Carmel. I *know* it. Why don't you just tell the truth

The DEATH of OBSESSION

and get it off your chest? This thing has got to be eating you up inside. Tell me what happened to her."

"I have no idea," he said softly. He propped his chin on the end of the rake. "You're making a mistake. Yes, at first I lied about talking to her. I did. But that's all. I talked to her on the phone. Nothing else."

"How do you think her pocketbook got here?"

Z shrugged. "Someone planted it, like you said."

"Yeah. Someone."

6.

Earth Farmer did not like to eat at restaurants because the food was never as good as what she could get at home. But David Kaplowitz had insisted on taking her out, and she finally decided on a sushi place in Hyde Park housed in an old fieldstone building. He picked her up in the BMW and she felt special. Thinking about David confused her. He was an exciting man—handsome and charming. But he was also mysterious and slightly sad.

The sushi restaurant wasn't crowded, and David got them a quiet table in the corner. He ordered a bottle of sake and they sipped at the rice wine while talking. When it came time for dinner, Earth opted for a vegetable roll dinner while David got the broiled eel. They drank and laughed, talking about everything and nothing. Earth found herself flattered and a little uncomfortable because he seemed to hang on her every word.

When the conversation faltered, Earth told Kaplowitz about Tasha and the Cardone girls. She tried to downplay her involvement, but after she was finished, Kaplowitz said, "That was so great of you."

She shrugged. "It was nothing, really. I love Tash. She's her own woman. I'd do anything for her. Anyway, the Cardones are punks."

Kaplowitz laughed. "You are something."

Earth ate her sushi slathered in spicy wasabi and exhibited incredible dexterity with the chopsticks. David fumbled with his own chopsticks and at one point turned to Earth and said, "Is there anything you're not good at?"

She smiled demurely. "David, you don't have to flatter me. I already like you."

He leaned forward, his brown eyes twinkling. "This whole thing has been crazy, you know, my mother disappearing and all. But then I got to meet you. So I guess good things can come out of bad situations."

The sake was making her flushed. "Oh, David, you're so smooth. You must have a trail of broken hearts all across New York City."

His cheeks reddened a bit. "Not really. Most of the women I meet are just ... so shallow." He laughed when he saw her intense gaze on him. "Look, I'm not saying I don't avail myself of good-looking women. But as far as emotional involvement there's no way. Until now."

"David, stop it," she said. She was not flirting; she was serious.

He reached across the table and took her hand. He was aware how hard and calloused it was, how much it showed her work ethic. She was an enticing combination of naïve farm girl and emotionally sophisticated woman. He could not easily figure her out, and that excited him. Holding that hand so tightly was as provocative to him as squeezing her breasts or massaging her thighs.

"Earth, I'm not bullshitting you," he said. His perfect face and searing eyes made her tremble inside. What was happening to her?

"Guys have been bullshitting my whole life."

He held her hand urgently. "Not now. Not me."

She didn't know how to answer that. She was light-headed from the sake and for other reasons she didn't want to think about. David Kaplowitz frightened her and aroused her. Pulling her hand away from his, she sipped at her green tea. The taste fortified her, brought her back to herself.

When the check came, Earth demanded to pay half. David said he had asked her out and paying was his obligation. "I got this," he said. When they left the restaurant she kissed his cheek softly and said, "Thanks," and he pressed against her with demands of his own.

"How'd you like to see a movie?" he asked her.

She shrugged. "I'm not much for movies," she answered. "I know a place where they have a jazz trio on Wednesday nights."

"Sounds perfect."

David didn't think the bar/restaurant looked very promising at first. It was in an outdoor mall in Wappinger, just off a commercial strip of Route 376, and the façade seemed plastic and crass. He was surprised how well appointed the place was inside, warm and snug with overflowing plant stands, classic Italian murals, and small, elegant tables bunched together to give the illusion that the place was always crowded.

"This is nice," he said as they sat down.

She nodded, didn't say anything. She was happy to shatter his stereotype that everyone in Dutchess County was a hick. *We understand what's tasteful we know about jazz we just choose to enjoy these things in a place that's not so smelly and crowded and a pain in the ass to navigate.*

The trio featured Diana Keyes on piano and vocals (yes that was her real name), one guy on the stand-up bass and another on the drums. They performed their own versions of jazz standards with surprising dexterity. David seemed entranced by the music, staring at the trio while its members ran through a series of tunes he loved: "I Didn't Know What Time It Was," by Rodgers and Hart; "Lullaby of Birdland," by George Shearing; "As Time Goes By," by Herman Hupfeld. The songs brought back days he had never lived through but wished he could have experienced.

They sipped drinks, him a cold limoncello, her a Baileys with no ice, and absorbed the music without saying much. At one point, he leaned across the table and kissed her on the lips, lingering for a long moment. "This is tremendous," he whispered. She could smell the lemony liqueur on his breath and the subtle hint of cologne on his body. His lips made her quiver and she was scared; things with this stranger were going too well. Was this how her mother had felt when she met Max all those years ago? Was this how love happened?

It was late when they got back outside to the car. The October night was chilled, raw wind hinting at the winter on the way. He revved up the BMW and Earth insisted that she needed to get home, but he kissed her again, this one deeper and more searching. She felt herself melting against him.

"Come back to my hotel," he said.

Breathless, she nodded.

When they reached his room, he was at first slow and gentle. He kissed the creamy skin of her face, ran his hands over her body with a tenderness that made her ache. She was passive at first, allowed him to lead the way. He unbuttoned her shirt and slipped his hand beneath her bra; she moaned, her nipples already so hard she couldn't stand it. They kissed passionately, tongues intertwining. She sensed how turned on he was, but he continued to move with restrained desire, making her want him all the more. At last, she ran her hand along his thigh and felt his hardness straining against the fabric of his pants. She rubbed it with long, smooth strokes.

They undressed each other deliberately, and when they were finally naked they touched and licked and nibbled with a fire that burned them both. He was aroused by her full, supple body. She was so unlike the underfed, skeletal women he was used to. She was soft and smooth and inviting. His fingers sought her crevice, found it damp, probed and played gently in the pliant flesh. Her sigh filled the room. She reached over, took him in her hand, and began pumping slowly.

"I want to taste you," he said, moving his head down between her legs. He opened her, slid his tongue into the wetness then pushed his face forward with a violence that shocked her. She grabbed his hair in both hands and pulled his head away.

"Gently, David," she said softly.

Her body went rigid and then she fell back against the mattress, instinctively closing her legs. He moved up to enter her, so swollen he ached, and opened her thighs roughly. He teased her at first, running the tip of his cock slowly along the opening. She closed her eyes and suddenly couldn't wait for him to finish. "C'mon, *c'mon*," she said. He mistook her urgency for excitement and plunged forward, enveloped in her hot wetness.

"Jesus, Earth," he whispered

David Kaplowitz prided himself on his sexual control, on his ability to hold off his own satisfaction until the perfect moment. But now, pumping urgently against Earth, he found himself spewing liquid into her quickly, the release so intense his entire body trembled against her flesh.

He kissed and caressed her in the moments afterwards, unaware that she seemed cold to his touch.

"I can do better," he said, laughing against her chest.

"It doesn't matter," she said. "I have to get home anyway."

Chapter Eight
In Search of the Perfect Orgasm

*You say faster so I speed up
But still I'm much too slow
I feel your innuendo.*
—Little Feat

1.

Even when I spent hours reading, I wrapped myself in a haze of smoke and drink. I was happiest when my mind was engaged in the intricacies of Dostoevski, Faulkner, and Garcia Marquez, or when I was working on a short story for creative writing class. Outside of the work, my mood fluctuated between ecstasy and misery in the blink of an eye. The reason, of course, was Crystal Cassidy. She had my life in her tiny hands and she never failed to twist it to her whims.

I tried not to think too much about how Crystal had bent me to her will. It was easier to smoke pot and drink beer and float in that half-space between consciousness and oblivion, to fill an afternoon and evening sitting with my suite mates, playing spades and listening to *Feats Don't Fail Me Now* while we puffed on joints and swigged cheap brew and laughed until we couldn't laugh any more.

Most times, the room was filled with an instant chill when Crystal returned from the library or her classes or wherever the hell she had been. She would glare at my friends and throw her books on the desk and instantly the game would break up and the guys would scatter. "Stoned again," she might grumble, without confronting me directly. My high would come crashing down and I would find refuge in a book.

The DEATH of OBSESSION

Occasionally, Crystal would return in a good mood and smile at everyone and join the party, choosing the next album and dancing around the room, sitting on laps and laughing with us and even taking a toke or two from a joint. Those were the rare happy moments when I believed it might really work between us. But that happiness was always short lived.

I knew in my heart that Crystal was still cheating on me, but I couldn't prove it, could never nail it down. She would disappear for hours and answer vaguely, if at all, when I questioned her about where she'd been. I heard stories, had friends try to give me gentle hints about her indiscretions. But ultimately, I didn't want to know. I didn't want to face the decision of breaking it off with her. I didn't want to be alone again. Opening that old door seemed intolerable.

The ironic thing was, the longer I stayed with Crystal, the more isolated I became from my best friends, Elise and Frank and Shank and Wendy. Crystal rarely wanted to hang out with them. She preferred to stay holed up in our room, drinking and talking and making love. I enjoyed those nights, too, but after a while I began to miss the parties and laughter and long talks with Elise.

But the sex with Crystal kept me riveted to her. She was well aware of that and used it to her best advantage. Our lovemaking remained intense, and she continued to find ways to bring it to new levels. She was creative and fearless in bed. There was so much I didn't know and so much she did. She had once told me that she'd lost her virginity when she was 14 years old. I found that kind of sad, like she had lost out on a part of her childhood. But she seemed to have no regrets about it. What she did have was a wealth of experience that made her an unequalled sex teacher. I was a willing pupil. I sat at her feet as if she were a guru of the sweaty moment.

The second half of my sophomore year was a blur, a fog of drugs and orgasms and the heartache of wondering where Crystal was and who she was fucking. I was exhausted, pretending everything was fine and knowing I was fooling no one. I was a pussy-whipped idiot and everyone realized it. Everyone but me.

2.

One of the ways I worked out my frustration was playing racquetball. Pounding that little rubber ball over and over helped me sweat out the poisons I was putting into my system and also offered me temporary relief from Crystal's curse; when I was concentrating on the game I couldn't think about her.

I was in the gym with Steve Antonios. We played together three or four times a week. It was fun because we were evenly matched. I was quick and could make circus returns, getting to balls that seemed out of reach. He was a powerful hitter who was also adept at deadening the ball in the corners. Our games usually went to the wire and always left us exhausted and glowing with endorphins.

I wasn't on top of my game that day but hung in there, losing the first game badly, winning the second game in a late rush, and going back and forth with Steve in the third game. Approaching the decisive point, he rocked a screamer that looked sure to get by me. I lunged to my left, laid out in midair, and snapped a backhand that clipped the bottom of the wall and fell in front of Steve before he could reach it.

"Nice," he grunted. "Lucky, but nice."

"Fuck you."

"Serve it, Z."

I was panting and bounced the ball several times, trying to catch my breath. I hit a low serve with a nice backspin, but Steve reached it and hit a dying swan into the corner. I anticipated a slam and was backing up. By the time I started forward, the ball was bouncing in front of me.

"Talk about luck," I said.

He smiled and got ready to serve. It was game point. He faked a finesse shot and battered one just above the service line, driving it hard into the far left-hand court. I ran hard and was just able to get my racquet on the ball, getting it feebly to the wall. He closed in and prepared for the kill, blasting the ball to the opposite side of the court. I changed direction quickly, dove to my right and managed

The DEATH of OBSESSION

to get the racquet on the ball, hitting it high off the wall. Steve was in perfect position and dumped the ball into the corner. I had no chance to reach it. I leaned against the far wall, gasping for breath and feeling good despite the loss.

"Nice game," Steve said.

"One more?"

He shook his head, long curly hair flailing across his head. "Can't. I got just enough time to grab a shower before Chu's class. How about tomorrow?"

"I'm open in the morning."

"I'm jammed until three. Friday at nine?"

"Definitely. Prepare to be beaten."

He laughed. "Sure, sure." He packed his stuff away and hurried out, waving to me as he headed out the door.

I left the court and sat on one of the benches in the hallway. I was glistening with perspiration and thinking about the rest of my afternoon. I had no more classes and that meant time for a long, hot shower and then a couple of bowls of pot while listening to music and maybe working on my latest short story. Crystal had back-to-back ninety-minute classes that were starting in about fifteen minutes, so I had time to myself.

I pulled on my sweatshirt and sweatpants, heading out into the chilly April day. The sun was pale in the northern New York sky. I walked slowly with my bag over my shoulder, still feeling the rush of physical activity. As I neared my dorm, I heard someone running and turned to see Shank pulling up beside me.

"Z-man, what's going on?"

I grinned, glad to see him. "Nothing, man. I just got finished playing racquetball with Steve."

"What're you doing now?"

I shrugged. "I'm going to take a shower."

"Yeah, yeah, then what?"

"I dunno. I was going to work on my short story."

Shank tucked his long hair behind his ear and put his hand on my shoulder. "A bunch of us are getting together in my room for a game of Risk and a few joints. Why don't you join us, man?"

I dropped my head, shrugged. "I don't think so, Shank. I can't."

"Sure you can."

"Naw, I just—"

"C'mon, man, everybody's gonna be there. It'll be fun. You remember fun, don't you, Z?"

I stopped and stared into his bright green eyes. He was mocking me and I knew he was right. What was I so afraid of? I had become such a worm I almost couldn't stand myself. "OK, let me grab a quick shower and I'll be over."

He clapped my shoulder again and said, "All right. Hurry up."

I got back to my room to find that Crystal had already left for class. I was relieved. After taking a few hits from my bowl, I stripped down and took a quick shower. The hot water felt good, and as I headed back to my room in my robe, I felt great. I took another few hits as I got dressed. My hair was still damp when I left for the third floor.

I followed the dreamy strains of Weather Report down the hallway to Shank's room. It was like old home week. Shank, Wendy, Charlie Maurice, and Elise were doing bong hits on the bed. Cramer was leaning against the window, drinking a beer, and Liz was standing beside him. Maggie was there, too, smoking a joint and blowing smoke toward the ceiling.

"Hey," I said as I entered the room.

"Z-man," Elise shouted.

"How'd you get away?" Cramer said.

"Suck me, farm boy."

Maggie passed the joint to Liz, who took it and drew in a lungful of smoke. Maggie smiled at me. I wished we were alone together then felt guilty for thinking it. I stared at her lips and remembered how soft they were. Shank passed me the bong and I took a huge hit, feeling my chest expand. Wayne Shorter and Joe Zawinul weaved saxophone and keyboards in and out of each other.

"This is great," I said after I had breathed out the smoke.

"You won't be saying that when I kick your butt at Risk," Maggie said.

"Never happen," I told her.

"Let's get to it," Shank said.

Before we got started, I asked Elise, "Where's Frank?"

"Oh, he's studying for a big physics exam. You know Frank, he's not happy unless he's working."

Shank set up the board on his bed. I got the black pieces, which were my favorites because they looked so badass. The other players were Shank, Maggie, Elise, Charlie, and Liz. Cramer and Wendy sat out but were vocal spectators. I got an early foothold in South America, an easy continent to hold, and a few moves into the game had secured myself a stronghold.

The dice rolled, the beer flowed, and smoke filled the room. Wendy hung over Shank's shoulder, holding a joint for him and handing him beers. Cramer massaged Liz's shoulders and kept telling her she could conquer the world. Outside the window, the light faded and it got dark quickly. Partway through the game, Sierra Enrique came in, kissed Charlie on the cheek, and took a couple bong hits. Shank's red armies were making progress in Africa and Europe. Elise had taken Australia and was building up her armies to protect it. Charlie and Maggie were battling over Asia—holding it was a tall order and worth seven armies per turn. Liz was scattered all over the board and was certain to be out first.

At one point, Shank got up to go to the bathroom and I quickly followed him. When we were alone, I said, "Listen, if you and I leave each other alone, we can be the last two left."

Shank grinned wickedly. "Sounds good. This'll be forever known as the Bathroom Alliance."

We laughed and headed back to the room. We both took bong hits and I opened another beer. I was feeling beautiful. Dice rattled on the board and Jeff Beck's guitar wailed through the speakers. I was sitting next to Maggie and she kept leaning on me and laughing. I really wanted to kiss her. And I was angry at her, too, because if she hadn't dumped me I wouldn't be with Crystal.

We all had the munchies, so we took up a collection and Cramer and Wendy went upstairs to the snack machine and bought bags of chips and candy bars. The game wore on. Liz went out, then Charlie, then Maggie. The party was winding down. Liz and Cramer left, and so did Charlie and Sierra. Maggie hung around, smoking more pot. Elise's armies were hemmed in and eventually succumbed to Shank's forces. It was just the two of us left.

"The Bathroom Alliance reigns supreme," Shank shouted.

Shank's red armies dominated the board. I glanced at the clock and realized that Crystal had probably been back in our room for a while. I swept my black forces off the board and said, "I concede."

"You bastards," Elise said. "You set this all up."

Shank laughed, grabbed Elise around the waist and hugged her while she pounded him on the chest. As they tussled playfully, I turned to Maggie and asked her, "What are you going to do now?"

The question seemed to fluster her. "Oh, I have to get back to my room. I've got a paper I've *got* to get done." She couldn't get the words out fast enough and I understood the message clearly.

"Yeah, I've got a ton of reading to do," I said, trying to save face.

Maggie stood, said goodbye to everyone, and disappeared through the door. I wanted to follow her. I wanted her to suddenly realize she still loved me or loved me again. But that was a ridiculous fantasy. She had never loved me, had, at most, been infatuated with me in a way that was too casual for my liking. When you spent the night with someone, snuggled against them in the half-light hours of the early morning, wasn't that serious enough?

I had to get back to my room. Crystal was there; or maybe she wasn't—an even more upsetting possibility. Perhaps she'd returned, saw I was gone, and went out to find her fun elsewhere. Suddenly panicked, I said, "I gotta get back," and headed out the door. Elise said, "Wait up," and followed me.

"Hey," she said as we walked, "that was fun."

"Uh huh."

"You should join us more often." She touched my arm and looked at me with those sharp blue eyes. "We all miss you hanging out with us."

I felt my cheeks turning red. I loved Elise and Shank and the rest and felt like I'd abandoned them. For what? "I know, El," I said softly. I couldn't think of anything else to say. When we parted, Elise hugged me.

My stomach churned when I entered my room and saw Crystal sitting on the bed, head buried in a book. She did not look up. Her face was a mask of indifference. "Hey," I said, but she didn't respond, acted as if she had not even heard me. I felt my knees trembling. Her eyes had the dead black look that terrified me, the look that said she needed no one but herself.

"Hey," I said again.

She finally glanced up from the book but remained silent. Anger emanated from every pore, penetrating me like cold steel. *Fuck this shit*, I raged silently, but I stood where I was, hoping to somehow win her favor. I sat down at the desk and, unable to think of an alternative, started plowing through Yeats' "Cuchulain's Fight with the Sea." Poetry was never my strong suit and Yeats' fascination with Celtic mythology demanded a familiarity with a cast of characters and places totally foreign to me.

I was a few verses in when Crystal said, "Where the hell were you?"

I was so glad she was talking to me I ignored the venom in her voice. "We were playing Risk in Shank's room."

"And doing bong hits, I'm sure."

"Time just got away from me," I added. "I almost conquered the world, but Shank ended up winning."

She had no interest in the outcome of the game. "Who else was there?"

"The usual suspects," I said. "Cramer, Liz, Wendy, Elise, Charlie. Oh, and Maggie."

Crystal glared at me, eyes narrowing. "Maggie?"

"Oh, Cryssie, come on."

"What's going on, Mikey? You want to fuck her again? Is that what you want? Because if it is, you can have her."

"Cryssie, it was just a game of Risk. Jesus. I love *you*."

She looked at me, her brown eyes suddenly wide. "Do you, Mikey?"

"Yes."

"Do you love me enough to stop getting stoned every minute of every day? Honey, if we're going to get married, I need to know you can be a responsible adult. You are smart and talented, Mikey. I don't want to see you waste that."

Married? Had I ever said anything about marriage? Where the hell had that come from? It was on the table now, though. So typical of Crystal. She made these leaps and put hooks into me every step of the way. She wanted to possess but refused to be possessed. I couldn't answer, so I said nothing.

She put down her book, her attitude suddenly softening. "Baby, I love you, but I get scared. Guys have let me down all my life. I know you're different, but I have to be sure."

A million words flashed through my brain, questions about her fidelity and the reckless way she spread her legs to more guys than I could count. But I found myself saying, "Cryssie, you mean everything to me." I wondered if I had somehow given her doubt. I thought about how, if she gave me the slightest opening, I would run back to Maggie. Did Crystal see that?

She opened her arms and said, "Come here, baby."

3.

Crystal was nothing but sweetness for the next couple days. She was with me every minute she wasn't in class, was upbeat and caring. She even took a few hits of pot with me and made long, slow love to me Thursday afternoon. Before I left Friday morning to play racquetball, she gave me a long, searching kiss and said, "Let's do something special tonight."

"What do you have in mind?"

She gave me a little smile and said, "Let's recreate the first night we met. I mean, let's do as much as we can the same."

It sounded a bit bizarre, but I was game. "OK. But how?"

"Well, we can't meet in Chad's room. But I'll go up into the rec room and you can come up and introduce yourself and we'll pretend we're meeting for the first time."

I laughed. "You're crazy."

The DEATH of OBSESSION

"It'll be fun," she said. She was so happy I didn't want to dampen her spirits.

"OK. Sure."

Her eyes twinkled mischievously. "That means we have to do it three times. That's what we did the first night, remember?"

"I'm up for it," I said.

She kissed me passionately and said, "I'm going to be busy most of the day. I'll see you tonight. Make sure you're ready for some action."

I was sky-high when I got to the gym. Steve issued a couple verbal challenges, but I didn't respond except to smile. I was so pumped up I was flying around the court, picking every shot he made. I played out of my mind. I took the first game easily and dug in hard to take the second game by a point. Steve decided he didn't want to play a third game. I had worn him out. "What the hell did you have for breakfast?" he grumbled as he left the court.

I hurried back to the dorm, took a quick shower, and headed for my South American lit class. My focus was sharp and I offered several excellent insights into Borges' complex story "Tlon, Uqbar, Orbis Tertius." Dr. Denise Daar, a tall blonde in her late thirties who exuded sexuality, kept complimenting me on my observations. "You have obviously put a lot of thought into this text," she said at one point.

After class, I revved up the old Buick and drove into town. I stopped at a liquor store and bought Crystal a bottle of vodka, then went to the grocery store and picked up some cheese and crackers and a few other snacks. The car was running very rough, and I was worried I might not make it back to campus. When I pulled into the parking lot and shut off the engine, I was glad I had no reason to touch the Buick for a while.

Back in my room, I hid the vodka in one of my drawers, set the cheese out on the windowsill and sat smoking a bowl of pot, listening to Miles Davis on the stereo. It had been a long time since I was so content. Maybe things with Crystal could work out after all. Maybe I wouldn't have to be alone again. I stretched out on the bed and drifted away to the cool strains of Miles' horn.

The next thing I knew someone was pounding at my door, rousing me from a peaceful sleep. "What?" I groaned. Woody threw open the door and popped his shaggy red head inside.

"We need a fourth for spades," he said in his usual loud voice.

"No thanks."

"Come on. Don't be a shit," he said.

I sat up and glanced at the clock. It was still a couple hours before Crystal would be back. I had no intention of keeping her waiting today. "OK," I told him. "Just for a while."

It was Stan and Woody against me and Thoms. We annihilated them in the first game as Woody screamed at Stan for tentative bidding and sloppy play. As we shuffled the cards for a second game, Woody pulled out a mirror with a gram or so of coke on it and said, "This'll get us going." It had been a while since I'd snorted, and the burn at the back of my throat felt good.

The cards fell their way in the second game, but I didn't care. I was riding the coke and thinking about the night ahead. As soon as we'd lost, I said, "Sorry, guys, I've got to run. See you later." I ignored their entreaties to stay and hurried back to my room.

Crystal wasn't back yet, so I decided to take another shower to be fresh for her. I leaned against the tiles and let the hot water flow over me. I sucked in the last few grains of coke as the steam cleared my nostrils. I don't know how long I was in the shower, but when I got back to the room, there was a note on the bed. I unfolded it and read the message: "Come and get me."

I dried off and dressed quickly. After a few hits from my bowl, I brushed my hair and splashed on some cologne. There was a knot of anticipation in my stomach, just like the first night I'd met Crystal. I couldn't imagine what had made her concoct this idea, but I was glad. It showed she was trying to add spice to our relationship. I wanted to believe that it meant she cared.

She was alone in the rec room when I got there, and she looked beautiful. She was dressed in the same green sweater and tight jeans she'd been wearing when we met.

She smiled at me shyly and I walked over to her tentatively, trying to play my part. Her brown eyes were sparkling.

"Hi," I said. "I'm Michael Zinarelli."

"Crystal Cassidy. Hi. Elise was telling me about you."

"What did she say?"

"That you were a nice guy and that you were good in bed."

"Did she really say that?"

She nodded. "Uh huh."

"Want to play some pool?"

"Nah. I'm not in the mood."

I took her small hand in mine. It was warm and inviting. "How'd you like to come down to my room and see my fish?"

She smiled. "Sure. I'll bet it's very relaxing."

I kissed her softly, arms enveloping her. She eased her tongue into my mouth and had my heart racing. I led her back to the room and locked the door behind us. We stood in front of the aquarium as we had that first night, talking aimlessly about the fish. I pulled the vodka bottle out of my drawer and said, "I got you a present."

She kissed me again and poured herself a plastic glass full of vodka, drinking down half of it in a few swigs. I asked her if she wanted to hear some music and she said, "Yeah. Can I pick?" Of course, she chose Grover Washington Jr.'s *Mister Magic*. I loaded up a bowl and took a few hits of pot while she finished her drink and poured another. When I offered her the bowl, she took a toke, holding it in her lungs.

We sat on the bed and I started running my hands over her breasts while we kissed. Her hand was on my thigh, then rubbing my cock through my pants. I gently pinched her nipple and she breathed, "Mikey." We undressed without any more preliminaries and my fingers found the wetness between her legs. As I massaged her clit, she whispered, "Baby, baby," over and over. She pulled away from me, leaned down and put me in her mouth. Her hair fanned out over my stomach and I watched her devouring me. "Jesus, Cryssie," I cried.

She was drenched when I entered her and I pumped furiously. She locked her legs around my back and bucked up to meet every thrust. It wasn't long before her pussy was squeezing my cock and she was saying, "Oh God, baby, I'm coming. I'm coming all over your hard cock." I arched my back and gushed fluid into her, grinding against her until I was drained.

I kissed her forehead, her nose, her full lips, then rolled off her. I could barely breathe. "You're a good boy," she said softly.

4.

I woke up Saturday morning in a contented haze, but immediately there was an emptiness in my heart. Crystal was not in bed. She was not in the room. I got up, threw on a pair of shorts, and walked down the hall. She was not in the bathroom, either. What the hell? I returned to the room and sat on the bed, trying to figure out where she could be. The gnawing in my stomach started. But no, she couldn't—not after the great night we'd just had. There had to be a simple explanation. She was at the dining hall getting coffee. (She hated the dining hall and why wouldn't she wake me up to join her?) She was at the library for an early study session. (What was so important that she had to study first thing on a Saturday?) She had some meeting she had forgotten to tell me about. (With whom and where?)

I sat at the desk and tried to read, but I couldn't concentrate. I smoked a bowl and waited for Crystal to show up. The morning dragged by and there was no sign of her. I got dressed, took a few more hits of pot, and left the dorm. I checked the dining hall, the library, the gym, Crystal's old dorm room. She was nowhere around. I asked a few people I knew if they'd seen her. No one had. It was like she'd disappeared from the face of the earth.

I went back to my room to check if she'd returned, but she hadn't. By this time it was early afternoon and I was frustrated and worried. I grabbed the keys to the Buick and went out to the parking lot. The car hesitated when I tried to start it, and when it finally did rev up, it chugged as if it were about to die. I drove down toward the lake but didn't see her there. I drove into the village, slowly cruising the streets and then stopping into a couple of bars to see if she was inside having a few drinks. The more I searched, the angrier I got.

As I headed back to campus the temperature gauge showed the engine running hot. Something was wrong with my radiator. I cursed Crystal and hoped the Buick would make it back to the dorm. It did ... just barely. I eased the old girl into its parking space and turned off the engine. My happiness of the day before had turned to dread. Cryssie had disappeared. My car was dying. I was a hapless idiot. "God damn you," I screamed inside the bubble of the Buick.

The room was still empty when I returned. I could not imagine where Crystal was. Everything had been perfect between us just last night. I was so frustrated I started pounding my fists on the desk until my hands were sore. *I can't do this anymore I can't stand it she's fucking killing me.*

I smoked until I was so stoned I nodded off on the bed. I don't know when Crystal slithered into the room, but she was sitting at the desk reading a book when I opened my eyes. It was dark outside. I couldn't believe she was there. At first, I was relieved. Then I was so pissed off I wanted to strangle her.

"What the fuck happened to you?" I croaked.

She turned and gave me a sheepish smile. "I was going the library early and I ran into Ruth. We got to talking and worked a lot of things out. She said she was going to see this guy named Trip Saunders who lives in the village. He went here a few years ago. She asked me to go with her so I did. We had a few drinks and hung out."

"Had a few drinks and hung out?" I jumped off the bed, feeling my rage return. "You were gone all fucking day. You couldn't let me know where you were? I was worried sick about you."

"I'm sorry, baby. I didn't think."

"You didn't think? You didn't *think*? Did you fuck this guy? Did he have a friend over there who you fucked?" I kicked her chair furiously and it toppled over, sending her sprawling to the floor.

"I didn't fuck anybody," she screamed. She pulled herself into a sitting position. Her lips twisted into a sneer. "God, is my pussy the only thing you care about?"

I didn't know how to answer her. Maybe that *was* the only thing I cared about.

5.

I could not bring myself to touch her that night because I knew, despite her protests, that she'd been with someone else. It was incomprehensible to me that she could screw another guy after the Friday night we'd had. What kind of person was she? Did she have any human emotion? I was revolted by her. But, as always, she was able to smooth things over. She almost had me convinced that nothing happened Saturday, that it was just an innocent afternoon with a friend. Crystal was a consummate liar. She was so good at it I'm not sure she even knew what the truth was.

I fed into her compulsive lying because I pretended to believe her. I *wanted* to believe her. I needed the truth to be that she had not cheated on me again, that she had not gone out right after our special night and took another guy's cock between her legs. How could such a thing be real? It was too painful and humiliating to consider.

We clung to our relationship, with its dizzying highs and crushing lows, and as spring break approached Crystal decided she wanted to come home with me to meet my parents. I was not sure that was a good idea. Crystal was not the kind of girl you brought home to Mom and Dad. She was the kind of girl you screwed the shit out of and kept hidden from polite company. But I had convinced myself I loved her. At least, I thought I might. So I agreed to bring her home for Easter.

Frank, who lived near me in New Paltz, had asked for a ride home, and in exchange I requested that he check out my Buick. Frank was handy with cars, so he said sure he'd take a look. His diagnosis was that the radiator was shot. He said he knew where he could get a used one for cheap. I called home and, after some begging, got my dad to send

The DEATH of OBSESSION

me a check for the radiator and the fluids to fill it. Frank spent several hours in the parking lot taking out the old radiator and putting in the new one.

When I told Mom I was bringing a girl home for break, she peppered me with questions. *Is she Italian?* No, she's a feisty Irishwoman from Boston. *Oh, that's nice. Is she Catholic?* All Boston Irishmen are Catholic, Ma. *Does she like baked ziti? I'll make my baked ziti.* I'm sure that'll be fine. *When will you be home?* Friday night. *She can sleep in your sister's room.* She'll love that. *What you do there is your business, but here she sleeps in a separate room.* Sure, Ma.

I hadn't told my parents about Crystal before because I didn't want them to know about her. I was uncertain how to explain my relationship with her. Being with Crystal was not like dating other girls. It was like jumping on the back of a mad bull and I had no idea how long the ride would last. Now I had no choice. I was bringing her back to Poughkeepsie and I had to make some explanations.

The trip home was interesting and kind of awkward. Crystal kept turning around in her seat and trying to talk to Frank, who was stretched out in the back and wanted nothing more than to sleep the whole way. He ignored most of her questions and comments, occasionally grunting a response until she finally got the message and turned around, staring through the windshield. Left alone, Frank snored softly. Crystal seemed peeved. At one point, she mumbled, "He's such a shit." She could not stand being ignored when she wanted someone's attention.

I concentrated on driving and tried not to think about the week ahead, about how Crystal might embarrass me in front of my parents, about how she might demand my undivided affection even though I had not seen my family in months. My spirits always lifted when I returned to the Hudson Valley, and as we passed the signs for Hunter and Woodstock and Kingston, I felt a quiet excitement. But it was when I turned off the Thruway at the New Paltz exit that I knew I was home.

Frank's place was off Route 32 in a wooded area where the lots were three and four acres. The house was far back from the road and couldn't be seen through the trees.

Frank told me to drop him off at the end of the driveway. "I'll walk the rest of the way," he said. "It'll give me a chance to get ready for my father."

"You need a ride back?" I asked.

"No thanks. El's coming down to visit partway through the week, and she's gonna bring me back."

"OK. Well, have a good break."

"You too. Thanks for the lift."

"Thanks for fixing the radiator."

He waved at me and started up the long drive. Crystal said nothing to him, having decided that Frank was a shit. He did not even glance at her as he walked away. I didn't understand what was going on between them and, at that moment, I didn't care. Driving across the Mid-Hudson Bridge, with the sun slanting behind the western hills and the river winding silver north and south, the familiar glow filled me with comfort. I was back in my valley.

Crystal seemed jittery as we approached my house. The mask of supreme confidence was slipping off her face. "You OK?" I asked. Annoyed, she nodded and lit a cigarette. I didn't want her smoking in my car, but I said nothing. She blew clouds out the cracked window then reached into her bag and pulled out a bottle of vodka. She hit on it a few times as we drove down Route 9, past the restaurant where I had my first job washing dishes and the movie theater in the outdoor mall where my high school girlfriend and I had gone on a snowy afternoon and been the only people in the audience.

The tension was thick by the time we pulled up to my house. Mom and Dad came out to greet us, giving hugs and helping us carry our bags inside. Crystal embraced my mother stiffly when they were introduced. Dad just smiled at her. My brother, Joe, and sister, Marie, were yakking nonstop. Crystal looked a little dazed. I'm sure she was not used to this kind of family intensity.

Since it was Friday, it was pizza night. Dad called and ordered two large pies, one plain and one with mushrooms. I went to pick up the pies, taking Joe with me. I asked him about school, if he was ready for the start of Little League, whether or not Marie had a boyfriend. Mario, the guy who had run the corner pizza shop forever, gave me a big hello when I entered. "Hey, how ya doin', Zina*re*lli?" he said, giving the name the most Italian pronunciation possible.

"Mario! What's up?"

"Ah, you know, same same, my friend."

The place was hot and noisy, but it was great being there. I couldn't remember how many slices I'd had in Mario's, how much banter I'd traded with the owner. I paid for the pies and handed them to Joe. On the way home, I asked my brother what he thought of Crystal and he said he didn't know. "I just met her," he told me. I thought that was fair and let it go at that.

Crystal had one piece of pizza and only ate about half of it. She kept asking me for orange juice and excusing herself from the table while she slyly poured vodka into it. My mother asked her if something was wrong with the pizza and she said no, it was fine. "Crystal never eats very much, Ma," I said, trying to keep everything cool. But everything wasn't cool. Tension filled the air.

My bedroom was in our finished basement and consisted of a corner partitioned off for me just big enough for a bed, a dresser and a small table that held my stereo. My father had put up the walls when I entered high school. Before that, I had roomed with my brother in our three-bedroom house. I was half asleep when I heard someone coming down the basement stairs at about 1 a.m. I knew immediately it was Crystal, and my stomach clenched.

She came into my room and sat on the edge of my small bed, giggling like a naughty little girl. She was wearing a T-shirt that came to about mid-thigh, and nothing under it as far as I could tell.

"Cryssie, what are you doing?"

"I wanted to visit."

"My sister—"

"Oh, she's sleeping. So are your parents." She looked at me wickedly and said, "Let's fuck, Mikey."

I hesitated. "You should go back upstairs."

She reached over and ran her hand along my thigh. Despite the resistance screaming at the back of my brain, I felt the familiar twinge when she touched me. "What's the matter, don't you want me?" she said.

"You know it's not that. But my parents will hear."

"They won't. And what if they do? You think they don't know we're screwing every night at school?"

"Cryssie ..."

She stood and lifted the T-shirt to her waist. She wasn't wearing any panties. I couldn't help myself. I wet my finger on my tongue and ran it along her slit. "You are so bad," I told her.

"That's why you love me."

6.

I woke up to the realization that I was cramped in my little bed. Crystal had spent the night. The next thing I was aware of was my mother clattering around the kitchen. My heart skittered. I didn't want to go upstairs. I wanted to turn over and go back to sleep until the week was over. Instead, I figured it was better to get this over with as quickly as possible, so I pulled on a T-shirt and sweats and headed up the stairs.

My mother ignored me when I reached the kitchen. She was making pancakes. Joe and Marie were sitting at the table. Marie blushed when I looked at her and she shrugged her shoulders. I poured myself a cup of coffee and said, "Morning, Ma." She said hello without any inflection in her voice, concentrating on the pancakes. I felt my stomach turning over.

As I sipped my black coffee, Crystal came up the stairs. My mother pretended not to notice. Crystal came to the table and sat beside me, taking my hand. "Mom's making pancakes," I told her.

"I'll just have a piece of toast and some coffee," she said. I could see my mother's shoulders tighten at the words.

"You don't want pancakes?" I asked, an element of begging in my voice.

"Nah, I'm not that hungry. Just toast and coffee."

My father came out of the bathroom, patting his freshly shaved face. "Morning everybody," he said. He looked at me. "What are your plans for today?"

"Crystal and I are going to West Point. She's never been there and she really wants to see it."

The DEATH of OBSESSION

"West Point, huh? That should be nice."

My mother put a stack of pancakes on the table and said nothing. I'm sure she expected me to spend my first day home with my family. I felt like a shit, but I thought it would be easier on everyone to get Crystal out of the house for now. I ate a couple of pancakes. My mother glared at Crystal while she nibbled a piece of toast and gulped down coffee. After breakfast, we both showered quickly and headed out.

I was able to breathe easier after we got on the road. It was a pleasant spring day in the valley. The sun was shining and as we drove over the Beacon-Newburgh Bridge we could see the river turn golden in the brightness. I was taking hits off my pipe and Crystal was sipping at her vodka bottle. We were not talking much until Crystal turned to me and said, "Your mother doesn't like me."

You haven't given her much of a chance. "She'll come around."

"I don't know."

You've done everything you could think of to piss her off. "Don't worry about it. It'll be OK."

Even Crystal, as jaded as she was, felt a sense of awe driving along the cliffside road toward the United States Military Academy. The rocks rose in sheer magnificence to our right and the river stretched far below us to the left. "Gawd, that's so beautiful," Crystal said. And it was. The view made me feel an intense love for the valley I called home. I knew I would never want to live anywhere else.

West Point didn't disappoint. Crystal marveled at the buildings that looked like medieval castles, at the views of the wooded valley below, at the cadets marching in perfect synchronicity across the parade grounds. "They're all so adorable," she said. I had no doubt she would open herself to any of them. The thought took the brightness from the day and depressed me—Crystal would never be what I wanted her to be.

My mother had spent the entire day cooking, and when we got home the table was filled with baked ziti, meatballs, sausage, and braciole. "Ma, this looks great," I said. "And it smells terrific." She smiled at me. Crystal said nothing. *Please compliment her please say something nice.* Dad handed me a beer and sat down, sipping his own. He asked about West Point and Crystal said it was gorgeous. She made no move to help my mother and offered nothing.

We started to eat and I grabbed some of everything. Crystal took a couple forkfuls of ziti and, after my mother's urging, a small meatball. She ate a few mouthfuls of the ziti and about half the meatball. I could see my mother fuming, and finally she told Crystal, "You don't eat enough to keep a bird alive."

Crystal shrugged and I interjected, "She's always that way."

"Is there something wrong with my food?" Mom persisted.

"Nah, I just don't got an appetite."

"Maybe you would if you didn't drink so much," my mother mumbled. I felt my face burning, but Crystal either didn't hear or pretended not to. She stood up, walked into the living room, and took a pack of cigarettes from her pocket.

"Please don't smoke in the house," Mom said sternly.

Crystal looked at her for several seconds without moving. Then she came to the table and said, "Mikey, let's go out on the porch." I wasn't finished eating, but I followed her out the back door onto the screened-in porch. Crystal lit a cigarette and puffed furiously, brows knit in anger.

"Your mother hates me," she said.

"She doesn't hate you," I answered cautiously. "But you haven't exactly gone out of your way to make her like you."

"You blaming this on me? She's been on me since I walked in the door. Your mother always gets her way, doesn't she?"

Just like you, princess. "Look, we're only gonna be here a few more days. Can't you just get along with her for now?"

"I don't put up with *anybody's* shit, Mikey. You should know that. My mother died a long time ago. She is not my mother."

I could hear my parents having an animated discussion inside, and although the words were muffled, I knew they were having a similar conversation to the one Cryssie and I were having: My father was trying to calm my mother down and beseech her get along with Crystal for a couple more days.

When we went back into the house, my mother looked at me and said, "We're going to ten o'clock Mass tomorrow." The next day was Easter and, although I was not very religious, I always went to church with my family on the holiest day in Catholicism. I turned to Crystal and said, "Is that OK with you?"

She put her hands on her hips and looked directly into my eyes. "I don't go to church, Mikey. You know that."

"Not even on Easter?" my mother asked.

"Never," she answered. "I'm not a hypocrite. Eastah's just another day to me."

My mother's face had turned so red I thought her head might explode. She was a passionate disciple of Jesus—though she talked about it more than she lived it—and she preferred to ignore the fact that I'd told her more than once I did not believe in organized religion.

"Then *you* stay home," my mother said to Crystal.

"Oh, I will. And I'm sure Mikey'll stay here with me."

Mom stood up, pushing away from the table. She was only a bit taller than Crystal, but she seemed to tower over her; Mom grew six inches in her rage. "He's going to church with us tomorrow, just like he always does."

"The hell. He'll do what he wants to do."

"Who do you think you are?" my mother screamed. "Stop trying to manipulate my son with *that!*" She pointed at Crystal's crotch. "You're nothing but a little whore who's trying to ruin my son."

Marie and Joe's mouths fell open. Dad said, "Toni, take it easy."

"Ruin your son! I made a man out of him. You should thank me. He's not going to spend the rest of his life with his nose up his mother's ass."

My mother raised her hand to Crystal as if she might strike her. Crystal laughed wildly and shouted, "Lay a hand on me and I'll call the police. I'm not one of your kids. You don't control me."

"No, you're not one of my kids," Mom seethed. "You'll never be a part of this family."

"That's what you think, *Ma!* Mikey and I are going to get married and there's not a damn thing you can do about it."

My mother turned toward me, her eyes wide with panic. "Is that true, Michael? Did you say you were going to marry her?"

I needed an answer that would satisfy Cryssie and keep my mother from having a stroke. I thought I was going to throw up. "I love her, Ma," I said. "Can't you two just get along, please?"

It was far too late for that, however. Crystal asked me to drive her to the train station; she would return to Boston for the rest of the break. Unsure what to do, I went down into my room and threw my things in my bag. When I got back upstairs, Crystal was out near the Buick, waiting for me. I could hear Mom in her bedroom, crying.

My father grabbed me by the shoulder as I walked out the door.

"Dad, I have to go with her," I said.

"Promise you'll call soon," he said.

"OK." I wrenched away from him, feeling I could no longer breathe in the house. When I got outside, air seemed to come more easily.

I got behind the wheel, started the car, and pulled away from my house. "Where are we going to go for the rest of the week?" I asked Crystal. "They won't let us back into the dorms until Saturday."

Crystal was puffing on a cigarette. "There are ways to get around that," she said.

Chapter Nine
Praying for Salvation

I don't believe in God, but I'm afraid of Him.
                           —Gabriel Garcia Marquez

1.

"Mr. Zinarelli, thanks for meeting me here."
Z looked intently into David Kaplowitz's finely chiseled face. He lifted the coffee cup to his lips and took a sip.
They were sitting in the coffee shop of the big Barnes & Noble on Route 9. The corner table they occupied was just big enough for their cups and the toasted bagel David was eating—butter, no cream cheese. Z was comfortable here. He had bought countless books in this store, had enjoyed countless cups of coffee while doing so. The place was crowded, as usual, on a Sunday morning.
"David, I only met you because I want to get rid of you. How can I convince you that you're wasting your time?"
"Mr. Zinarelli—"
"For God's sake, call me Mike."
Kaplowitz took a bite of his bagel and chewed slowly. After a moment, he said, "I can't figure out why you're lying to me, Mike. Are you trying to protect my mother? Or is it that you just don't want anything to do with her and you want all this to go away?"
"Tell me about your mother. About your life together."
Kaplowitz sighed wistfully, but his eyes seemed to burn. Z was unaccountably afraid for a second then shook it off.
"Let's see ... she's been married three times. Her first husband, Adrian Kaplowitz, was a professor at her grad school. He's my father. I don't remember much about those

years. I was still young when she left him. Or he threw her out. I'm not sure how it happened. Then there was the colonel. Christ, that lasted about eight months. And finally she hit the jackpot and married Richard Stallman. The guy can burn money. He's an ugly little gnome, but he's filthy rich. And of course, between the husbands there were guys, so many guys. You know what she was like. *Is* like."

Z sipped coffee and thought for a moment. Into the strained silence he said, "That must have been tough for you."

He showed his perfect teeth, but it wasn't a smile. "It wasn't the happiest childhood. But I lived through it. It made me stronger."

Z leaned forward. He had to ask the question. "You think I killed her, don't you, David."

"Yes. And if you didn't, you know what happened to her."

"You're wrong. The last time I talked to her ..."

"You were with her, Mike. You were with her right before she disappeared. What happened to her?"

Z shook his head. "I don't know, kid. Really."

"And you don't give a shit, right? You'd be happy if she was dead."

Z stared at him. His heart was pounding hard. He felt he was sweating too much to hide it. "No. Whatever happened between us, I wouldn't wish her dead."

"Wish her dead? How about *make* her dead?"

"I'm no saint, David, but I couldn't kill anyone. I wouldn't."

Kaplowitz raised his voice, venom spewing from him. "Do you know what you did to her, Mike? You ripped her heart out. I remember her drinking tumblers of vodka and talking about you, saying, 'David, I only really loved one man in my life. Mikey. But I screwed that up.' You destroyed her."

Z shook his head involuntarily. "It wasn't my fault."

"Wasn't it?

"Look, I admire your devotion to your mother. But you need to look for her somewhere else. I don't know what happened to her. There's nothing here for you."

David was silent. He stared across the table without emotion.

"Or maybe there is something you're interested in here. Maybe you like the scenery. Especially the scenery across the street from my house."

The young man breathed out a laugh, shook his head. "You got me, Mike. Yeah, I am infatuated with Earth Farmer. Can you blame me? But that's not why I'm hanging around. You know that."

"Do I?"

Kaplowitz finished his bagel without hurry and took a few sips of coffee to wash it down. He did not appear to feel awkward in the silence. He was, Z thought, very composed for someone who was probably 30ish, give a year or two. Neither man spoke for a while.

Finally, Kaplowitz said, "What was it with you two?"

Z sat back in his chair. There was no easy answer to that one. Indeed, what *was* it with him and Crystal? After three decades her name still sent shockwaves through his body. That was his problem, not hers. Try as he might, he had never fully gotten past that time of straddling orgasmic heaven and ball-busting hell. It had confused him, how much he could love and hate a person at the same time. Their relationship had been a war in which both sides were decimated—atomic warheads detonated.

"I'm not sure what it was," he said after leafing through several possible replies. "Neither of us was able to get a handle on it, that's for sure. We were definitely not good for each other."

"Still, you should have married her."

Z shook his head. "Never."

"Was it really that bad?"

Z didn't answer. He just stared straight ahead and remembered trying to snuff the life out of Crystal Cassidy.

2.

Exhausted, Z sat back and drank in the quiet of the newsroom. The only sound was the sports editor, Eddie Mangini, tapping away on his keyboard. Z's night was finished and he was getting ready to head out. He tried to clear his mind of Otto Hellinger growling at him, of Molly Thaves glaring at him silently as she passed through the newsroom. Was it so long ago that she praised his work? That she looked at him as a valuable member of the staff? Now it was clear she wanted to break him.

As if reading his thoughts, Mangini said, "This is all such bullshit, Mike."

Z glanced up and saw the burly Mangini staring at him for a response. "What's bullshit exactly, Eddie?" He didn't want to get into this conversation, not now when he was just about to leave.

"The sports section took a huge hit in the last readership survey," Mangini said. "Is that my fault? We don't get half the scores we used to into the paper, thanks to these new freakin' deadlines. That's the real problem and everybody knows it. But Molly wants me to come up with a plan to 'turn things around.' And not some three-paragraph write-up. She wants something 'comprehensive' on her desk by Monday noon."

"Yeah, that sucks," Z replied.

"She tells me she wants more high school sports coverage, but who's going to do it? They've taken everybody away from me. 'Get some interns,' she tells me. It takes more time to train interns than it's worth. I have to rewrite most of their copy. It just ... it's damn frustrating."

"I feel your pain, buddy."

Anger welled up in Mangini and he abruptly started to shut down his computer. "The hell with it," he said. "I'm not staying here all night working on this shit." He tossed some papers into his bag, slung it over his shoulder, and headed for the elevator. "See you tomorrow, Mike."

"Goodnight, Eddie."

Alone in the newsroom, Z did a mental survey of tasks he needed to complete before leaving. Everything was finished. He began the shutdown of his computer, logging out of programs, closing his e-mail, and in a minute the screen turned blue, offering two small boxes for his sign-on and password. Tomorrow he would start the day by filling in those boxes for the nth time. In a moment of heavy sadness, he considered how worthless it all seemed. What had he ever really accomplished?

The DEATH of OBSESSION

He stood, put on his jacket, and headed for the back stairs. The emptiness of the *Sun* building closed in on him. He felt slightly sick, heat building behind his ears and running across the back of his neck. Sweat collected on his collar. He stopped partway down the stairs, leaned against the metal handrail, and sucked in a deep breath. Was this all nerves or was something actually wrong with him? It had been a while since he'd had a check-up—Anna was constantly nagging him to do so—and there was no guarantee he was not wracked with cancer or a clogged heart.

Outside it was cool, a slight breeze blowing up from the river. The chill refreshed him a bit, though he still felt wobbly. He headed toward his car parked at the far end of the lot. *God I just want to get home I'm too old to be working nights I've paid my fucking dues.* A siren wailed somewhere in the distance; he could not tell if it was a police car or a fire engine or an ambulance. His first thought was that he might be missing something important. But he didn't care. Caring about his job had been ripped out of him by Molly and Otto and the corporation that had gutted the *Sun* simply to keep the stock prices from plummeting.

As he walked past the big green dumpster, Z was vaguely aware of a flash of movement. Before he could react, someone was standing in front of him. His heart jumped into his throat. He shouted.

"Jesus, Zinarelli, take it easy," a familiar voice said.

Z peered through the darkness. After a few seconds, he said, "God damn, Delson. You trying to give me a heart attack?"

The detective chuckled. "I thought you reporters were supposed to be tough guys."

"What are you doing here?" Z said gruffly.

"I need to talk to you."

"Ever hear of a telephone?"

"I was right here," he said, nodding over his shoulder, "so I figured what the hell." City hall, which included the police department, was across the street from the *Sun* building.

"Yeah, so what do you want?"

"I'm worried about you," Delson said.

"I'm touched," Z answered, but there was more concern than sarcasm in his voice.

Delson stood silent for a moment, his hawkish nose outlined against the nearly full moon. "Don't be," he said. "I have to be unbiased. Just like you, right?"

"Right. So why are you worried about me?"

"If you didn't kill Crystal Cassidy—and I'm still not sure you didn't—someone's going through a lot of trouble to make it look like you did."

"Aha," Z said, pounding his fist against the dumpster. "I told you."

"Just listen," Delson told him. "It's time for you to tell me everything, Zinarelli. Right now. And I mean the whole truth."

Z folded his arms across his chest in a defensive posture. Then he relaxed and dropped his hands to his sides. "Crystal called me a few weeks ago, out of the clear blue sky. We talked for a while and then a few days later I called her back. You have to understand the kind of intense relationship we had. I just wanted ... I don't know what I wanted. To put it to rest, I guess."

"I'm not your wife, Zinarelli. I don't give a shit. Keep talking."

Z pursed his lips then continued. "She told me she was going to be in Putnam County on business and she suggested we have lunch. I should have said no, but I wanted to see what she looked like after all these years. We met at Margherita's and talked for a while. That was it. We didn't go to a motel and I sure as hell didn't sleep with her. I may be a dumb ass, but I'm not that dumb."

"Why the hell did you meet with her in the first place?"

"It's hard to explain," Z said. "You ever have a love affair that was really wrong, but you just couldn't get away from the woman?"

Delson laughed. "Yeah. It was my ex-wife. She still drives me nuts."

"Me and Crystal ... there's no easy way to talk about it. We don't have enough time. But when she said she wanted to meet with me, I had to. I just had to see her once more."

"So you didn't sleep with her."

"No. No way."

The DEATH of OBSESSION

"What was she doing in Poughkeepsie?"

"I have no idea. I didn't even know she was in Poughkeepsie until you told me she went missing here. I'm telling you, we met for lunch in Carmel and that was it."

"What did you talk about?"

"Old times. What's going on in our lives now. Nothing special."

"She say anything about her husband?"

"Not really. I know he's some rich dude. She didn't talk about him much. Why? What's going on?"

Delson leaned forward and spoke quietly. "This guy Richard Stallman, he's nobody to fuck with. He's not just rich, he's influential. Friends in high places. I don't know if he suspected his wife was cheating on him, but if he did ... well, I wouldn't want to be her. Or the guy she was cheating with."

"It wasn't me!"

"Maybe he thought it was. I don't know. All I know for sure is that we've been getting these anonymous tips. About you being in Carmel with Crystal Cassidy. About her purse being down near the river. And everything's pointing to you, Zinarelli. You get what I'm saying?"

Z nodded. "Yeah, I get it."

"Somebody saw you two together in Carmel. That means somebody followed you there. They were either following her or you. Zinarelli, it comes down to this: There's gonna come a time when they will force me to arrest you and the DA's gonna be under pressure to get an indictment against you. With or without a body. It's a matter of time. So I hope you've come completely clean with me."

Z's stomach was churning. He was afraid. "I've told you everything, Detective. I swear to God."

"I don't believe in God. I believe in evidence."

"I didn't kill her. I'm not even sure she's dead. Are you?"

Delson shrugged. "Then where the hell is she?"

"Maybe she figured the same thing you did, that Stallman was after her. Maybe she just took off."

"Without her pocketbook and all her credit cards? That doesn't make any sense, Zinarelli. How could she disappear without any money?"

"Crystal's real resourceful. I wouldn't sell her short. Maybe she put money aside somewhere. Maybe she's the one who left the pocketbook near the river. I'm telling you, Delson, you never know with her."

The detective took a pack of cigarettes out of his shirt pocket. He shook one out of the deck, put it in his mouth, and torched it with an old-style metal lighter. "One thing I've learned in this job," he said, "you never know with anyone."

3.

David Kaplowitz stretched lazily in his hotel bed, looked around the plain, clean room, and slumped back down against the pillows. He kicked the blankets off, stood, and made sure to get his blood circulating. Jumping jacks, pushups, sit-ups. Staying in razor-sharp shape was an obsession and, in his eyes, a necessity. Physical perfection led to happiness. He always felt on top of things. Nothing caught him off guard. Strong body, strong mind. He was nothing like her, and the thought made him laugh. Discipline, focus—these were the keys to his life. It was absurd to be dragged down by weakness. If the mind could conceive it, the body could be molded to deliver it.

He stripped out of his sweats and took a short, cold shower, soaping himself quickly. The icy water cleared his mind. He understood what the rest of the day would bring. The journey was nearly over. It had been a challenging one. But now he was on the verge. He was proud of how cleverly he had pieced everything together. Still, there was more work to be done.

He stepped out of the shower and let the water drip from his naked body. The chill air jarred his skin, but he stood perfectly still, refusing to dry himself with a towel. The water beaded, was absorbed into the atmosphere while he watched himself in the mirror. He was not surprised that women found him appealing. He *was* appealing. It was not hubris, simply fact. He was lucky in that way.

The DEATH of OBSESSION

One of the happy byproducts of this adventure had been meeting Earth Farmer. She had been attracted to him from the first, he knew, but he also found her fascinating. There was a genuine chemistry between them. Their conversations had been interesting, the magnetism that drew them together strong. He had wanted to keep the pull she exerted on him separate from what he was here to do, but it was difficult. She was a force he had not expected to contend with. He would use it to his advantage somehow, though. That's what he did.

The end was close now. There was no doubt.

He reached down into his bag and pulled out a small book. It was his mother's diary. Still naked on the bed, he opened it to a familiar page and started reading.

> *I thought I loved Adrian Kaplowitz. I know he didn't believe it after a while and who knows maybe I never did love him. It has always been hard for me to stay focused on one man but I tried hard to stay loyal to Adrian. I'm not even sure what I originally saw in him. Maybe I just wanted someone and there he was steady and rocklike and looking at me in a way that told me he was mine if I wanted him. It was always so easy for me to know which guys wanted me and even more to make guys want me who did not even know it. My sex has been my best weapon in life, my pussy is what's kept me alive. I have to be honest with myself. I've been smart, I can be charming if I want to be but people have always pissed me off and in the end I could make them pay if they were women. I could make their men want me and have me and if they were men I could control them with their orgasms. That's my talent, that was the way I kept the world from devouring me. Sure I hurt people, sure I caused some pain but I was in pain too. I was hurt along the way and where was my hero, where was the man who would drag me out of the hole I had fallen into. Does anyone think about that? Does anyone care how much pain I was in? No, we all have to take care of ourselves. That is the only thing I've learned in my life. Nobody else will do a thing for you. It is every person for themselves.*

I thought Adrian was the one who might save me. I thought he truly did love me enough. He was a young professor and I was a grad student trying to get my masters in developmental psychology and god he was brilliant. Adrian was a quietly confident man when it came to his knowledge of what he was teaching. He was not handsome the way some guys made me damp before they ever touched me but he had something else and I was so tired of living my life chasing physical attraction. Jesus, I thought there had to be something more and then Adrian smiled at me in class and said Miss Cassidy what do you think about that and I knew. I knew he wanted me. Maybe he did not even realize it himself but there it was and I worked my way into seeing him after class and soon we were seeing each other every day. It was only a matter of when I would lead him to bed. He was a smart man, a brilliant man, but he had no experience with women, he had no idea how to touch me, how to get me where I needed to be. He might have been a virgin, I have no clue because I never asked him, so I took control and that was fine. If I had not totally seduced him we would never have gotten together, but I made it happen. He was clumsy and fumbling and he didn't make me come, he didn't know how. I took him in my hand and then in my mouth and he was shivering and moaning and I got on top of him and put him inside me and it was maybe a minute before he was shooting into me. I could feel it and I knew I had him and I pretended to enjoy it, grinding against him and letting out a shriek like I was a porn star playing my part and he believed it. He had no clue. I made him think he was the best cockmaster in the world. We had sex the next three nights and he proposed to me as I lay in his arms, wishing he could give me an orgasm, even one. I said yes. I wanted to be married. I wanted something substantial in my life, but it was not right. I manipulated him so easily it was almost criminal. Adrian, I'm so sorry. I wish I could tell you, but you won't talk to me, and how can I blame you?

After we were married, I tried to teach him. I tried to get him to understand what I needed in bed, but he didn't want to work at it. He didn't want to try anything new, no matter what I suggested, no matter what I initiated it ended up the same way. I don't think I had one orgasm with him, which was pathetic and it was only a matter of weeks before I met a guy in the library. He was tall and a little angry, with long hair pulled into a ponytail, and we went back to the cottage I shared with Adrian and we smoked a joint and this guy ripped my clothes off and fucked me so hard I could not stop coming. I drenched his cock. He must have thought it was a year since I'd been fucked, but I didn't care. I wanted him to keep fucking me forever and when it finally ended, he splashed so much jism into me I thought I might faint and I kept milking his cock until we both fell asleep.

God help me, he was not the last one. After that I don't know how many guys on campus I fucked. It was too many to keep track of. When I found out I was pregnant I pretended to be happy and told Adrian we were going to have a baby, but what I did not tell him was I had no idea who the father was. Adrian was ecstatic. He told me how much he loved me and I felt like a shit. I didn't want to betray him. I felt worthless, but what could I do? I decided to put my pursuit of my masters on hold because I didn't want to go to class with my belly sticking out, so I stayed home and read books and watched daytime TV and got more and more depressed. I fucked a janitor while I was pregnant and a guy who mowed the lawn and some other guys I don't even remember. I swear to god the kid was about coming out of me and I was still fucking someone, anyone. I wanted to feel like somebody wanted me. I wanted to know I still had my power. When the kid was born, Jesus, the worst agony I had ever felt, we named him David after Adrian's father. I didn't care about the name. The truth is I didn't even care about the kid and now I hate myself for what I did to Adrian and what I did to my son.

When the talk and the rumors reached Adrian he was so devastated I thought he might die right then and there and I cried and pleaded with him to forgive me but he couldn't. He hated me and he hated my child. He was so hurt. After Adrian things happened so fast I can't even think about it. There was the army colonel and the FBI computer whiz and so many others it makes my head spin and yeah okay I married the colonel. Christ almighty that lasted eight months and I drifted from thing to thing and then there was Richard with all his money and power and I finally thought this was it. But goddamn it, there was too much history. We can't get away from what we've done, right Mikey? We're doomed by our own actions. We can only pray for salvation.

Kaplowitz snapped the book shut. He stared at the ceiling with a grim look on his finely chiseled face. "Isn't that right, Mikey?" he said softly.

4.

When Z got home he found his wife sitting on the bathroom floor, staring into space.

"Anna, what's the matter, honey?"

Her big brown eyes, the ones he had fallen in love almost thirty years ago, searched out an answer in his face. He wanted to believe he still loved her that much, but he didn't know anything about himself any more. "Mike, what the hell is going on? The truth."

He hesitated. He was not certain if it was for dramatic effect or because he didn't want to speak. "I need to tell you everything."

"Then do it."

He put the lid down on the toilet and sat heavily. "I did see Crystal. I had lunch with her a couple weeks ago. She was in Carmel on business and we met there."

Anna groaned and leaned back until she was sitting against the wall. Her face turned rose. "That bitch has been in my life since I met you. You know that, Mike? I'm tired of living with her hanging over my head."

"She's not hanging over your head," he said.

"Yes, Mike, yes she is. Everything in your life goes back to her. How you relate to women. How you relate to your family. How your old college friends look at you. You dumped her thirty years ago, but she's still got her claws in you. There is no escaping that bitch."

"We had lunch. Once. That's all, Anna. I should have told you, but I knew how you'd react. Nothing happened. We ate sandwiches. That's it."

She bent her head, put her hands over her face. Through her hands, she said, "Why? Why did you meet with her?"

He sighed. He wanted a few shots of bourbon. "I don't know. I just had to. It's not that I wanted to sleep with her. I wanted to look her in the eyes and ask her why she did what she did to me. I'm getting old, Anna, and I thought maybe I wouldn't have another chance."

She slapped her hand on the tile floor. "Why the hell do you care so much? Hasn't our life together meant anything?"

He touched the side of her face. "Our life together, raising the girls, means everything to me. What we've built is real. The rest is a bad dream."

Anna looked up at him. Her face, fleshier from the years, creased with worry lines, was still as pretty as he remembered it from their first meeting. He wanted to tell her that, but he could not form the words.

"I'm glad you finally told me the truth, Michael," she said. "Because I knew you saw Crystal."

He stared at her. She always knew when he was lying.

"Now let me tell you the truth about something." Her voice was so soft he could barely hear her. He leaned forward as she said, "She came to the house looking for you a few days after you had lunch with her. She didn't realize you were working, I guess. I almost shit myself when I answered the door and she told me who she was."

Z's mouth was gaping open and he made an effort to close it. He pressed his teeth together so hard his jaw hurt. "Jesus, Anna."

"She told me everything. How you two had started talking again, how you'd met for lunch. She said she was happy to renew your old friendship. That's what she said, Mike. She was happy to renew your friendship. All I could think was that she wanted you back, that she was going to seduce you again."

"No. Never again."

Anna eyed him uncertainly. There was obviously a larger issue on her mind. He waited. "She grinned at me and said we'd probably be seeing a lot of each other. Mike, I couldn't take that. I won't take it." Tears started to spill quietly from her eyes. "I wanted her dead, Mike. God help me, I wanted her dead."

His breath was coming shallow and strained. He fought to control his voice. "What happened then, honey?"

"I threw her out. I screamed at her. 'Get the fuck out of my house.' I wanted to kill her. I swear to God."

The words slammed him so hard he felt himself drawing back into a vacuum where there was no sound or feeling. Then his blood started to flow again and he chuckled humorlessly. "But you didn't."

She threw herself against his legs and hugged desperately. After all this time was she still so unsure of herself, of him? Life was a constant series of doubts and reassurances. That's really what love was, he thought: letting the person you loved know every day that they were treasured and appreciated. Human beings were so emotionally fragile. He wondered why.

He reached down and drew his arms around her. "Anna, you are the love of my life. Don't ever forget that."

"Michael," she said. Her voice sounded far away. "I've always wondered if you would have rather married her. Maybe that's silly, I don't know. But I don't think you ever got over her."

He wanted to blame this surfeit of emotion on the tension of the past few days. It was more than that, though, and he knew it. "You're wrong," he said. "I would trade every day I ever had with her for our life together. Jesus Christ, you saved me, Anna. Don't you understand that?"

She was crying even harder now, tears pouring down her face. His chest ached at the sight of her tears.

"Back when we were together, I almost killed her once," he said, ignoring the shock that registered on her face. "I was so close to killing her it scares me. I swear to God I could be doing a life sentence right now. A few more

The DEATH of OBSESSION

seconds and she would have been dead." He laughed grotesquely. "Maybe I should have done it."

"Michael," she whispered.

"But I walked away, Anna. I just walked away. And I started a new life without her claws in my back. I know our life hasn't been perfect," he said. "But I've done my best. You and the girls are my life. There's nothing else."

She stared at him with glistening eyes, too overcome with emotion to speak.

5.

Earth Farmer was supposed to be splitting some firewood, but she stood motionless before the pile of logs, contemplating her life. The axe lay at her feet. She felt foolish, almost dirty, because of her encounter with David Kaplowitz. She had rushed into sleeping with him, and she couldn't understand why. Yes, he was handsome, but she had had handsome suitors before. Was she so desperate to fall in love that she had jumped into bed with him? The sex hadn't even been very good. In fact, it had left her frustrated. She found him brusque and uncaring in bed, concerned only about his own satisfaction. She should have taken her time, not spread her legs so readily, but now it was too late.

Earth picked up the axe and slung it over her left shoulder but didn't start chopping. David had seemed ecstatic when he dropped her off after their night together. He kissed her on the cheek and said, "I'll see you soon, baby. Tonight was terrific." He seemed to glow. But in her eyes it hadn't been terrific. The more she thought about it, the more it made her sick. It was partially her fault for leading him on. She should have known that Max and Cyndey happened once in a lifetime. Even the relationship between Anna and Mr. Z, as imperfect as it was, was something rare.

She had pressed too hard to have David be that man for her. But it wasn't right. She had known that before she slept with him. It was frightening because he had wanted it even more than she had. He was so needy it alarmed her. As cool and sophisticated as he tried to portray himself, he was really just a little boy who wanted to be loved. Maybe he was more like his mother than he cared to admit—emotionally crippled and hoping someone could save him. She would have to be honest with him, would have to tell him that they had plunged too quickly into this. It wouldn't be pleasant. She understood that clearly.

"Hey."

Earth turned around and saw Tasha walking across the yard. Her dark hair was pulled back into a ponytail and her face was red from the breeze.

"Whatcha doing'?"

Earth looked at the logs, then back at Tasha. "Splitting wood for the stove," she said.

"Doesn't look like you got too far."

Earth smiled. "No. I'm just getting started."

"Can I help you?"

Earth looked dubious. "You ever done this before?"

Tasha shook her head. "Not really."

"Why don't you watch me for a while and see if you think you can handle it. How's that sound?"

"OK."

Earth hefted one of the logs, set it on end on top of the stump where they cut their wood, and swung the axe deftly. The wood crackled and split almost completely down the middle. She jerked the blade out and finished the job, sending two nearly symmetrical pieces onto the grass.

"Cool," Tasha said.

"It's easy when you get the hang of it."

Earth put another log onto the stump and prepared to chop. She was aware of her young friend watching her.

"Boys are jerks," Tasha said before Earth swung the axe again.

Earth chuckled. "They sure are."

The words came spilling out of Tasha's mouth: "I like this guy named Riley Evans, and he told my friend Courtney that he likes me. But when I try to talk to him, he totally says nothing. It's like his lips are glued shut."

Earth set the axe down and looked Tasha in the eyes. "The problem with most guys, Tash, is that they're not very together. They try to come off all cool, but they're more scared than we are."

"Yeah?"

"Oh yeah, Tash. Trust me on this one."

"What should I do?"

Earth put her hand on Tasha's shoulder. "Keep talking to him. Make him feel like he's in charge. Guys need to think everything is their idea." She tickled Tasha on the ribs, bending her over with a giggle. "But we know the truth. It's the secret all women know. We let men think they rule the world."

"The only man you can trust is your father," Tasha said, as if reciting something she had heard from Anna.

"You can say that again."

Chapter Ten
Encounters with the Evil Seductress

Sometimes you wake up from a dream. Sometimes you wake up in a dream. And sometimes, every once in a while, you wake up in someone else's dream.
—Richelle Mead

1.

As the end of spring semester neared, I still was not on speaking terms with my parents. I had to decide where I was going to spend the summer because I had no intention of going back to Poughkeepsie right now. I talked briefly to Shank about returning to Connecticut with him. He said he was sure his parents wouldn't mind, but I didn't feel comfortable about it. Elise offered a spot on her couch in Potsdam; she suggested, however, that I go home and make nice with my parents. I was mulling over what to do when Crystal informed me that I was spending the summer with her Boston.

"Is your father going to be cool with that?"

"I already asked him and he said he was fine with it."

"What am I going to do in Boston all summer?"

She grinned. "Drink beer and fuck me," she said.

I laughed and tried seem happy about spending the summer in Beantown. But as April melted into May, I found myself more and more anxious and unhappy. What the hell was I doing? All of this was getting out of hand. At least half a dozen times I made an attempt to call home and reconcile things. It didn't happen, though. Either I lost my nerve or I got angry again thinking about how my parents tried to control me. And what would I do in Poughkeepsie for three months? Fret about what Crystal might be doing.

The DEATH of OBSESSION

I finished my finals early in the last week and was ready to let loose. After my last exam—in Eastern Philosophy, which I aced—I came back to the dorm and smoked a couple bowls of weed, listening to Fillmore East and drumming on my bed. Crystal had a psych final the next day and was studying with Jenny Fisher, who, I was told, had aced every History of Psychology test in the spring semester. Crystal was not her friend and, as far as I knew, rarely spoke to her, but somehow she had latched onto her at the critical moment. I was finding out how typical of Crystal that was.

I was stretched out on my bed, letting the strains of "Stormy Monday" wash over me, when Elise came through my open door and shouted, "Wake up, Z, there's partying to be done."

I sat up slowly, academic exhaustion and a cloudy brain dragging me down. "El, what's going on?" I said without enthusiasm.

"C'mon, Z," she ordered. "We're having a thing for Woody. He got the word today that he's not coming back next semester."

I knew it was coming, but the reality snapped the high out of me. "That sucks," I said. "This place isn't going to be the same without Woods."

Elise sat on the edge of my bed and nudged me with her elbow. "He failed every class. I think he even failed a couple he didn't take. He had his fun, Z, but now comes the time to pay the piper, you know?"

"He should get credit for some of the other shit he did," I said. "Like diving out that third-story window into the snow bank. That takes talent, El."

"No argument here. But the guy's grade point average is decidedly south of a D. How could they let him stay?"

She was right, of course, but I didn't want to see Woody go. I took a hit off my pipe and handed it to Elise, who sucked down a big hit and blew a cloud into the ceiling. We finished the bowl without saying much more. "So where is this shindig?" I asked her finally.

"Shank's room."

"Where else?" I couldn't help asking: "Is Maggie gonna be there?"

"Come on, Z!"

"It's just a question."

She shrugged. "When's the last time Maggie missed a party?"

Shank's room was a madhouse. There were so many people when we arrived we had to squeeze our way in. The room was foggy with smoke. Woody was sitting on the bed taking a bong hit. Stan was sitting next to him, his face drooping with disappointment. Replacing Woods as a roommate was going to be an impossible task. Was there anyone else quite like him? I couldn't imagine it.

"Woody," I said. "This whole thing blows."

He took another hit and laughed crazily. "You don't know. Wait till Raymond Sweet Senior gets here to pick me up." He shook that fiery red hair and bounced up and down on the bed. "It's death, I tell ya. I'll never make it back to Woodstock alive."

"Maybe you could go home with Cramer and hide out with his chickens," Billy Thoms said.

"I'd rather face death."

Everybody laughed. I took my turn at the bong and sucked in a ferocious hit. My head expanded; Shank had put something special in the bong. He always seemed to have an exotic variety of smoke on hand when it was required. Everyone in the room was blown away and chattering in a dozen different conversations. I watched Maggie sitting on the floor, talking to Wendy, her face flushed and animated. I stared at her without trying to hide my fascination. I wanted to crawl down on the floor next to her and wrap my arms around her. That would have resulted in total humiliation, not to mention possible castration had Crystal found out, but at that moment I didn't give a damn.

"Hey," I shouted over all the voices, "let's see who can tell the funniest story about Woody."

Everyone thought that was a tremendous idea, and since he roomed with Woods the whole year, Stan was handed the honor of going first. He was normally so reserved you didn't know he was around, but losing Woods seemed to fuel something in him.

"First night, I wondered what the hell I'd gotten into with this guy," Stan said. "He wouldn't shut up, and when he wasn't talking he was making these weird noises. I was ready to go home. I just shut up and let him do all the talking. What else could I do?" Everyone was laughing, but Stan seemed a little sad about it all. I realized in that split second that he was losing one of the best friends he'd ever had. And he knew things would never be the same between them.

"It was near the end of the first week and my mother sent me a care package. Mom's that way. Inside was a chocolate cake, wrapped tight in plastic wrap. I took it out and showed it to Woody, and he grabbed it away from me and took a huge bite out of it, right through the plastic. I stared at him for a few seconds ... I didn't know what the hell to do ... and then I started laughing so hard I almost pissed my pants."

The story was funny, and I chuckled, but it also made my stomach clench. I understood then, even as a 20-year-old, that there was no going back—that no matter how much laughter and camaraderie there was, time moved inevitably forward. Stan's hilarious first week with Woody would soon be nothing but a story he would tell to his friends and family and maybe, someday, his own kids.

That seemed so incredibly moving I thought I might cry. Or maybe it was just Shank's pot.

2.

When the party broke up I found myself in the rec room playing pool with Maggie. I don't remember how it happened, but I know it was the happiest I'd been in a long time. She was throttling me at eight-ball, although I must confess I was not really concentrating. I was watching her slender fingers wrap around the cue and her tongue poke slightly from the side of her mouth when she shot.

I was perched on one of the uncomfortable green chairs when, after missing a shot, she plopped down on my lap said, "Your turn."

I didn't want to take my turn. I wanted to sit there with her nestled in my lap until time stopped. Instead, she stood abruptly and said, "What's the matter, Z? Afraid to take your shot?"

Woozy from pot and beer, I thought maybe this was my opening. I kissed Maggie softly on the lips, wrapping my arms around her. She didn't resist, but when the kiss ended she backed away from me and said, "Z, don't. I don't feel that way about you. Just be my friend."

I have all the friends I need. I stared into her glossy brown eyes and said, "Maggie, that's asking a lot. After what we had ..."

"I like you, Z, I really do. But that's it."

"Mags, it hurts," I said, thinking that one last stab at honesty might do something.

She cocked her head, eyes wide through her thick lenses. "I'm sorry. I'm sorry if I let you think there was going to be more." She rested the fingers of her right hand on my cheek. The touch felt warm. "Z, I can't love you just because you want me to. Can you understand that?"

I was about to answer when the rec room door slammed open and I saw Crystal standing there. My heart froze. Maggie jerked her hand away from me and took several steps back. Crystal was breathing so hard I thought flames might shoot out of her nose. I couldn't think of anything to say so I stayed quiet and waited. Maggie edged farther away from me, looking at Crystal the whole time.

"We were playing eight-ball," Maggie said.

Crystal laughed cruelly. "His balls belong to me," she said. "Get that through your head. You are ancient history."

"Crystal, I'm not—"

"You think he'd go with you instead of me? I've been giving him the best sex of his life. Why would he go back to you when he has me?" Her deep brown eyes were blazing and I could see the vein on the side of her head throbbing. I was afraid. Not afraid of losing her, afraid she might take a cue stick and thrash one or both of us.

"Cryssie, for God's sake, we were just playing pool," I said. I wrenched up my voice into stiff anger. "What the fuck is wrong with you?"

The DEATH of OBSESSION

Her eyes shifted from me to Maggie and back to me. The gnarled anger in her face slowly relaxed as her breathing returned to normal and she seemed to recapture control. "Mikey, let's go back to the room," she said.

As soon as the door to my room closed, Crystal pushed me in the chest with both hands as hard as she could. I stumbled backward onto the bed. "Is that what you want, Mikey? A tight-ass bitch like Maggie? Then have her."

"We were playing pool," I said as if it were my only defense. "That's all, babe."

She moved toward me, head thrown back with fierce pride. "And what if she'd asked you to go back to her room? Would you have gone?"

"No way," I answered, maybe too vehemently. "I have everything I want right here, Crystal. Maggie is just a friend."

"I don't like you being friends with her," she said, more softly. "I think she wants to get back with you."

"No, she doesn't. We've both moved on from that. Cryssie, I swear you have nothing to worry about. Haven't I proved how much I love you?" I hated myself for pledging my undying love when I knew how many other guys she'd been with, how many times she'd made a fool of me. But she had a spell over me and I couldn't shake free of it. I longed for her approval.

She came and sat on my lap, kissing the side of my face, stroking my beard. "I don't know what it is about you," she cooed. "I've been with handsomer guys, stronger guys, taller guys ..."

"Yeah, that makes me feel good."

"... but you have gotten so far into me it's ridiculous. I've never loved a guy like I love you, Mikey. It's crazy." She put her lips against my ear, kissed me there, and whispered, "Can I tell you something? You are the best lover I've ever had. I don't know why. You reach me in places nobody ever has."

Fortified by her words, I pulled her down onto the bed to demonstrate my prowess.

3.

The semester was over and I was getting ready to spend the summer with Crystal in Boston. The prospect of living in Boston for three months was unsettling, especially to someone who had spent his whole life in the Empire State. I didn't see any alternative, though. I was not going home. I had not spoken to my parents since Easter. I was stubborn and was more proud than I should have been.

I was packing up my room when Elise knocked softly on the open door and came inside. I melted a little when I saw her. Her yellow-brown curls flowed around her flawless face, and those sky-blue eyes were riveted on me. "Hey, Z," she said. I smiled at her and waved her into a chair.

"What am I going to do with these fish?" I asked her.

She shrugged. "Have a fish fry."

"You're a cruel woman, Elise Mathieu."

Her white teeth grinned at me. "You want to smoke a little pot?" I asked her.

"Sure."

I filled a bowl and handed it and a lighter to Elise. She took a hit and gave me the pipe back. I sucked in some smoke, held it in, and blew a cloud toward the open window. El was staring at me and I wondered what she wanted. I decided to let her get to it in her own time.

"Where's Crystal?" she asked.

"She's getting her crap out of her old room. When are you leaving?"

"Tomorrow morning. What about you?"

"The same." I lit the pipe again, toked on it, passed it to Elise. She accepted it and took a hit.

Elise shifted on the chair, looking a little uncomfortable. *Here it comes.* I could smell her clean hair and body powder despite the pot smoke in the air. "Z, Maggie told me what happened between her and Crystal," she said.

I hesitated then snorted out a laugh. "It was no big deal."

"That's not the way Mags tells it."

"Well, Maggie's overreacting."

El watched me without replying. I could see by her ironic smile that she did not agree with my assessment. Naturally, she would take Maggie's side. But she didn't understand Crystal's point of view. Even I hadn't understood how insecure Cryssie was about my relationship with Maggie.

"Crystal's worried about losing a guy like me. Can you blame her?"

I was looking for a laugh, but instead El said, "Then she should treat you better."

My mouth dropped open. I had no idea how to answer that. Elise's words hurt, mostly because of the clawing truth in them. I was not ready to acknowledge that, however. I set my jaw and stared back at her.

"Z, I know I should mind my own business, but you're my friend," she said. Abruptly, she laughed in the goofy way that seemed to dismiss everything. "What am I talking about? I'm going out with Frank." Her azure eyes sparkled and I realized why I found her so wonderful.

"Frank's a good guy," I told her.

"Z, this is not good for me. I feel responsible for you being with Crystal," she said. "I *did* introduce you."

I laughed. "Introduce us? You practically threw us into bed together."

"I was trying to get your mind off Maggie. I didn't know you'd take it so serious."

"Yeah, well, I guess that's one of my problems," I said. "I have a hard time with casual involvement. The truth is, El, I'm just a goddamn romantic trying to disguise myself as a cynic."

She laughed again. "Oh, Z, that's what I love about you."

4.

I was driving toward hell with Crystal beside me. She was dragging on a cigarette and sipping vodka from a small bottle. For most of the ride, she was quiet. She didn't seem any happier than I was to be going to Boston. Every time I tried to start a conversation she would grunt a few words in reply and then sulk into silence. I couldn't help but think she regretted asking me to spend the summer with her.

At one point, she said, "You're going to stay in my room. I don't give a shit what my father says."

"I really don't mind staying in the guest room—"

"The hell with that, Mikey. We're engaged."

It made my head swim when she said things like that. I didn't consider us engaged. No way. I hadn't given her a ring and had no intention of doing so. What was her rush to marry me? Did it give her some sense of security? Honestly, I looked with horror at the possibility of being married to Crystal. It would be like putting on a blindfold and racing on a motorcycle at 100 mph—inevitable disaster. The question I couldn't answer—or maybe refused to answer—was why I stayed with her if I felt that way.

We swept around Albany and passed from New York into Massachusetts on I-90. The day was gray and it was raining intermittently. A perfect reflection of my melancholy mood. I tried to focus on the fall semester, on seeing Shank and Elise and everyone again, on laughing and smoking and playing Risk with them. It was, I feared, going to be a long, ugly summer. I was pretty sure Crystal's father and brother were not happy that I was going to be leeching off them for three months. And I only had a couple small buds of pot left and no easy way to buy any in Boston. I couldn't very well ask Crystal to hook me up since she would rather I didn't smoke at all.

It wasn't long before we started seeing signs for Boston. The highway was no different than the ones I drove in New York, except almost all the license plates were unlike mine. The green signs, the tree-lined stretches, the hills and vistas were all similar. Instead of comforting me, the sameness freaked me out. I might have been driving in the Hudson Valley—but I wasn't. I was not going home. That meant I would not accidentally run into Devon Shea or Christine Wendel; I would not laugh with my sister and roughhouse with my younger brother; I would see none of my high school friends, would not have beers with them at Frank's Bar & Grill until we were so drunk we sang, loud and obnoxious, to jukebox tunes. What the hell was I doing?

The DEATH of OBSESSION

Crystal had fallen asleep and was slumped against the passenger side door. I carefully plucked the vodka bottle from her lap, unscrewed the top and gulped down a few mouthfuls. The bottle was almost empty. I reached into my pocket and pulled out my pipe, lighter, and small bag of pot. I had learned the skill of filling a pipe while driving and I did so as we penetrated deeper into Massachusetts. After three or four heavy hits off the bowl and another gulp of vodka I turned up the radio and tried to relax. I opened my window all the way to blow the smoke out of the car. I breathed in the rippling air and felt the top of my head opening.

My surroundings warped into something surreal. The sun broke through the clouds creating a spiritual canvas of yellow, blue, white, and gray. I laughed at God's artistic touch. Why was He trying to impress us? Buildings rose out of the landscape, breaking the horizon with shocking abruptness. Steel, glass, and stone constructed at impossible angles. Golden light shimmering off mirrored surfaces like beckoning beacons. Everything flooded into my head and it all seemed so much I wanted to pull off to the side of the highway and take it all in.

Crystal stirred, yawned, opened her eyes. "We there yet?"

I said nothing. I wasn't sure where we were. I wasn't even sure we were still in Massachusetts—or, for that matter, still on Earth. I picked up the directions Crystal had written out for me and stared at them. I couldn't understand what they meant.

"Christ, Mikey, pay attention," Crystal snapped, fully regaining her senses. "Ya gotta take the next right."

I jerked the car into the right lane, cutting off a maroon Cadillac; the driver leaned on his horn and screamed something out the window. I'm sure it didn't help that I was sporting a New York license plate. I zoomed down the exit ramp without noting what the sign said. For all I knew, I was taking a turnoff onto Jupiter.

"Take a left at the light, Mikey. You got it? *A left at the light!*"

I took a couple deep breaths. "Stop yelling at me."

"I'm not yelling ... bear right here. Jesus, Mikey, what is wrong with you?" She lit a cigarette and started puffing furiously. She felt around the front seat for her vodka bottle and found it with a sip or two in it. Cars seemed to swarm around me, closing in on all sides. Driving in big cities made me want to vomit.

When we finally reached Crystal's house in South Boston, my nerves were ringing like a church bell. "South Baastin" was where you lived if you were Irish, according to Crystal. So here I was, a Guinea among Irishmen for the next three months. Crystal lived in a smart-looking, two-story home, yellow with red trim, on East 7th Street. It looked recently painted, crisp and angular like a New England home. The houses were packed closely together and there were no driveways anywhere I could see.

"Find a spot as close as you can," Crystal said. "Parking's always a pain in the ass."

Luckily, there was a spot not too far from the house. I eased in and Crystal immediately wrenched open the door and got out, stretching her back. "God, it's good to get out of that fuckin' car," she said.

I started to open the trunk, but she stopped me. "Leave the shit for now. We'll get it later," she told me.

I obeyed because I didn't know what else to do. I had a feeling I was going to be doing a lot of that. She threw open the front door, which was unlocked, and shouted, "Hey, we're here."

The entryway was impressive, with a brick-face wall on one side and polished wood floors. I noticed a bronze umbrella stand near the front door and a large, colorful abstract on the far wall, which was painted a neutral cream. The entry hall opened into a large living room with a modern-looking, black wood stove tucked into the corner. The furniture, a massive sofa and an overstuffed chair, were beige. Everything seemed impeccable.

William Cassidy was standing at the edge of the entryway. He was an imposing figure, with a barrel chest, thick neck, and powerful arms. His legs were spindly, though, and appeared too small to hold up the rest of his body. He had a disheveled head of curly hair, black with shocks of gray scattered throughout. His dark eyes were

The DEATH of OBSESSION

unfriendly, and his nose looked as if it had been broken a time or two. I was immediately intimidated by him.

"Hi, Daddy," Crystal said.

"You're finally here," he answered.

"It's a long fuckin' drive," she said. "Give me a break."

I could not imagine talking to my own father that way and I wished she wouldn't do it, either. At least not when I was around.

"Dad, this is Michael," she said casually.

I stepped forward, trying to sound respectful. "Nice to meet you, Mr. Cassidy. Thanks for letting me stay here."

He didn't utter a sound—not a word, not a grunt—and looked from me to Crystal and back to me. I wanted desperately to be back in Poughkeepsie. I don't think I've ever felt so awkward.

"What are were having for dinner?" Crystal asked her father. "I'm starvin'."

"Whatever ya wanna make," he said. "I'm going to Candace's."

"On my first night back? Jesus fuckin' Christ!"

He shrugged. "We got the whole summah," he said, as if this were a curse. He walked away and went up the stairs.

"Thanks a lot, you shit," she yelled after him.

I'm not sure, but I swear I heard him laugh.

5.

I didn't meet Crystal's brother until the next morning, when we were having coffee at the kitchen table. He had stayed huddled in his room all night. Apparently, Mr. Cassidy had never come home from his girlfriend's house because there was no sign of him. Crystal was unconcerned about her father's absence. When Conor came down the stairs and into the kitchen, he looked at both of us with a blank stare then poured himself a cup of coffee.

"You must be Michael," he said to me. He made no move to shake my hand.

"No shit, Con. Where were you all night?"

He shrugged. "I didn't feel like comin' outta my room."

It was strange; he didn't really resemble his father or sister. He was medium height and very slim to the point of being delicate. He had an abundance of freckles, and his brown hair was long and straight. Thick glasses perched on his small, rounded nose.

"Well, we didn't miss you, that's for sure," Crystal said. Exasperated, she added, "You are such a fuckin' weirdo."

"Look who's talkin'."

She sipped at her coffee, staring off into space. I kept my head down and tried not to think about how long the summer was going to be. The coffee was very strong and I drank it black, no sugar. The bitter taste braced me.

"Mikey's never been to Baastin before," Crystal told her brother. "We should show him around a little."

"I'm not goin' anywhere," he said. "Make me some eggs."

"Go fuck yourself," she snarled. "Make your own eggs."

She got up from the table and stormed up the stairs. I sat there, embarrassed, for a minute, finishing my coffee. Conor didn't look at me and I didn't look at him. I stood, washed out my cup and left it in the sink. Then I followed Crystal up the stairs. I didn't know what else to do.

6.

Crystal and I spent the day lounging around the house, drinking booze from her father's extensive liquor cabinet, and watching TV. We made uninspired love early in the afternoon. When I protested that her brother might hear, she said, "I hope he does." She took me on a short tour of the neighborhood, saying hello to a few people she knew and introducing me to the small grocery store a couple blocks away. We shared a Coke and walked back to her house.

The sun was peeking in and out all day, and we sat in her fenced-in yard for most of the afternoon. She put on a pair of shorts and a tank top and sunned herself in a lounge chair. I was rereading *Crime and Punishment* and spent several quiet hours with Raskolnikov. Could a man justify reprehensible actions or would they always leave a stain on his soul he could not erase? That was the

The DEATH of OBSESSION

question. Weak individuals always had an explanation for why they perpetrated evil. But really, most people knew the difference between right and wrong. Still, they usually acted in their own self-interest because they felt it was their due. How far would people go, though? As far as murder?

At about five, Crystal announced she was going in to take a shower. Left alone in the yard, I walked the perimeter of the fence, scanning for neighbors. Nobody was outside, though. It was quiet for a late May day. No music was playing, no one was shouting, there weren't even any noisy kids. It was like being in a bubble.

I sat back down on the deck stairs and started to read again when Conor came out of the house. He was dressed in neat jeans and a green polo shirt tucked in just so. His long hair was tucked behind his ears. At first he walked around the deck, ignoring me. He was, I was already detecting, a strange bird. After a while, he sat down next to me, so close we were almost touching, and said, "Hi."

"How ya doin'?" I asked, feeling very uncomfortable.

"Me? Fine, fine. How about you?"

"OK."

He locked on me with his hazel eyes, which seemed to shift constantly between green and brown, and said nothing. I was nearly squirming under his gaze. To defend myself, I said, "Crystal tells me you're going after your master's. What are you studying?"

"The philosophy of mathematics."

I had absolutely no answer to that, so I said, "Really? Sounds interesting."

He shrugged. "It's way too esoteric for most people. My father thinks I'm a freak for pursuing a master's in something nobody gives a damn about. He said if I was interested in math, I should have become an engineer or an architect. Those are things he can understand."

I had dabbled in some heady philosophy classes, so I was not totally out of my element. Trying to impress him, I said, "I read Russell's *The Principles of Mathematics*. It was deep water, but I think I got most of it."

"It barely scratches the surface," he said. "If you want to take a bigger bite, read Hilbert's *Principles of Mathematical Logic*. It's a good starting point."

"Um, sure, I'll keep that in mind."

I turned back to my book, hoping he would stand up and move away from me. Instead, he stayed glued to me and said, "Ah, reading Dostoevsky, I see. Quite a thinker in his own right, although he relied too much on the spiritual."

I was in my own ball park now. "One of his main concerns was the soul and how it's affected by the trials of human existence. Are we spiritual beings or animals or something in between? And how do we reconcile all that? So of course he was concerned with the spiritual."

"I understand that, but the only way to solve that dilemma is through pure logic."

"He would have said there's no such thing as pure logic."

"Then aim for the purest we can attain."

"We are not human without our emotions and impressions," I said.

"Maybe so, but we can't figure out what we are and where we belong in the universe without the discipline of logic. Everything we say, everything we do is meaningless without understanding."

"Maybe understanding defies logic," I said.

He smiled at me, showing a row of yellowing, uneven teeth. "You're a smart guy," he said. "What are you doing with my sister?"

Before I could answer, he stood up and went inside the house.

7.

Mr. Cassidy got home around six-thirty and as soon as he walked in the door he poured himself a tumbler of whisky with a couple of ice cubes. He gulped it down before saying a word and poured himself another. Crystal, who had a glass of vodka in her hand, asked him what we were doing for dinner.

"You been home all day," he said. "You plan on cookin' somethin'?"

"We'll do takeout," she said. It was not a request, it was an order.

He sighed. "Whadda ya want? Chinese? Italian? Burgers from the diner?"

"Let's do Italian," she said.

He looked at me as if I had somehow demanded Italian because my name was Zinarelli. Truth was, I didn't much like Italian takeout. It could never match my mother's cooking. I averted my eyes from him and said nothing.

"Get the menu from Giacomo's," he told Crystal. "They deliver, right?"

"I think so. But me and Mikey can go pick it up if you want."

"Whatever."

Crystal called her brother down from his room and we passed the menu around. I decided on a chicken parm sandwich. "That's all you want?" she asked me, and I told her I wasn't all that hungry. She wrote down everyone's order and called it in, opting for delivery because the wait wouldn't be that long.

We all sat down at the kitchen table. Mr. Cassidy was working on his third drink already, and Crystal was keeping up with him. I sipped at a beer. I had sucked in a few hits of pot in Cryssie's room right before her father got home, so I was feeling OK. Conor was drinking orange soda.

"Daddy," Crystal said suddenly, "Mikey can't be sittin' around the house all summah. Can you fix him up with somethin'?"

I didn't like the sound of that. Mr. Cassidy was the general manager of a construction company and I dreaded what he might have in store for me. He grumbled, shifted in his chair, and gave me a sour look. I wasn't sure if he hated me or his daughter or the world in general.

"I got a job over in Roxbury right now," he said. "I guess I can use him as a gofer. It don't pay that much, but hey, beggars can't be choosers."

"Mr. Cassidy, I appreciate—"

"Six bucks an hour," he said. "That's the best I can do."

Six dollars an hour was, like, three times the minimum wage—for what sounded like basically a do-nothing job. What was I going to say? "Mr. Cassidy, really, that's very generous."

"Forget it," he said. "Tomorrow's Saturday, so why don't ya start on Monday."

When the takeout arrived, Mr. Cassidy pulled a wad of bills out of his pocket and tossed a few at Conor. "Go pay the boy," he said.

As soon as the food hit the table, Mr. Cassidy starting wolfing down his pasta like a starving man. He finished quickly, stood up, and said, "I'm goin' to see Candace. Don't wait up." With that, he was out the door. Crystal stared after him for a long time, obviously unhappy with his abrupt departure.

"I hate that bitch," she said.

"She's nice," Conor said.

"Shut up."

"You shut up. She makes Dad happy."

Crystal's brown eyes were smoldering. "Yeah, he's happy. He's happy to be getting' pussy from a younger woman. Wake up, Con."

"Jesus, Crystal, you are so crude. What the fuck is wrong with you?"

"Oh, I forgot, Con, you don't know anything about pussy." She was leaning forward so far she was in his face. "If you were a fag, at least I could respect that. You'd be sucking cock and I could understand it. But you ... you are nothin'. You don't want women and you don't want guys. What do you want, brother? You want to fuck a quadratic equation?"

He stood up and glared at her for a few seconds, measuring his response. Then he walked away without saying anything.

"That was pretty harsh," I said.

She jerked her head around and attacked me with her eyes. "Mind your own business, Mikey," she said.

The DEATH of OBSESSION

8.

On Monday morning, Mr. Cassidy drove me to the job site. We didn't talk at all during the drive. His crew was putting up the metal skeleton of a warehouse. They had erected the first floor and were getting ready for the second stage. He introduced me to the foreman, a pot-bellied Jew named Mort, and then got in his Cadillac and drove away to another job.

The place was swarming with over-muscled tough guys in wife-beaters and worn jeans. Several of them wore Red Sox caps. Mort didn't bother to introduce me to anyone. A couple of guys came up to me and asked my name and what I was doing there, but mostly everyone was too busy to bother with me, which was good. I felt so out of place it was ridiculous. My first was job was to get the morning coffee. I wrote down everyone's requests and walked across the street to a deli, where I patiently repeated each order: coffee black; coffee light, two sugars; tea with honey, etc. By the time I got back, everyone was scaling the metal. A huge crane was swinging I-bars into place and the workers were bolting them in as fast as they could.

The sun was hot overhead and everyone was sweating and cursing and laughing at private jokes. I stayed close to Mort, waiting for him to give me instructions. But he didn't say much to me. "Pick up that wrench and hand it to Kelly." "Move that toolbox out of the way." When lunchtime came, I took orders from everyone and ran over to the deli, edging my way to the front and calling out sandwich after sandwich. When I got back, I was proud that nobody complained about a screw-up.

As the guys sat around eating, I became a focus of interest.

"So, New Yaark, you like the Yankees?" a guy named Duffy asked me.

"Actually, I'm a Mets fan," I said.

Everyone laughed. I felt my face turning red.

"No shit," Duffy said.

I wanted to remind these New England douche bags that Boston hadn't won a World Series in a thousand years, but, being in enemy territory, I said nothing.

Another of the scholars, a juiced-up muscleman called Maz, grinned at me as he tore into his ham and cheese with spicy mustard, and said, "So you're goin' out with Cassidy's daughter. That right?"

"We've been dating for a few months," I answered carefully.

"She's a nice girl," Maz said and laughed wickedly.

"Oh yeah, we *all* know how nice she is," someone said from the back of the pack. Everyone howled.

I was ready to start swinging and let shit fall where it would. But before I could move, Mort yelled, "All right you stupid fuckers, back to work. We got a building to put up. And let me tell you something else, I hear anybody else talk about Mr. Cassidy's daughter that way and I'm gonna rip 'em a new asshole."

"We're just fuckin' around," Duffy said.

"Yeah," a few other voices chimed in.

"Fuck around on your time. Move!"

There was a general grumbling, but everyone stood up, wolfing down the last bites of their lunch, and headed back to work.

9.

I thanked God when the end of the week finally came. The odds that I would get through the summer without killing someone or being killed were slim. I wished the Soviets would detonate an atomic bomb over Boston. I would stand in the middle of Fenway Park and call the destruction down with a smile on my face.

When I got home from work Friday evening, Crystal informed me that she was going out with a couple of her high school friends. "I hope you don't mind," she said. I did mind, but what could I do? I told her it was fine and I would find something to do. I had gotten my first week's pay from Mr. Cassidy, in cash, and I was feeling flush. It amounted to more than two hundred dollars.

Before she went out, Crystal asked me, "Mikey, can I borrow a few bucks? You got paid today, right?"

I thought she had a lot of nerve taking money from my first paycheck, but I said, "Sure. How much do you need?"

The DEATH of OBSESSION

"I dunno. Whatever you think," she said.

I handed her two twenties and she looked at the bills sitting in her hand. After a minute, she said, "How about another twenty, just in case?"

In case of what, I wondered. But I gave her the bill. She kissed me on the cheek and headed out the door as someone beeped the horn for her. "Thanks, baby," she called as she left. I had a flash of my future with Crystal: me handing her money as she hurried out the door for some rendezvous.

I mapped out my miserable Friday night. I'd order some takeout, smoke judiciously from my dwindling stash of weed, drink some scotch from Mr. Cassidy's liquor cabinet, and watch mindless TV. Crystal's father was already on his way to Candace's house, and we were not likely to see him for the rest of the weekend. It was hard for me to believe that Cryssie was leaving me alone at the end of my first work week.

I was sitting in front of the television watching the local news when Conor came downstairs and asked me what I was doing for dinner. I told him I was ordering Chinese and he said, "Can I get in on that?" I said that would be fine and we pored over the menu for several minutes.

Conor called in our order while I filled a glass with ice and then poured scotch in. He drank orange soda while I tried to get drunk as quickly as I could. I watched the news about the reopening of the Suez Canal by Egypt. I flipped the channels and found a rerun of *I Love Lucy*. I sat for a while and laughed. Conor stretched out on the floor and watched with me.

The food came and we ate in the living room, watching *Sanford & Son*. We put the leftovers in the fridge. I kept knocking down scotch, hoping to get into bed early and fall asleep. Maybe Crystal would wake me up when she got home and we'd make love. Conor and I were watching *Chico & the Man* when he looked over at me and said, "Do you have any pot?"

I stared at him for a moment and said, "Why?"

"I'd like a hit or two, if you do."

"You smoke pot?"

He grinned sheepishly. "Once in a while. I feel like it tonight."

I went into Crystal's room and took my smoking materials out of my bag. I pinched a bit off a bud and put it in the bowl. Back downstairs, I handed the pipe to Conor. He smiled and took a hit, choking as soon as he got it into his lungs. "Sorry," he coughed. He tried to hand the pipe back to me, but I waved for him to take another toke. This time he was able to hold it in.

We smoked for a while and raided the liquor cabinet, Conor drinking cognac and me sipping scotch. He giggled uncontrollably at silly sitcoms. I found myself liking him a lot more. It wasn't long before he was wasted, eyes glassy and far away. I quickly discovered that he was a gabber, unable to shut up when he was stoned. He talked about unintelligible math theories for a few minutes, but then turned to something more personal.

"My father doesn't give a damn about us," he said. "You can tell that, right? Even before my mother died he didn't want much to do with us. After she died ... shit, he might as well have died with her."

He looked at me, but I said nothing.

"He never had much use for me anyway. I wasn't the tough guy he wanted me to be. I sucked at baseball, at basketball, at everything he wanted me to be good at. And Crystal, Christ, he just stays as far away from her as he can. She's too much for him. He lets her do whatever she wants as long as she leaves him alone." He laughed bitterly. "We're some family, huh?"

"I'm sure it's not that bad," I said. "All families have problems."

He shook his head. "You don't know. You really don't know Crystal. I like you, Michael, so I gotta tell you somethin'. And I mean this. Get in your freakin' car and get the hell out of here as fast as you can. Don't look back. She is as bad as it gets. She's my sister, but I can't lie. Every time I see her it reminds me how bad she is. Michael, I'm tellin' you what it's like."

I thought about everything she had put me through and felt the force of Conor's words. It was making me a little sick.

"You know how many guys she's brought into this house? I can't count 'em. And she'll disappear for days and Gawd knows where she is or what she's doin'. I heard stories about her that would make you vomit." He leaned his head back and stared at the ceiling. "She's evil, man. She's one of those female demons who come to you in your sleep and sap all your strength."

"A succubus," I said.

"Yeah, yeah, that's it, a succubus."

"That's pretty harsh, Conor." I felt I had to at least try to defend her.

He drew his eyes down from the ceiling and focused on me. "I'm gonna tell you something you can never repeat. I'll deny I ever said it. But it's the Gawd's honest truth." He took a gulp of his cognac, swallowed slowly. "One night when she was about sixteen, Crystal snuck into my room and started ... touching me under the blankets. I was asleep but I got ... aroused, you know, I thought I was dreaming. But then it started getting too real and I opened my eyes and there she was, with her hand on me. I screamed, 'What the fuck are you doing?' and I shoved her, hard. She fell off the bed, and you know what she did? She started laughing. She said, 'You just passed up the best pussy you'll ever get.' And she walked out of my room."

I stared at him, dumbfounded. "Maybe your mother's death affected her more than anybody knew," I said. I couldn't think of anything else.

"She was fucked up before my mother got sick. She's nasty bad, that's all. She broke my mother's heart. I think she was relieved to die."

10.

With a hollow in my chest, I waited for Crystal to return. Midnight came and went and there was no word from her. I lay down on her bed, fully dressed except for my shoes, and tried to read. My head was swimming, though, and the words kept running together into senseless phrases. I don't know when I drifted off to sleep, but it was late. I slept uneasily, sweating and thrashing. I sat bolt upright when the sun was barely above the horizon. Crystal was not home.

"This can't be happening," I said to the window. But I knew it was.

How could she bring me all this way only to abandon me in an unfamiliar city—stranger in a strange land? I wanted to punch something. Instead, I stretched back out on the bed and assured myself there was an explanation. She had gotten shit-faced with her old pals and had fallen asleep at one of their houses. She'd be calling as soon as she woke up. She would not, I decided, intentionally leave me alone here with her brother. I didn't fall back to sleep, but drifted in and out of consciousness. I was haunted by Conor's story from the night before. He had to be a lying sonofabitch. He was a freak, anyway. There was no way Crystal had tried to seduce her own brother. And if she had, why the hell would he tell me about it?

The sun punched up over the houses to the east and light flooded in the windows. The sky was a mellow blue with small puffy clouds acting as accents. I and went downstairs and filled a glass with scotch, drinking it down greedily. Conor was nowhere in sight. I turned on the TV and watched Saturday morning cartoons, grunting out an occasional laugh at the absurdity. Nine, ten, eleven o'clock passed and the phone did not ring. I was by myself. Conor was obviously avoiding me and Crystal was ... where the fuck was Crystal?

The later it got, the more I drank, until by noon I was floating just this side of reality. Every so often, I would take a hit of weed to keep my head right. But I was losing my grip. I kept waiting for the phone to jar me back to the world, but there was nothing but silence. At one point, I thought about going to Conor's room and pounding on the door, but that would entail talking to him and I was in no shape for that. I went out back and walked around the yard for a few minutes then returned to the living room and kept drinking until I thought I might pass out. No such luck, though. My brain would not turn off.

With nothing else to do, I decided to visit the Museum of Science, which I had heard was a huge deal. I smoked more weed, drank another glass of scotch and headed out.

The DEATH of OBSESSION

I knew I shouldn't have been driving, but I didn't care. It took me a while to find the museum. I got trapped on one-way streets, jammed in weekend traffic, led astray by confusing signs. By the time I reached the museum, an impressive structure overlooking the Charles River Basin, it was late in the afternoon. I debated whether or not to go in but decided that since I had worked so hard to find it, I might as well enter.

My head was in the clouds and I was feeling sick from drinking scotch all day. I paid my admission (I have no idea how much it was) and started walking aimlessly, eschewing the site map that was offered. The museum was a blur of dinosaurs, huge magnets, fossils, and crackling electric charges. Since it was a Saturday, the place was mobbed and kids were running everywhere, screaming "Look at this, Mom" or "Come here, Dad." At one point, I stood in front of one of the massive, southwest-facing windows and stared out at the smooth blue waters of the Charles. It soothed my soul a bit and made me wish I was looking at the Hudson.

An hour or so into my visit I was exhausted, coming down from my high and weary of dodging unruly children. I trudged outside feeling shaky. I wanted to lie down, but there was no way I was returning to Crystal's house yet. I walked away from the museum, leaving my car in the lot, and traveled without any idea where I was going. Cars whipped by me, occasionally beeping angrily as I weaved out into the road. A small seafood restaurant attracted my attention, and I went inside. I was dressed in shorts and a T-shirt and my hair was matted with sweat. The hostess eyed me suspiciously when I asked for a table for one, then I changed my mind and said I'd sit at the bar.

The place was a typical seafood shanty with nets hanging from the ceiling and plastic lobsters pinned to the walls. I ordered a beer and a dozen steamers. The bartender nodded and walked away without saying anything. The beer was cold and I sucked it down greedily. By the time the clams arrived, I was ready for another Budweiser. The sounds of families enjoying their fish dinners, glasses clinking, and forks scraping, made me unaccountably sad. I was alone.

I ate about half the clams, finished my second beer and left a twenty on the bar. I wasn't sure I'd find my way back to the car, but I did. Getting to Crystal's house was another matter, and there was a moment of absolute terror when I had no idea where I was and I was so close to vomiting I almost pulled over. But I kept driving, saw some street names I thought I recognized, and eventually worked my way back to her house. By this time, it was after eight o'clock.

I squeezed the car clumsily into a parking space and stumbled into the house, waiting for Crystal to descend on me and ask where I'd been. The place was silent, though. I pounded up the stairs thinking I'd find Crystal in her room, but she wasn't there. I could hear Conor down the hall, pacing around his room. His door was closed. The thought that Crystal was still out enraged me. "You fucking bitch," I said. I pounded the bed several times because I didn't know what else to do.

My head was pounding, my stomach churning. I stretched out on the bed and repeated, "Fucking bitch." I took a few deep breaths, trying to calm myself. Without knowing how or when it happened, I passed out.

11.

I awoke in a cold sweat, startled and unable to figure out where I was. It was pitch-black except for moonlight peeking through the window. I had no idea what time it was. One thing I knew: I was alone. Climbing off the bed, I turned on the light because the darkness was eroding my soul. I couldn't get what Conor said out of my head. Had his sister actually tried to seduce him? *Jesus Cryssie Jesus Christ what the hell is wrong with you?* I had to be insane to be involved with this girl. Everyone I knew was trying to tell me that. Even her own brother.

Without thinking about what I was doing, I started throwing my stuff in my bag. I had some boxes to carry downstairs, and as soon as I started packing the car, I felt better. I was going back to Poughkeepsie. I was going home to apologize to my parents and get my life back on track.

This whole thing had been a nightmare. Maybe Conor was right. Maybe she was a succubus.

All that was left in Cryssie's room was my duffle bag, and I took the stairs two at a time to get it. By this time it was almost four in the morning. There was silence in Conor's room and I had no intention of saying goodbye to him. I would be glad never to see him again. I couldn't wait to get the car started and be on my way. With any luck, I could be home by breakfast.

I was crossing the living room when the front door opened and Crystal walked in. She was startled to see me and stood looking at me for a moment. Her hair was disheveled and her face was drawn and pale. I wondered when she'd slept last. She looked like she'd spent the last thirty-two hours getting fucked by every player on the Red Sox.

"Where are you going?" she asked finally.

I couldn't help it: I laughed. "What do you care?"

"Mikey—"

"I'm going home," I told her before she could say anything else.

"Don't go."

"Don't go? DON'T GO! Fuck you," I snarled. "Where have you been since Friday night?"

Her face began to glow red. "I needed some time to myself. I was with my friend Erin. I'm sorry, Mikey."

"You couldn't call and let me know you were still alive?"

"I know I should have called."

"Who were you fucking, Crystal? Or should I ask how many guys you were fucking? I'm done, you whore. Understand? I am DONE!" I was working so hard to control myself I was trembling with the effort.

She took a couple steps toward me, but I moved back. "Don't."

She started crying, tears falling silently from her brown eyes. "Michael, I love you. I wasn't with another guy. Erin and I got drunk and—"

I moved so quickly I shocked her. I lunged forward and slapped her across the face so hard her head jerked. Eyes wide, she stared at me.

"You got fucked, Crystal. I am not stupid. Stop treating me like an idiot. Oh my God, you are nothing but a liar and a whore." I slapped her again and she stood firm, head held high, waiting for another blow.

"You can't hurt me, Mikey. I love you too much."

I shook my head, fire flowing through my entire body. "You are a sick bitch. You know that? You need help."

Her dark eyes focused on me like lasers and she offered a tiny smile. "You know you love me, Mikey. You know I made you feel better than any girl ever has. Don't lie to yourself. You want me. You want me right now."

I was terrified because she was right. I did want her right then. And if I had succumbed, I might have ended up a sapped and twisted victim. Something pulled me back, though. I slapped her again so hard she fell to the floor. I hated myself for hitting her. For the rest of my life, I would live with the stain of using violence against her. I never forgot it, never reconciled it.

She snorted a laugh at me. "You are so needy, Mikey. I had to have some fresh air. You were suffocating me."

"Suffocating you? I gave up everything for you—my family, my friends. And you have the fucking gall to say I'm suffocating you?"

"It was a trade, Mikey. The best pussy you ever had for the rest of that shit. Wasn't it worth it, baby?" There was something repulsive in her demonic smile. Was I going insane or was she gnawing at my soul?

I moved without thinking. I grabbed her by the hair and dragged her onto the sofa. She didn't fight me. "Suffocating you? You want to see suffocating you? Fuck you!" I snatched up a sofa pillow and pressed it down over her face. She didn't fight at first, letting me have my way, as if her compliance would show me that she really was dedicated to me.

When I wouldn't stop shoving the pillow into her face, though, and she couldn't catch her breath, she began to panic. Her feet thrashed and her arms flailed and she wanted me to get off. But I was just as determined to end this once and for all. I was going to kill her. I was going to expunge this demon. Who else could? It was up to me. If I didn't kill this thing it would continue to torment unsuspecting men. She stopped struggling, let her arms fall out to her sides. Thank you, God, it was almost over.

I don't know what made me stop. Abruptly, I yanked the pillow away and stood up, unhinged at what I'd nearly done. I stared at her, my mouth wide open. She sat up and gasped for air.

"What the hell have you turned me into?" I whispered.

"What have you turned yourself into?" she wheezed.

Chapter Eleven
Leap of Faith

Love is all, it gives all, and it takes all.
—Soren Keirkegaard

1.

Z kept pounding down Jack Daniel's, trying to get his mind to turn off. But it wouldn't. He could not stop thinking about that Wednesday afternoon.
"No, I don't think about the good times," I tell her. "Mostly, I wonder why you did the things you did to me. Honestly, Cryssie, I still don't understand why you wanted to hurt me so much. That has haunted me all these years." I know it sounds corny but I figure this will be my only chance to say what I've had bottled up for three decades.
Her face turns steely cold. I remember the look. It makes me shiver. "Poor little Mikey. Always the victim. You always wanted to blame me for everything, but it wasn't all my fault, Mikey. You're the one who left me, remember?"
"Jesus, Cryssie, are you kidding me? Do I have to remind you how many other guys you slept with while we were together? If you had even tried to be faithful I might have stayed with you."
"That was all in your mind. You were so insecure, Mikey. You just wanted a devoted geisha girl. I'm not the one who broke you down, Maggie was. I'm the one who built you back up. You never appreciated that."
I sit back, amazed. She refuses to take any responsibility for skewering me. She's putting the blame back on me. "You are unbelievable, Cryssie. You really are. Are you saying you never cheated on me?"
"Yes, I slept with other guys while we were together. But I always loved you. I always came back to you. Why was

that so hard for you to accept? You couldn't just love me, you wanted to possess me. I couldn't be possessed, Mikey. I never could be. Not for my whole life. You wanted to make me something I wasn't."

I realize this is going nowhere. I need to go home and stop trying to recapture something that never existed. Before I can say anything else, Crystal glances at her Michele Tahitian ceramic white diamond watch (at least $1,200) and says, "I don't have to be anywhere for a few hours. Let's forget the rest of this bullshit and enjoy each other for old time's sake."

I stare at her, so numb from twenty-seven years of marriage I'm not sure what she's getting at.

"You know I was never one to mince words, Mikey. I want you to take me to a motel. You're still the best lover I ever had."

I feel myself turning to jelly. I can't answer that. "I'm not in the kind of shape I used to be."

"Who is?" She glances between my legs, making me feel even more uneasy. "I'm sure that still works."

I squirm uncomfortably in my chair. "Listen, Cryssie, I'm flattered—"

"Please don't tell me you love your wife, Mikey. I don't care about that. I just want to be with you to remember old times. Don't you ever think about those nights we had together?"

Faced with the realization that I could actually fuck Crystal again if I wanted to, I am petrified. Isn't that why I really came here in the first place, to see if we could restoke that fire? But she hasn't essentially changed in thirty years. Maybe I haven't either. But I have changed enough.

"Cryssie, I can't. How could I go home and face Anna if I did?"

She smiles at me, but it is a frigid turning up of her mouth. "Ah, Mikey, always the noble boy. That was always your problem. You wanted everybody to be as noble as you saw yourself."

"I'm not noble. I just have to live with myself."

She reaches into her pocketbook, takes out her credit card to pay the bill. "Have you been happy, Mikey? Have you been happy with your Suzie Homemaker wife, living in your little house in Poughkeepsie and working for the local paper? When was the last time you had an adventure?"

"Today."

She laughs, genuinely amused. "You are a sad case, Mikey. Don't you miss the way I made your heart pound?"

"I don't have to walk along the edge of a chasm to feel alive, Cryssie. I guess that is one thing I learned from you."

"I'm not finished with you, Mikey."

"Yes you are, Crystal. Yes you are."

"We'll see," she says with an evil grin.

I am thinking that, all those years ago, I should have held that pillow over her face for a few more minutes.

2.

The BMW pulled into the Farmers' driveway and idled there for a few minutes, the driver going through various scenarios in his head. When David Kaplowitz opened the door, he appeared smooth and confident. He reached into the backseat, pulled out a guitar, and slung it over his back. He looked like a handsome Bob Dylan, dressed in tight jeans and leather jacket. He was feeling good.

With supreme self-assurance he pounded on the front door of the Farmers' home. At first, there was nothing. He waited calmly. After a moment, Air Farmer opened the door, a slightly younger version of her sister: wheat-colored hair pulled back into a rough ponytail, blue eyes focused on him like lasers.

"Hi," she said.

He offered her the perfect-toothed grin. "Hello," he said. "Is Earth around?"

Air edged away from the door, shouted over her shoulder, "Earth! Somebody here for you."

Earth felt her stomach roiling as she approached the front door and when she saw the figure of David Kaplowitz it made her chest clench. She had hoped this would not happen so soon, that it might take place over the phone after he returned to New York City. But now that he was here it had to happen.

"Hi," she said softly.

The DEATH of OBSESSION

He showed her his white teeth, his eyes shining. "Earth, how are you, darling?" Before she could answer, he said, "I wrote a song for you. You want to hear it?"

She felt slightly sick. This was going to be more difficult than she thought. She wanted to shrink away from the doorway but understood this had to end here. "Let's go out back and talk," she said in as neutral a tone as she could manage.

"Sure."

They walked into the backyard and crunched through fallen leaves to the stone bench at the very back of the property. Earth felt her heart palpitating as if she were running a hundred-yard dash. When they had settled onto the bench David abruptly swung the guitar around from his back and began to strum chords.

"Let me sing you the song," he said.

Earth reached out and put her fingers across the guitar neck. "David, wait. Let's talk first."

The light in his eyes went out. He yanked the guitar away from her grasp and frowned. "OK, what?"

"David," she began, "this is really difficult. I mean, you're a great guy. But I just think we rushed into this."

"Rushed into it?"

She felt her cheeks turning bright red. She couldn't control it. "I ... we shouldn't have slept together so fast. It was my fault, David. I know I led you on but I realized afterwards that we went too fast."

Kaplowitz appeared calm at first. He strummed a few chords on the guitar and began humming. Then he stopped abruptly and she could see the clouds in his deep brown eyes. "So you were just playing with me?" he asked.

"No. It's just ... David, it's all going too fast."

"Too fast." He laughed bitterly. "You're the one who wanted it to happen. Do you deny that, Earth?"

Feeling closed in, she stood up and walked a few steps away from the stone bench. Even though she was in her own yard, she was afraid. It was the first time she had ever felt afraid there. "I don't deny anything," she said. "But I have the right to change my mind, David."

He tore the guitar off his shoulder and tossed it onto the ground with a twang. "You think you can play with people's emotions like that? It's not fair, Earth. It's not right. You make someone fall in love with you and then you change your mind."

"What?"

"I love you, Earth. You made me fall in love with you."

Even in the brisk autumn air her forehead was dripping. *God I screwed up what the hell was I thinking this is ridiculous.* "David, you barely know me," she said, trying to sound reasonable. "How could you possibly be in love with me?"

"After the other night, how could I not be?"

She took a deep breath. This had to end now. "David, the other night was a mistake. It shouldn't have happened."

"A mistake?" He seemed incredulous. "No, Earth, you're wrong. It wasn't a mistake. It was wonderful. It was a beautiful coming together to two souls. Jesus, didn't you feel that?"

She was afraid to answer, but she did. "No. Honestly, David, what I felt was two strangers groping each other in the dark. And that's not enough for me."

He kicked at his guitar on the grass but missed it. After a few seconds he gathered himself and said, "What was it, Earth? Wasn't I good enough for you? Wasn't my cock big enough? Didn't I have enough stamina for you? Was it all about the goddamn performance?"

"David," she said quietly, "you need to leave."

"Earth, please," he implored her. "Who turned you against me? Was it him? I'll bet it was that sonofabitch."

Confused, she was not sure how to answer. "What are you talking about? Nobody turned me against you."

"Don't lie to me," he growled. He was getting angrier by the second. "It was that bastard Mike, wasn't it?"

"What does Mr. Z have to do with this?"

"Yeah, that's what I'd like to know. What does he have to do with you and me? He just wants to ruin my life like he ruined my mother's life. Don't you see it? Now that he's killed my mother, he wants to destroy *me.*"

She backed away from him. It was obvious now that he had become completely unhinged. She was ready to turn and run back into the house when her father walked out the back door and headed toward them, looking stern. Max Farmer was dressed in his coveralls and had his long hair pulled back into a messy ponytail. His thick chest and powerful arms seemed to pulsate as he marched forward.

"Is everything all right here?" he roared.

One look from Earth told him it was not.

"You better go now," he said to Kaplowitz. David started to say something, but Max cut him off. "There's no discussion about it."

Kaplowitz hesitated several beats, considering what to do next. Max stood over him, offering no choice. With an angry grunt, Kaplowitz stood up, snatched his guitar from the ground, and walked away. After she heard the car door slam, the engine rev, and the BMW drive away, Earth sobbed, "Daddy," and buried her face in Max's chest.

He hugged her tightly and said, "It's all right, sweetheart. I won't let anything happen to you." But he knew it was a promise he could not keep.

3.

What Michael Zinarelli liked most about his house was its location. Aside from the Farmers across the street, he had no neighbors. To the right was a state-designated wetlands, a small swampy area that filled with water whenever it rained and in dry times was all reeds. There would never be any building there. Behind the house and to the left was the wooded buffer zone for the county resource recovery plant. Again, barring a drastic change in circumstance, no structures would be put up on that land.

To Z, it was a perfect situation. His house was five minutes from any convenience, yet it was like he was living in the country. For the most part, he hated neighbors. Really, what he could not tolerate was other people's noise. When he and Anna were first married and living in an apartment complex, he was constantly aggravated by pounding music and loud voices and the screams of children. The first time he saw the house that was so close to everything and yet so far away, he fell in love with it.

As for the Farmers, he could not have chosen better neighbors. They were quiet and respectful and never hosted parties. They were content to spend their days working their garden and reading on the front porch and cooking large pots of soup. He hoped they would never move out of their house.

Sitting in the pressure cooker of the *Hudson Valley Sun* office that day in October, Z had no idea that his little slice of paradise was being scouted for weaknesses he had never had reason to consider.

4.

Detective Barone was shuffling through paperwork at her desk and feeling tired. Most days she enjoyed her work, but today something was nagging at her. She leaned back in her chair and ran a hand through her short yellow hair. She thought about going home to her boyfriend, Edward, and having him give her a full body massage. He had talented hands and the patience to do a thorough job. Always, she rewarded him for his efforts. Sex with Edward was satisfying and, at times, explosive. Barone was not a beautiful woman, she knew that, but she liked the way she looked—she was healthy and strong and wasn't a cookie-cutter Barbie—and, just as important, Edward liked the way she looked.

She was hours away from her massage, though, and the back of her neck was aching. The details of this Crystal Cassidy case were bugging her. She couldn't put her finger on why. The pocketbook found in the rocks along the Hudson had obviously been planted there, but what was the purpose? To indicate she was in the river or to point blame at someone specific? Her car had been found in Poughkeepsie, but her husband said he had no idea what she was doing here. Much of the evidence seemed to indict Michael Zinarelli, but Barone had a gut feeling that he was not a killer. She had met several killers during her career and he didn't strike her as having the bloodlust. Still, anyone could be pushed over the edge. That was something she had learned in her 15 years as a police officer. Under the right circumstances, anyone could kill. Even the Dali Lama.

The DEATH of OBSESSION

Barone leaned back in her chair, hands behind her head, and thought she needed to question Zinarelli's wife again. If she knew Cassidy and her husband had renewed their old relationship, that would certainly give her motive. She wouldn't be the first woman driven to murder to keep her family together. Barone was considering how she might approach Anna Zinarelli for another interview when Steve Delson's phone rang.

Her partner snatched up the receiver and said, "Detective Delson."

Pause.

"Yes, sir, we are taking her disappearance very seriously. I can assure you we are doing everything we can."

Pause.

"Well, there hasn't been an arrest yet because we don't have a really strong suspect. And, honestly, we don't even have a body, so it's especially difficult to arrest someone for murder."

Pause.

"That's all circumstantial, sir. It's difficult to arrest someone for murder on that kind of evidence ... That's right. Even if the DA was able to get an indictment, a good defense attorney would shred the prosecution's case."

Pause.

"No, I'm not an attorney." Delson made a face into the receiver. "Listen, I have to go. If we get any news, we'll be sure to get in touch with you." He hung up before there could be any reply.

Barone chuckled. "Nice. Who the hell was that?"

Delson stared at her, silent at first. Then he said, "Come on."

5.

David Kaplowitz was very careful. He parked his car in the lot of a fast-food joint several miles from Z's house, making sure to pull into a space in the back of the building. Walking slowly along the road he kept his head down and tried to seem inconspicuous. His only worry was that Earth or someone in her family might be in their front yard, but the yard was empty as he passed. Quickly, he darted around to the back of Z's house.

The house was built into the side of a steep incline, and the door to the basement was at the back of the house at the bottom of the hill. Kaplowitz waited near the door and listened intently. No sounds came from the house. It was early afternoon and he knew Z was already at work; Anna was at work, too, and the girls were in school. Having scouted the house, Kaplowitz knew that Tasha was the first one home in the afternoon. She got off the bus and let herself in. Sophie got home at least a half hour later; sometimes she did not come home until dinnertime.

Kaplowitz looked around then began kicking the basement door until it splintered away from the jamb. It wasn't long before he was in the cluttered basement. He mentally chided Z for not keeping the room in order. Tools were scattered across the crowded work bench, empty boxes were piled against one wall, and various items that had obviously been unused for years took up the rest of the space. Kaplowitz believed messiness was a sign of weakness.

He tromped up the basement stairs and tried the door that led into the house. It was unlocked. He pushed it open and there he was inside Michael Zinarelli's house. A small smile creased his lips. It seemed he had been waiting for this his whole life. *Payback is a bitch, Mike.* He walked into the living room, sat on the sofa, turned on the television. There was still a while before Tasha would be home.

Breathing more easily, Kaplowitz reached to the back of his pants and pulled the Glock from his belt. It was sleek and black, and he admired the 9mm weapon as if it were his salvation. He had bought it from a friend in the Bronx and practiced for months in an empty warehouse, squeezing the trigger, feeling the recoil until he was so comfortable with it there could be no question. He set the gun on the coffee table.

After a few minutes of watching cartoons (he couldn't stand to watch anything else), Kaplowitz walked into the kitchen and rifled the cabinets until he found Z's bottle of bourbon. He brought the bottle back into the living room and sat down on the couch again, taking tugs from the

The DEATH of OBSESSION

Jack Daniel's. SpongeBob SquarePants was filling the room with his annoying machinegun laugh, and it made Kaplowitz smile. He had always loved cartoons. He recalled his mother sitting him in front of the TV and turning on *Teenage Mutant Ninja Turtles* to keep him amused while she ... did whatever she did. Leonardo, Michelangelo, Donatello, and Raphael had kept him company when he was at his loneliest.

Kaplowitz took a long swig from the bourbon and stared at the television. He reached out and ran his fingers along the Glock. It felt cool and real.

6.

Tasha Zinarelli was happy when she got off the bus. She had talked to Riley Evans at lunch and he had ended the conversation by asking her to Friday's dance. Earth's advice had been perfect. Tasha had initiated the conversation but then had let Riley take the lead. She smiled, tilted her head, threw in a comment when it was necessary. But she allowed him to control the situation and that had given him the confidence to ask her to the dance.

When she had told Courtney about it, she had been so envious she'd slapped Tasha on the arm and said, "No way." And they'd laughed about it and barely ate any lunch, talking about what Tasha should wear and whether she and Riley would dance a slow dance together.

Tasha couldn't remember the last time she'd been so lighthearted. Maybe never. She ran to the house, slipped the key into the lock, and swung the door open. As she stepped inside, the first thing she saw was someone sitting on the sofa. Her heart caught. What the hell? When she recognized the person she said, "What are you doing here?"

David Kaplowitz sat forward and grinned at her. "Come on in," he said.

When she backed toward the door, he picked something dark and menacing off the table and pointed it at her. "I said come in." She shivered and stepped forward. She didn't know what else to do. She had never had a gun pointed at her before.

"What are you doing in my house?" Tasha asked him.

His smile seemed like it was meant to intimidate her. "Whatever I want," he said. After letting that sink in, he added, "You're going to do exactly what I tell you to do."

She nodded slowly. Her stomach was turning over and she could barely breathe. She felt like screaming but didn't want to make him angry. All he had to do was pull that trigger.

"Now," he said, "pick up the phone."

7.

Water Farmer set the receiver down and yelled, "Earth, it's for you."

Earth was hesitant to answer the phone. She was afraid who might be on the other end. When she asked her sister who it was Water shrugged and said, "Sounds like Tasha."

Relieved, Earth picked up the receiver and said. "Hello."

Tasha's voice sounded tight, on the verge of breaking. "Earth, it's me, Tasha. I need your help."

"What's wrong, honey?"

"Can you come over here? Right now?"

Earth's nerves began to tingle. "OK, sure, Tash. Is everything all right?"

"Just come, please. By yourself."

Earth looked out the front window. There was no car in the Zinarellis' driveway. Her parents weren't home. "What's going on, Tash?"

"Earth, just please come over."

She could hear the panic in Tasha's voice. "I'll be right there," she said.

8.

When his line rang, Z wanted to ignore it. He was editing stories for tomorrow's paper, going through them much too fast and hoping he wasn't letting any mistakes get by. He was up to his eyeballs in copy, but he had to pick up the receiver. Otto Hellinger was glaring at him; it was editorial policy always to respond to readers' calls as promptly as possible.

"*Hudson Valley Sun.* Michael Zinarelli."

Z was surprised to hear Earth Farmer's edgy voice on the other end. "Mr. Z, hi, it's Earth."

What can she want? "Hi. Is everything all right?"

"So far. Listen, Mr. Z, we need you to come home."

"We?"

"Me and Tasha."

"Earth, I'm very busy right now. What's going on?"

"It's kind of hard to explain ..."

He heard a scraping as if someone had wrestled the phone out of her hand. The next voice sent icy fingers down the back of his neck. "I've got Earth and your daughter here, Mike. You have half an hour to get here before I lose my patience and somebody gets hurt."

"Where ...?"

"Walk into your backyard, almost to the back, then turn left into the woods. Keep walking until you find us."

"David, I'll be there. Don't do anything crazy."

"And come alone, Mike. If I even whiff a cop around, everybody's going to die. Earth, your daughter, you, me. All of us."

"You're in charge, David."

"Goddamn right. Now get your ass over here."

Z laid the phone back in its cradle and stared straight ahead, his heart pounding wildly. He couldn't think straight. His hands were shaking and he could barely draw a breath. *Tasha!* If Kaplowitz hurt her in any way ...

Z turned toward Hellinger, who was on his phone explaining in an exasperated voice, "If your boyfriend doesn't want to be in the paper, he shouldn't get arrested for robbing a convenience store ... Yes, it is our business. It's public information."

"Otto, I have to leave."

Hellinger held up his beefy finger. "Look, miss, I'm trying to explain to you how it works."

"Otto, I have to leave now." Z was already on his feet.

Hellinger said, "Hold on a minute," then put his hand over the mouthpiece. "What the hell's going on?"

"Family emergency. I have to leave."

"We're jammed ..."
The stony look on Z's face stopped him. "I'm leaving."
As Z walked away Hellinger said, "Call me later and let me know what's going on."
Calling Hellinger was the last thing he was worried about.

9.

I'm paying for the way I indulged myself when I was young all the smoking, drinking, snorting, fucking, licking throwing myself into everything like there would be no tomorrow but there was a tomorrow and tomorrow and tomorrow and the petty pace just crept on and on if I knew I'd live so long I'd have taken a deep breath and asked the universe for the strength to live like an ascetic. But I didn't. Now comes the universe's revenge. My Tasha! If Kaplowitz puts a hand on her he will die or I will die trying to get my hands on him.

Z raced up the stairs to his bedroom, pulled open his top dresser drawer and fished out the knife with the smooth white handle. His father had handed him the knife days before he died. Michael Zinarelli Sr. had carried the pocketknife everywhere like a rabbit's foot, and when he gave it to his son Z knew his father was surely dying. Z had no idea where his father had gotten the knife, but he suspected it was a gift from his own father. At least, Z wanted it to be the case. It would fit into his family mythology.

Z glanced at his watch. He still had twelve minutes until Kaplowitz's deadline. He unfolded the knife and tucked it into his belt, fluffing his shirt over it. There was little chance he would actually get to use it against a gun-toting madman who was more than twenty years younger. But maybe it would bring him just enough luck to save Tasha and Earth. That was all he wanted. Z did not care what happened to him. He had lived his life, had experienced more than a lifetime's worth of love and laughter, of hate and darkness, of transcendental moments.

The DEATH of OBSESSION

The realization that he would die this day made Z numb. Oblivion might sometimes seem sweet, but life was the better alternative. All death had to recommend it was eternal rest. His father had reminded him of that. And there came a time when everyone was ready for that rest. But Z understood now that he was not ready. As much emotional pain as he carried around, he still wanted to smell sweet spring mornings and watch his daughters grow up and to laugh at silly memories with his brother and sister. He did not want to be gone. He did not want to become just a memory, like his father.

Z steeled himself, walked quickly down into the kitchen, and looked for his bottle of bourbon in the cupboard. It was not there. Ignoring that, he walked out the back door onto the deck and followed the stairs into the yard. He glanced at his watch again. Seven minutes. He had to hurry. With long strides he headed to the back of his property, and just before he reached it he headed left and crashed into the brush. The ground was soggy and his shoes were sucked into the mud. His emotions went blank. As had happened often in his life, Z nearly shut down when faced with calamity. All he wanted now was to get Tasha and Earth away from Kaplowitz.

Half-naked branches clawed at him as he walked. Scruffy undergrowth grabbed at his legs. He put his hand to the knife. Strangely, he had never walked this far into the woods near his house. *The familiar is never as familiar as we think. Jesus, every minute is unique every breath is different. How could I forget that?* Z laughed at himself with a grunt. It seemed ridiculously appropriate that he would die because of Crystal Cassidy. It might have happened thirty years earlier.

When he walked into the small clearing, Z froze. Kaplowitz was standing behind Tasha with his arm locked around her throat. The barrel of the Glock was against her head. Tasha was white with terror, her green eyes wet. Earth stood beside them, softly saying, "It's gonna be OK, honey."

Z's first instinct was to rush him, but he mastered himself and said with forced calm, "I'm here, David. Let her go now."

"You're just in time, Mike. I was afraid I was going to have to shoot her."

"I did what you asked. Let her go."

"She'll go when I say she goes!" Kaplowitz growled. "I'm in charge here, in case you didn't notice." He was sweating heavily despite the chilly October breeze blowing. He shoved the gun harder against her head.

"OK," Z said, holding up his hands to show his acquiescence. "Tasha," he said. She was staring down at her sneakers, shaking. "Tasha, look at me." She slowly raised her head and put her terrified eyes on him. "I'm going to get you out of here. Just try to stay calm."

Defiantly, Tasha said, "Dad, I'm not afraid."

"You should be," Kaplowitz said. Then to Z: "How are you going to get her out of here, huh, Mike? How are you going to manage that?"

Z swallowed hard. "By giving you what you want, David. Me. I'm the one you want so let's get to it."

Kaplowitz shook his head. His brown eyes were wild, almost pulsating. "You're not going to take this away from me, Mike. This is my moment. This is the time when everybody gets theirs."

"David, please ..." Earth whispered.

He snapped his head toward her and gritted his perfect teeth. "I'm getting to you, bitch. Wait your fucking turn." He jerked the Glock away from Tasha's head and snapped it across Earth's jaw, sending her spinning to the leaf-covered ground. Tasha screamed. Z took a step forward but held himself back. He knew he could not cover the distance between them quickly enough.

"What are you doing?" Z asked him.

"She used me, Mike," Kaplowitz said earnestly, as if confiding to a friend. "She made me think she was in love with me. Then she pissed on me. You expect me to ignore that? I'm finished ignoring things. She is going to pay for ripping my heart out."

Earth crawled to her knees, holding the side of her face. Her blue eyes were filled with tears of pain.

"If you kill us, you're never going to get out of here, David," Z said.

The DEATH of OBSESSION

Kaplowitz laughed grimly and put the Glock against his own temple. "I don't plan on getting out of here," he said.

"David, come on. Let Tasha go and then we can settle this. She's just a kid and she's not involved at all. Getting your revenge is one thing, but hurting an innocent kid is another. Right?"

"Don't try to bullshit me, Mike. You are an evil sonofabitch. You killed my mother. You killed her!"

Z took a deep breath. Things became so clear to him his head seemed to expand. "What if I did kill her? You should be thanking me. The way she sucked the life out of your father. She left him empty and half-dead. And then, what, she dragged man after man into your house. You spent your whole life embarrassed by her, right? And then, finally, when it looked like everything was calming down and she married Richard Stallman, she started to fuck that up, too. He was good to you and she treated him like shit. Like always. Hey, look, if I killed her I did the world a favor. I got rid of something vile."

Kaplowitz stared at him for a moment, eyes wide. He tightened his grip on Tasha's throat. Then he flashed a nasty grin. "I despised her. How could I help it? I took as much as I could, but when I found out she was talking to you again that was the end. Of all the people in the world for her to hook up with ... Jesus! After the way you ruined her life, for her to go after you again was too much."

"You saw us when we had lunch, right?"

Kaplowitz nodded slowly. "When she told me she was having lunch with you, I followed her. Yeah, I saw you two together. Sitting on that deck looking out over the lake like it was old times. Like she wanted to screw you again. I could not tolerate that, Mike. Can you understand that?"

"Nothing happened. We ate lunch and went our separate ways."

Kaplowitz pointed the Glock at Z and dragged Tasha back a few steps while keeping the grip on her throat with his forearm. Tasha whimpered. "Yeah, well it wasn't over for her because I followed her to Poughkeepsie. She went to your goddamn house. That was the day she had to die. I could not take her becoming obsessed with you again."

"David, my daughter doesn't have to hear this. Let her go back to the house. Her and Earth."

"Shut up!" Earth was still massaging her jaw when Kaplowitz kicked his leg out to the side and sent her face-down into the ground again. She was crying softly. "I was waiting for Mom when she got home. Richard was out. I killed her right when she came through the door. I didn't want to hear anything from her filthy lying mouth. I had it planned out perfectly. I spread a plastic drop cloth on the floor and when she stepped on it, she looked at me with a question in her eyes before I bashed her fucking brains in with a brick. She was twitching for a few seconds and I hit her again, really hard, and she stopped moving. I wrapped her up in the plastic and then covered that with a cheap rug I'd bought and carried her downstairs like she was a carpet. Nobody saw me. Nobody thought anything of it. I put her in the trunk of my car and that was it, she was gone."

"Where is she?" Z asked.

"Where nobody will ever find her. I drove her car up to Poughkeepsie, parked it near the river and walked to the train station. Then I took the train home. My plan would've been complete if I could have gotten that stupid ass Delson to arrest you for her murder. But he was either too ignorant or too smart to do it. It would have been perfect. The ultimate irony."

Z shook his head. He was trying to gauge how quickly he could pull the knife from his belt and launch himself at Kaplowitz. "You tried too hard," he said. "Planting that pocketbook was too much."

Kaplowitz shrugged. "Well, I'm gonna get you anyway, Mike. So I win."

Z edged forward, trying to keep Kaplowitz engaged in conversation. "What did I ever do to you, David? Why do you hate me so much?"

The wind picked up and half-fallen trees rubbed against each other, creaking and moaning like woodland ghosts. No one spoke for several seconds and for instant it seemed like a normal October day in the valley: fluffy clouds against piercing blue sky, cool breeze wafting up from the river, birds hopping from branch to branch. Z took everything in with a swelling in his heart.

"You should have married her, Mike," Kaplowitz said. "You should have been my father. I got so sick of hearing her talk about you when I was a kid and I thought you *were* my father. She needed you, Mike, and you abandoned her and it ruined her life and ruined my life."

Z laughed cruelly, staring into Kaplowitz's eyes. "You are dreaming, kid. Crystal ruined her own life, and almost ruined mine, too. She was nothing but a self-centered whore and you know it. That's why you killed her."

"Shut up."

"It had nothing to do with me. She was just a worthless little bitch and you're her worthless son."

Kaplowitz turned bright red. He pointed the gun at Z and, howling with rage, pulled the trigger, firing a shot into Z's leg just above the knee. For a split second Z felt nothing, but then white hot agony flowed up and down his leg. He wailed and thought he might pass out.

"No," Tasha screamed. She wrenched away from Kaplowitz's grip with adrenaline-fueled strength, no longer afraid for herself, and ran to her father. Sobbing, she knelt beside him.

"You stupid ass," Kaplowitz said. "What made you think you could get mixed up with someone like her and just walk away?"

Z barely heard him. The ocean was crashing in his ears and he saw nothing except Kaplowitz pulling Earth up by her hair. He wanted to plead for her life but he knew it would do no good, knew that it would only feed Kaplowitz's sick need to punish them both.

"David," Earth moaned. "Please."

He tightened his grip on her hair and pulled until she was crying out. "Shut up." With the Glock in his hand, he stroked her cheek gently. "You were a sweet little fuck, Earth. I'm not immune to that. So I'm going to do you a favor. I'm not going to torture you. I'm going to kill you quick so I can concentrate on this sonofabitch." His black eyes glared at Z. "I'm going to have fun with you."

"David," Earth pleaded.

He put the gun against her temple. "Enough of this shit," he snarled.

Kaplowitz was not focused on Z, who was writhing on the ground, blood running freely from his leg. He did not see Z slip the knife out of his belt and grip it firmly in his right hand. For a heartbeat or two, Kaplowitz hesitated, smelling the clean scent of Earth's hair and flashing briefly on their lovemaking. It was just enough time for Z to lurch forward and bury the blade as deeply as he could in Kaplowitz's thigh. He figured it would be his last act, and he wanted it to count. He gripped the handle with the last of his strength and kept shoving it forward.

Kaplowitz howled and threw his arms out to the side, releasing Earth. The Glock tumbled into the undergrowth as his hand involuntarily jerked open.

"Run," Z screamed at Tasha. When she hesitated, he said. "Goddamn it, go!" She took off through the trees while Earth rolled away from Kaplowitz and dove into the bushes.

Kaplowitz growled like a wounded bear. With amazing strength and a superhuman imperviousness to pain, he yanked the blade out of his leg and held it up, examining his own blood as if for the first time. "Don't worry," he said to Z. "She's not going to get away. Nice try, though. I didn't think you had it in you, Mike."

He limped forward, the knife poised to strike. "This has been a lot of fun, but it's over now."

The Glock erupted, echoing madly in the quiet woods. Kaplowitz's eyes widened in shock. He staggered a couple steps, then turned slowly and saw Earth standing a few feet away, the gun leveled at him. He took a step toward her and she fired again, hitting him in the chest. He stumbled back, blood exploding from the heart shot, and crashed to the ground, eyes staring sightlessly at the roof of branches above their heads. At first, Earth did not move. She seemed appalled at what she had done.

A moment later, she was at Z's side, lifting him into a sitting position. "You're going to be OK," she told him. Blood was pouring out of his leg and she knew she needed to get help immediately.

The DEATH of OBSESSION

Suddenly, she began weeping, water washing down her face while her shoulders heaved. He draped his arms around her as if she were his own daughter. He felt ashamed he had ever thought of her in any other way.

"Thank you," he said softly. "Thank you." The pain took him away and all he saw was blackness. A sense of complete peace washed over him. He felt his father taking his hand and leading him away, but then he realized it was Earth's calloused hand and she was shouting at him.

"Mr. Z, you stay with me," she screamed. She gritted her teeth. "Goddamnit, don't you dare!"

The pain returned sharply. He squeezed her hand. "I'm not going anywhere," he mumbled. "Not yet."

She put both hands over the wound and pressed with all her might, trying to staunch the flow of blood.

A moment later, he heard Tasha screaming, "Over here, over here," and Detective Steve Delson came crashing through the brush with his partner close behind.

"Call for an ambulance," he said to Barone. "Now!"

10.

Leg propped on the coffee table, Z sat watching afternoon cartoons on television. He was chuckling at Popeye's exploits. Why, he wondered, was the sailor man so attached to a woman who ran off with the first hunky dude who came along, only to call for Popeye's help when things got dicey? Anna came into the living room with a cup of tea and set it on the table.

"Olive Oyl is nothing but a whore," he told his wife.

She shook her head, but a tiny smile crept across her lips. "You are a very sick man, you know that?"

"I don't want any more tea," he said. "How about a shot of Jack?"

"No Jack," she said sharply. "If you behave yourself, I'll let you have half a glass of wine with dinner."

"Aw, Anna ..."

"You are going to stop drinking so much," she said. "Even though you're a pain in the ass, you're *my* pain in the ass, and I want you around for a while." She leaned down and kissed the side of his face. "We have a lot of things to work out, Michael. When you're feeling better, we're going to see a marriage counselor."

"OK," he said. "But you know I love you, girl." He pulled her down against him.

Her brown eyes were wet. "Let go of me," she said. "I have something in the oven." She stood up and, as she left the room, looked back over her shoulder as if to make sure he was really there. She had taken a week off from work to nurse him after his release from the hospital.

"Oh," she yelled from the kitchen. "Molly called before. She wanted to know how you were doing."

"She just wants to know when I'm coming back to work," he grumbled. He was on medical leave and had months before he had to think about returning to the newsroom. He was not sure he was going back at all. He had changed irrevocably over the past few weeks. Being so close to death did that to a person. But he had time to think about his future. For now he would just breathe and laugh and try to learn to live without Jack Daniel's.

He reached for the tea, took a sip, and put it back down, making a face. This would take some getting used to.

He stood up carefully and gripped the cane he had propped next to the sofa. "I'm going out onto the porch for some air," he called to Anna. He slipped on a jacket and opened the front door. The November day was nippy but not too unpleasant; the sun was shining and felt good. He limped out onto the porch, dragging his leg and its soft cast. He didn't mind. He just kept thinking about what might have happened.

Across the street, Earth was standing in her front yard, staring up at the sky as if studying the clouds. He waved to her, but she didn't see him. Her mood had been mercurial since the incident, swinging between elation and despondency. In his mind, it was understandable. She had killed a man. He couldn't imagine how heavily that would hang around someone's neck. But he remembered the rage in his hands as they pressed the pillow against Crystal's face all those years ago, and he understood.

Z crossed the street slowly, leaning hard on the cane. The doctor had told him he needed to walk a bit, even if it

The DEATH of OBSESSION

hurt. He would be starting physical therapy soon. It was a long road back, but he was fortunate. He could have lost the leg. Even though he would likely walk with a limp for the rest of his life, even though the leg would ache on rainy days, Z felt lucky. Luck, he decided, was a strange thing—all relative.

When Earth saw him, she offered a thin smile, a smile that softened his heart. He wished he could somehow make things better for her. But he knew that was impossible. He had enough trouble helping himself.

"Hey, Mr. Z," she said. "How's the leg?"

He tried not to stare at the angry purple bruise on her jaw. "Well, my dreams of an NBA career are gone."

She giggled quietly. "That's too bad. I heard you were a mean defender. Tenacious."

"I've been called worse." A silence settled in between them. They listened to the cars and trucks racing along Route 9 about a mile away. Kids at the daycare center up the block shouted as they played outside in the mild November weather. Life moved on all around them, but it was difficult for them to grasp it.

Z reached out tentatively and touched her shoulder. "How are you, Earth?"

At first, she averted her eyes. "I'm OK," she said. He waited. She looked at him with eyes so blue they could have melted him. "Mr. Z, I don't know what to feel right now." She breathed deeply and turned her face toward the sky. "Sometimes I think I'm the one who died out there."

"You didn't," he said passionately. He grabbed her by the upper arm and shook her slightly. "We're both alive because of what you did. Do you understand that?"

She groaned bitterly. "When I close my eyes at night I see his face, Mr. Z. It won't go away."

Earth had been exonerated by the DA, who, on the strength of Detective Delson's report, had declared her actions self-defense. Even though she had been forgiven by the law, she couldn't forgive herself.

"Listen, Earth, David screwed up his own life. He was the one responsible, not you. Just like his mother. She screwed up her life and a lot of other people's lives."

"But you don't hate her," Earth said. "You kinda still love her, don't you, no matter what she did."

Z made a face. "I loved being twenty. I loved being young and having all the possibilities in the world stretching out in front of me. Like you, right now, Earth. I let what Crystal did to me cripple me for a while. Don't make the same mistake. You have so much potential. Don't let this bastard ruin it."

"You were lucky to meet Anna," Earth said.

Z's lips turned up into a gentle smile. "It was the luckiest day of my life," he said. "You'll meet somebody, too."

She shrugged. "Maybe."

He said, "One thing I've been meaning to ask you. When did you learn to shoot a gun?"

She pursed her lips then said, "That was the first time in my life I touched a gun. It doesn't take a genius to shoot a gun, Mr. Z."

Z laughed. He reached out and embraced Earth, who returned it briefly. "No," he whispered into her ear. "It doesn't."

They disentangled quickly and he started back across the street. "I'll talk to you soon," he said as he limped toward his house.

"Hey, Mr. Z," she called as he reached the other side of the street. He turned and looked at her. "You're a good guy, you know?"

He felt like crying but said, "Nah," and kept walking.

Back inside the house, he slumped onto the sofa in front of the television. His leg was pounding. He picked up the prescription bottle, shook two Percocets out into his hand, and washed them down with tepid tea. He turned a game show on TV and sat in mindless suspension for a while. The sound of Anna puttering around in the kitchen was comforting.

The squealing brakes of a bus made him aware that the girls were coming home from school. A minute later, Tasha came bustling into the house, all noise and energy. She kissed her father on the cheek, something she had recently taken to doing. He conjured an image of her dressed for the dance that Riley Evans took her to. It made him soft inside, thinking about it. Time was passing. There was no way to stop it. There was no way to go back. But he was still alive and she was still alive, and that was something. Maybe it was everything.

"How's it going?" he asked.

"Pretty good," she answered breezily, and ran up the stairs to her room, calling, "Hi, Mom," as she did.

About the Author

Ray Fashona is a longtime journalist who has written and edited for several newspapers and magazines. This is his first novel.

He lives in the Hudson Valley with his wife and two daughters.